OTTOLINE ATLANTICA

Other novels by the same author

RIBSTONE PIPPINS

CAVAN

OTTOLINE ATLANTICA

Helen Wykham

MARION BOYARS
LONDON – BOSTON

First published in Great Britain in 1980
by Marion Boyars Publishers Ltd
18 Brewer Street, London W1R 4AS
© Helen Wykham 1980

ALL RIGHTS RESERVED

Australian distribution
by Thomas C. Lothian
4-12 Tattersalls Lane, Melbourne, Victoria 3000

British Library Cataloguing in Publication Data

Wykham, Helen
　Ottoline Atlantica.
　I. Title
　823'.9'IF   PR6045.Y440/

ISBN 0 7145 2686 X Cloth edition

Any paperback edition of this book whether published simultaneously with or subsequent to the casebound edition is sold subject to the condition that it shall not, by way of trade, be lent, resold, hired out or otherwise disposed of without the publisher's consent, in any form of binding or cover other than that in which it is published.

No part of this publication may be reproduced, stored in a retrieval system, or transmitted, in any form or by any means, electronic, mechanical, photocopying, recording or otherwise, without the prior written permission of the copyright owner and the publisher.

Photoset by
Specialised Offset Services Limited, Liverpool

Printed and bound in Great Britain by
Redwood Burn Ltd, Trowbridge & Esher

In memory of my father
DOUGLAS
and in public acknowledgement of
a gift he once gave me.

*Nature seeketh to have things that are
curious and beautiful ... Nature is covetous, doth more willingly
receive than give, and loveth to have
things private and her own.*

Thomas à Kempis, *Imitation of Christ*
Fourth Book, chapter 54

THIS BEGINNING is not a beginning and there is no story to follow it. There is only one thing of which you may be certain – only one thing of which I am certain – and that is the island. The island is in the West (of where does not greatly matter), somewhere where the great Atlantic fetches in on this side. You may have visited it, I live on it. You may find that I am it; I do not promise to make this clear, for I am not sure to what extent I shall ever know. You may find out, and maybe I shall not! There will be no story because nothing ever happens here. It cannot.

The island lies on the edge of the great Atlantic; it is isolated from anything you could call a mainland by miles of sea, and a boat comes twice a week in summer and once a week in winter. The island is called Coimheadach, which, as near as I can put it into English sounds, is pronounced 'Ku-*vedda*-(ch)'. I mention this, not really for your sake but for mine, because I would not like to think of you in Penarth or you in Bexhill saying the name wrong. I do not know how many people live on the island now – a hundred or so, perhaps, or less – and I do not know how many people have lived here. They die, but it is not always easy or necessary to know when. The island has been here for a long time, and we who live here do not know why we stay.

Mostly we are stock-raisers. We keep cattle, and then we eat the cattle. The cattle have been here for a long time, too. I do not know why they stay, either; except that I suppose they cannot go, any more than we can. In the simple terms of these mobile, unlocalized days when strangers are familiar and no one says, 'Where do you come from?' any more, we could certainly step onto *St Ursula* next Thursday and arrive somewhere else by Thursday night. But in fact we would not arrive anywhere, because we would not have left. We – being the island, the islanders, the narrator of the book, the central figure in it – we would still be the island, wherever *St Ursula* docked.

The island came into us before we were born. It came up the umbilical in our mother's blood; in what she ate, in the air she breathed, in the postures and temperatures Coimheadach placed around her and to which there was no alternative. Herbs grow differently where there was once a dwelling, a hearth, a pathway, a stone slab, a dung heap, a grave. When we buried Auntie Bridie we put her little calcium bones down on the granite bedrock. Because of those little bones and nails richer grass will grow where Auntie Bridie lies.

Coimheadach is strewn about with patches of succulent grass where the balance of acid rock and base-rich deposits is more favourable than is general on the island. There is very little soil here, so the depositions are very close to our feet as we walk. Sometimes we know what has made a certain little patch. This is how we live, kicking out a place to dance among the ankle bones.

Around the island seal circle. We have eaten them, used them well and kept our distance from them. Some think of the seal as people of the sea. They are not people: they are animals, although it is true that we resemble them in many ways; and knowing that they are there, marking us inside a boundary, puts a distance between us and others of our own kind on other islands or on the mainland. They surround us with an alien existence; they island us again.

I am writing this from inside the island – this Coimheadach. I – the I that my mother and brother Christopher would recognize, that there are pleasantly hand-tinted photographs of and who am currently the narrator of this book – I am also the island, because the island wells up in me, in my body, in my dreams, in my coughing. I have no existence outside the island; I have no fact but Coimheadach. When I die my bones, too, will go down on the granite, but while I live – and I do live – it is up here in me, racing under my skin, gripping my knee joints, pounding down my thighs. Where I am, is Coimheadach. So, too, while I live, Coimheadach is I (Coimheadach is also every I who is living now, who is one of us here. But we do not live very long, and the shape of Coimheadach alters little through the aeons), and the words which come from me to you are a miscellany out of Coimheadach. To contain that miscellany I take on many rôles; that of myself, as my husband or Edward or Mansel might recognize me, which I have called by one of my many names – Ottoline – so that the things I do and say and wear are immediately recognizable to them – as Mark said once, 'A cue for laughter.' Ottoline is myself, certainly, and Ottoline, like me, is Coimheadach.

But, being Coimheadach, I am also those who have been Coimheadach before me, and their rôle, too, I hold in front of my face on a long stick, and in their place I posture and figure. I use a mask here to identify resemblances rather than distinctions; the mask is very like Ottoline's face in certain moods; like my face, too. It is true that I have often picked up a cigarette and found myself holding the stem of the mask, but the face on the mask and my own face are not unalike, and it may not matter greatly, except to a classicist.

And I take up, too, the place of the narrator of this book, because in the nature of written work there has to be a narrator and he is a control such as you might have in a laboratory experiment. It is against his substance as a secular figure, subject to causality in time and place, that the availability of Coimheadach is to be measured. It is through his existence that I am able to address you, 'gentle reader', and exploit my obsessive desire to parade Coimheadach up and down Church Road and Westminster Road and Dyers Lane; a narrator like a child's ribbon-man in the street with sweet, vulgar wares which are forbidden by the governesses I used to have, but the odour of whom I must drag up Sengenydd Road and down Mosney Strand, TO ATTRACT THE ATTENTION OF YOUR CHILDREN.

I

... AND without warning. Coco from a cardboard coffin, Ottoline Atlantica, split the night in her black crêpe de chine pyjamas. Shooting out a hand she wrenched at the ivory damask so that the zany sun exploded in the window as the lining ripped with the sound of gunfire. Crump! shouted the miniature guns of morning, a salvo of direct hits on Ottoline Atlantica. Wide-eyed, Ottoline stared at the morning. She had never seen THIS morning before ...

'Hell and damnation,' she moaned, falling back. Exhaustion burst in her head, splinters of inability tore her limbs out of activity. She shut her eyes again, pretending that the morning wasn't; but the bed-curtains, rakish and *déshabillé*, dishonoured her, betrayed her to This Morning, would not cover her. In pulling them back she had created this morning. She lay against the pillows (she slept with four behind her and two on the right side to lean against; they made her breathing easier for she smoked too much) unable to cry since she had produced her morning. If someone had woken her, she would have cried easily and comfortingly, blaming them and cursing them and recovering from the loss of night while she did so. Now she lay, like a captured marshal, in black crêpe de chine, glaring at the defeat she was responsible for.

Ottoline's mother (who was the only woman on record to have driven a four-in-hand through the Spanish Arch at a gallop and who had had brassy hair and a taste for sweet port) had been larger than Ottoline all round, so that her pyjamas, ordered by post from John's, Maddox Street, for 16s 3d in 1912, were loose on Ottoline, and the proud Brandenburg fastenings sagged and wrinkled across her frame so that she looked weak and puny, an old woman struggling with fatigue. Aware of it she moaned again, more loudly and less convincingly. Her hand, lying loose and wrinkled on the bed cover, was thin, the nails tinged with blue and broken out of their sweet filbert shape. In distress she opened her eyes, slyly looking at nothing but the pathetic, old woman's hand resting upon the pale crotchet that was so old that no one knew any more how old it was. The sun struck two little tears from the corners of her eyes, and the touch of them, cool and salty, rent her with pity for the little old woman whose hand was now blurred like the hands of drowned children beneath the wavering, violet sea –

A-CUSH-la, a-CUSH-la, whispered the Atlantic on the rocks below the window and Ottoline Atlantica to the wavering hands of the drowned.

That such indistinct and aqueous shapes should be forced to grotesque labour; that a child's hand, broken and pale, should be thrust into the turgid cement and forced to twist and writhe upon the handle of the trowel, to beat and slap and grasp, so gentle and darling a hand – larger and more beautiful tears moistened her cheeks, and their cool dew settled in the garden of her soul. Perhaps, she thought, it had been indignation that had brought Christ bursting out of the tomb in the garden like that, giving that poor Roman guard Quintus, the fright of his life, trampling down the lilies and knocking boulders about – really, GARDENING! Resurrected, Ottoline Atlantica widened her violet eyes deliberately and the tears vanished.

Hell and damnation (and, unlike Christ, she was no longer concerned with either of them), how the morning onshore winds did drag up across the sand the moans of the children, and hers, and her daughters'. It laid them in the fuchsia tree at dawn to toll in her vivification with the knell of their little bloody bells! A christ, she jerked to the Ting-a-ling-a-ling of morning bells, Christ cursing the labour, the return to the endless dusty vineyard, the parched garden.

'Hell and damnation!' she screamed at her daughters, at her daughter Auschwitz who pulled the bell with a hand contrived of weird flutes made of old bones wherein the wind drifted witlessly and whose notes were stamped out by the applauds and the shifting of phlegm in adult throats. Four corners to my bed, four daughters at my head, at the head of the old sea bitch on the rocks weighting the bellies of the children with mica, felspar, quartz, who had asked for bread and received only the mass of Materia Mundi, *prima mater, mamma, mamma, feed us.*

Still jerking, Ottoline Atlantica dragged herself up on the pillows and snatched at the packet of cigarettes, fumbling and grasping and tearing until one was lit. It was dry and stale in her after the night's abstinence, but she suffered it, knowing that the next one would be better. The pictures of the drowned children and the Auschwitz children and the old women pulling ploughs and lancing their own fistulae with iron potato knives settled in her and grew detached. In time they would revert to cartoon strips, buried down in her own private mythology, gathering dust off the confused and untidy scraps of her day-book down at the bottom of her mind. Some other morning they would be disturbed again, flutter to the surface and be reburied. These were the mornings. These were the names of morning – Auschwitz, and Liverpool, Los Millãres and Coimheadach.

Ottoline looked again at her hand. It was a hand that functioned, that worked, that manipulated tools; no more. Today it would work cement. Today it would mend a drain, relieve Coimheadach of taint. Her ambition and her purpose drove the hand to the cement with as much power as any lash made of an old mule's knotted pizzle. That's a nice description of a mind at work – an old mule's knotted pizzle!

Today she would put the old hand to work, cementing up the drain and loosening the roots of the fuchsia which Great Aunt Hatt had planted to disguise the noxious elements at the outlet from the *necessarium*. Since she had no servants capable of performing the task, and since her son Sigerson was of no account, she would do it herself rather than call in Rory from the harbour. She would not admit to Rory, after all these years of contiguous living, that she had drains, let alone unhealthy ones. Rory's prudery would besmirch her freedom to nurse her own. For the abbey was her own, was her brother, was of her flesh, or she of its stone. The relationship between Ottoline and her house was as close and as rancid as incest.

Coimheadach Abbey lies at the westernmost end of the island. The harbour is at the east, riding out in the direction of the mainland, yet it is in no way the outpost of the mainland; it is the beginning of Coimheadach. At the first bump on the jetty *St Ursula* is prepared for the return voyage – she docks backwards, turning before she comes alongside.

The whole of the harbour is low, built not for the Mail Boat but for the black boats and the smacks and trawlers and hookers, and the steps and walls are faced with smooth rectangles of dark flagstone which are quarried from this end of the island. The flags were laid down as muds and silts of calm waters in the springtime of the green plants whose shadowy fossil-lines still lie in the stone as once they stood in the reflecting waters. The haven, the houses, the hearths of Coimheadach have all been shaped of this flagstone; the narrow roads of the township are paved with it; the bauns and bothies and folds built out of it. The soil which covers it is deep and rich, and the pastures fat. It forms a little ramp, jealously owned and jealously inherited, of two hundred acres or more which slopes eastwards and finally dissolves away under the leeward sea, and the town is carefully placed just beyond its limit. For its limit is the violent edge of the granite. And that granite which burst up from beneath, surged up and smashed open the gentle muds, reared high above the placid strata and flung its shape into the Atlantic skies, is the essence, the very matter of Coimheadach.

It is on the granite, on the westernmost sea-foot of the granite mountain which is the island, that the abbey stands. It is within the abbey walls that Ottoline, called Atlantica, holds her Fool's Synod.

There is no further west to travel.

In the spring of 1135 Mihilanus had been placed by his father in the care and tuition of the monks of Cluny; at Cluny, as Mihilanus later expressed it, his 'soul had been painted'. The shades dyed into it were the deep, luxurious tones of ecstasy and perpetual, hypnotic devotion. Within the unceasing, omnipresent, omniscient discipline of Cluny, the adolescent scholar found areas of expression which almost amounted to intellectual masturbation, so profound and physical was his relief and exhaustion on completing his exercises, and also the solid certainty that wherever his artistic and inquisitive mind might lead him, at the end all things had the purpose of expressing his belief and adoration of God. He knew, with Rock-of-Peter certainty, that Cluny, in burying him in God, buried him alive and entire and that Cluny would use every particle of him from his clever, draughtsman's fingers and the power and pressure of his developing testicles to his passion to love and be loved beyond the limit of expression. Saving only that Cluny admitted no limit to the expression of the glorification of God.

This ideally stable existence was broken apart by the white, pure wind which blew out across Europe from Clairvaux. There, when Mihilanus was still a gangly youngster, obsessed and super-sensitised by the infinite variety and unending gratification of God-glory, he was sent. His mother's brother's spiritual adviser felt the strength of the new, spring wind out of Burgundy, and so Mihilanus was taken from the sensuous rapture of Cluny and put to the rigours of St Bernard's new discipline. What wind may have seemed fresh and pristine to the monks who followed Bernard willingly was as hoar frost and freezing, billowing fog to the young Benedictine. At Clairvaux, then later as a man at Savigny the reformed hours of the 'White' monasteries crept about him, insidious as frost-bite. The hothouse momentum of his desire and ability seized up; his talents shrivelled and tightened; his glorifying hands drew only letters and stern, light structures. He became recognized at Savigny as an architect, and his stiffening fingers drew not tiers of steps to God but prisons for himself: rigid, straight, luminous prisons, exposed and exposing in a bitter masochism. For the beauty of his designs he was sent with Gilles, the Norman, from Savigny to found the new daughter-house in the West. There, in the Atlantic storms and old, cold rains he built for Gilles the most stringent of all his gaols: Coimheadach Abbey.

O, he built it on conventional lines – it is quite easy to find your way around Coimheadach; coming under the great gate, the chapel ruins lie, conventionally, on the left. The roof is gone now, except for the bit over the chancel, and the upper parts of most of the columns have broken off. There are no doors or windows; the floor has been taken up many years ago, dug and spread with cow-dung, and it makes a wonderful rose garden. The bushes grow very tall, partly because Ottoline never prunes them and also because they are enclosed by such high walls. Some of them are almost as tall as a man – at least they are as tall as a twelfth-century monk. From the north side of the chancel the night-stair ascends to the upper storey of the east range, which is what you see opposite you when you enter through the great gate. The upper floor was the dorter, the sleeping quarters for the monks, and the existence of the night-stair enabled them to trot down to the chapel for nocturnes and lauds without going down the main stair and across the side of the court in the open. Beneath the night-stair there is a little arched passage – the slype – which gives access from the court to the graveyard which lies beyond the east range, outside the confines of the court. They used to carry the coffins of the dead monks out of the main door of the chapel, up the side of the court and through the slype. The passage is very dark and low, and the flagged ground is constantly damp. Some livid fungi and acid-toned mosses sprout from the walls; it echoes and stinks of urine and hens, although there is no particular reason for this. At its far end the slype bursts out of the walled confines into the graveyard, which catches more sun than any other part of the abbey, being unwalled to the east and only partly sheltered to the south. Beyond the graveyard there is a barbed wire fence, and beyond that there is the mountain where the sheep run. In winter, they come down and press against the wire, which has little scurries of torn wool on the barbs.

Ottoline and Sigerson have their bedrooms in the old dorter. It was Mihilanus who built the high, blind windows with their three lights, which look out across the graveyard into the rising sun. Mihilanus built them. The floors are carpeted. There are wooden walls, put in five hundred years later at vast expense for wood is costly out here – we have not one living tree on the island now –

but the work was done with an apparent lack of conviction. Instead of the deep, glossy solidity and substance which wooden walls of that period usually suggest, redolent of thick velvets, madrigals, *louis d'or*, wenches and seaman's pitch, the interior walling at Coimheadach seems but a poor, light thing. It is obvious where measurements have been incorrect and different woods inserted to fill gaps between panels and the cold stones; the positioning of the windows is eccentric to the shape of the rooms; the cast of the original ceiling exotic to the new small shape. It remains, the dorter which Mihilanus built, a great stone space uneasily partitioned into bits.

In the room nearest to the slype Ottoline dozes and dawdles. In the lobby adjoining it, which leads into the first tread of the night-stair, she has had a great wooden window thrust into the wall: a bulging, backwoods edifice which hangs out over the point where the slype runs out into the bright graveyard; a small, unstable, creaking crow's-nest of a place, where the paint is peeling in layers off the rotting frames of the windows, where the glass panes are cracked and spider's webs sling drab hammocks across ill-angled corners. There she grows indoor plants; a profuse, vulgar, fleshy heap of them, piled in splitting pots without regard to type, texture or colour. Their over-sweet perfume eddies like hash in the draughts, stale and decadent. In here Ottoline has her card-table, which she litters with her bills and accounts, paying carefully those creditors who seem most likely to do her down. Here also is a ravelled wicker chair in which she sits; so ancient and uncared for that the flat, mutilated cushions are sunk and sifted between the pale rush-work, never shaken, never moved except by her own fidgeting body. In here she torments her two whippets, smokes her sour little cigarettes and listens endlessly to the crackling wireless, as large as a coffer.

Sigerson has his room further along the dorter. Ottoline has designated the area between them as a 'guest room'. Both she and Sigerson know that no 'guests' ever come to Coimheadach. Ottoline cannot bear to hear the sound of another's sleeping. It reminds her of Pinell, her husband, and the brief years he spent in her bed. Not even the sound of her son's movements is permissible, let alone that of his dreaming. Sigerson is not allowed to keep any possessions of his own in that room; in this way she effectively guards against his intrusion as surely as if she had locked the door. To Sigerson, it is more effective than any lock.

Below the unhappy dorter lies the vast chapter, a long thin cavern of a room. The great Orcadian chimney is lightless, and damp soot clings to its walls; the dog-grate, though elegant, is too small, and in any case there is never wood to burn in it. It stands somewhat to one side of the hearth area, and in the centre a heap of silver ashes lies on the naked flagstones where the turf now burns in its stead. On one side a great high-backed chair stands, facing obliquely down the room so that Ottoline may rest her feet near the turf, but her eyes stay gazing down the dim length, resting on the length. An untidy sofa occupies the other side of the hearth, its back broken, its depths a-scurry with black beetles, fleas, bed bugs. Behind Ottoline's tall chair there is a carved teak table from Macao. Because it is carved from a single piece of wood it has not split or warped. It is elaborately decorated with long, proud horses' heads and serpentine dragons. The scant light which penetrates the chimney glazes their round, hard eyeballs. On the table there stands an ornament. It has an iron stand, a geometric, criss-cross plinth, inset with reduced human face-masks with huge lips and elongated elliptical eyes. Upon the plinth there is a column of black leather, eighteen or nineteen inches high, coming to a smooth cone at the top. The surface is shiny where Ottoline strokes it, surrounding it with her small hand which she runs caressingly up and down. About two inches from the top there is a white bone band. Above the band the leather is rough. Once Sigerson brought from England a set of fairy lights as a Christmas present for Aelebel, but Ottoline stole them from her servant sucking-sister and draped them over the black leather ornament. On festive nights when she is drunk or crazy she lights them up and giggles at them.

The rest of the room is much as Mihilanus set it. What furniture there is is pricelessly ancient, dark and unpolished, or just big, dark and unpolished; chests, campaign chairs, an easel with a discoloured rendering of some black Lethe, two tapestries depicting a pale Leda in successive stages of her discomfiture (one of these so curled by the damp of the wall behind it that Leda's flaccid, indoor buttocks and the swan's icy white down are juxtaposed in an impossible relationship. Ottoline giggles at this, too); a lacquered cabinet displaying some lumpy Rhenish glass, two whaling harpoons crossed on the wall above a lace jabot and a pair of minute lemon-yellow doe-skin gloves in a frame, the backing stained and blotched with age; a cold Etrurian urn and a stuffed armadillo in a glass case. Several skewbald sheepskins, a dun pony skin and a Kazak carpet make little islands on the flagstone floor. None of these articles makes any impact on the room. As with the dorter, it remains a stone space. Mihilanus' stone space.

Beyond is the hall. It is nothing, just a tall enclosure from which the wide, pale stairways mount to the upper storey. Five men, with their swords, could walk up it abreast. The centres of the treads are more worn than the sides; the proud O'Treanns and their servants making deeper ruts over the secular centuries than the monks before them had done, slipping on their cold, sandalled feet, slyly, humbly pressed against the dank walls.

Still westwards from this, and beneath Sigerson's end of the dorter, the warming-room is perhaps the nearest approximation to a 'room' which the abbey possesses. It has been turned into a combination library and sittingroom. Most of the stone walls are hidden behind bookcases, which are, rather surprisingly, crammed and choked with a wild array of printed matter. Yellow-backed novelettes of the Twenties break up the sequence of Jane Austen; original translations of Freud and Malinowski rest horizontally on the top of Dorothy Sayers and Gogol; Ian Fleming and Geoffrey of Monmouth encapsulate collections of cigarette cards, programmes for Diaghilev's ballet, newspaper cuttings on brucellosis and pamphlets on the cultivation of yams. The floor is softened by a maltreated and dog-stained carpet from one of the minor Creuse workshops, an ancient Portuguese mat hangs on one part of the stone wall not hidden by books and a *gros-point* tapestry of *Robin et Marion* conceals the remaining section.

It could be said that Mihilanus is less destructive here than anywhere else; his influence has been so largely smothered over the years that what he built no longer twists the attitudes of the living as it does in the rest of the house where the strength of Mihilanus is greater, it seems, than the strength of time. Time-present, whenever that present may be, lost its grip on Coimheadach Abbey after Mihilanus finally went. Paradoxically, it is Sigerson who haunts the warming-room, where there is so little of Mihilanus left, and Ottoline who crouches and snivels and blasts by the dog-grate in the chapter, as if she took no notice of Mihilanus, as if living with him were no combat, no more restricting than living with the whippets or the green stains inside the window frames.

Beyond the warming-room the south range of the abbey runs in a T-shape. Within the square of the court the refectory with its own entrance door and shallow steps is now the dining-room. It makes an awful dining-room because the food is always cold by the time it gets there; and the diners are always cold because the sun never gets there, and even in summer there is moss in one corner of the flagged floor. The silver — some of which is unfrocked ecclesiastical and rather difficult to use with scrambled egg or pickled herring, some of which is Mexican and impossible to use with anything, and some of which is more conventional and has been used for so long that it is bent and battered out of shape — is all covered with acid-green and blue stains, gritty on the tongue, except where immemorial eggs have left lustrous colours like burnished flame: reds and oranges and deep umbers. There is a genuine Aubusson here, with bald patches where O'Treanns have sat in immutable hierarchies and tracks where the generations of servants have passed from chair to chair. Cats have plucked threads beneath the distaff end of the table; dogs have torn holes beneath the remainder, grappling for bones and chunks of cold fat.

Worst of all here are the portraits hung from the stone-faced walls. There are seven of them, some very large indeed, some merely enormous. At the beginning of the last century a younger O'Treann left the island and went to Edinburgh to study medicine. There, because of his manner and his expertise with a throwing knife, he became something of a nine-days' wonder and was invited to a number of the grander Edinburgh houses, all of which boasted formidable numbers of bad portraits. Greatly impressed by this method of brightening the walls of large dark houses, the young

O'Treann bought himself the services of one of Edinburgh's less scrupulous painters. Dressing himself in a number of different costumes from different ages and of both sexes, O'Treann posed seven times as his male and female relatives and forbears, and the painter, who was lacking in imagination, painted him seven times: in wigs and helmets, in ruff and beauty spot, with and without milky breasts, spotted hounds and inaccurate globes. The devastating result of this expensive exercise now embellishes the walls of the refectory. Ottoline's grandfather used to remark that it made a hundred pounds a year difference to his butling bills, as visitors were inclined to think that they must already have drunk more than a sufficiency before the great wines ever reached the table. It was amongst these seven pairs of identical and slightly cast eyes that Sigerson was to refuse mince pie for breakfast.

The east end of the refectory, or factory, leads into a long passage, off which open many doors with conventual iron grilles across eye slots in each. Behind the doors are the gun-room, conserving-room, preserving room, hanging-room and laundries, and the far end of the corridor expands into the cells of the infirmary, altered and divided up in the thirteenth century out of the original great hall which Mihilanus had built for the sick, so many of whom died of the flux, no matter what ailment had brought them there in the first place. The infirmary faces out across the graveyard to the projecting east end of the abbey church itself. Beyond the other, west, end of the refectory lie the kitchens where Aelebel lives. This is a complex of dairies and larders and store rooms. Beneath it the cellars are only three feet high, for this was as deep as the monks could dig into the rock. It is necessary to crawl down there. The entrance is now boarded up, but this was done hastily and no one knows what was down there when the work was begun.

The fourth range, within which the gate is set and which faces the chapter and warming room, is now used as outbuildings, full of spades and hens and sheets of rusted corrugated iron where the brew house was. In that part to the north, or left, of the gate as you enter, which became the later abbots' private dwelling, the O'Treanns had made their mews. Here a mouldering brougham, two phaetons and a private hearse trickle rotting paint and wood motes onto the cobbled floor. Ottoline's cattle, the Land Rover and the bloody-minded yellow pony now shelter in winter where the proud hackneys and Cleveland Bays once stood, and the whippets moan and scream where the elegant Carriage dogs basked in the warm straw. The corrosion on the harness buckles has eaten through the stiff leather, and the saddlery could no longer take the weight of a man hanging himself. In a stone cupboard on the wall a dried out bottle of horse iodine and a blistering iron support yellowy cobwebs across the flagstone shelves where Brother Thomas kept his herbs and where, before him, Mihilanus kept his nibs and brushes. Nor does Sigerson ever come in here, although Ottoline does; wandering around with a slight frown as though she were looking for something she once left here.

Sigerson O'Treann, only son of Ottoline, had lived all his life with Mihilanus. He knew Mihilanus before he ever read the monk's letters in the flat, brown book. He had been born, headfirst towards the threefold windows, straight into the hands of Mihilanus. The lines which the monk had created and made material were the lines which had confined and supported him; sheltered him from wind and rain, held him back from the dreadful sea; shielded him from any illusion of personal significance or individual substantiality. He grew up breast to breast with Mihilanus, but without ever knowing his face. It was not until he read the *Letters from Coimheadach* in which Mihilanus mercilessly strafed every wall he ever built that Sigerson found his understanding of Mihilanus.

On first reading the *Letters* Sigerson was aware only of a sort of echo; a sensation he likened to watching a radar bleep yet being unable to determine the object causing it. But the bleep was not a mechanical thing: it was a human mind, making words which he received off the printed page. The fear he was aware of in himself seemed to rise back at him off the page from a great distance. For a long time he did not make any analytical effort to determine its shape let alone its source, until one Saturday in the summer of his Tripos exam when he saw suddenly that his own love for history might only be an alignment of hatred against Coimheadach and that his hatred for Ottoline was in part a hatred against her possession of

Coimheadach, the Coimheadach which somehow he knew was able to break him. Again and again he thought of Ottoline and her house and of himself and his living. And he saw at the same time the same duality in the revelations of Mihilanus. The hatred the monk poured out against the bitter salt place he had built became nothing other than the only way left to express, and so achieve, the consummation of coupling with its opposite.

Sigerson had found his ally. That which had been a fascination became now, for Sigerson, an obsession. He read and re-read every extant word of Mihilanus. He wormed his way into the words, the syntax, the minutest twist of expression, until he could draw up from Mihilanus an exact reflection, an intimate imitation, of every twist and contortion of his own emotions. Then, he discovered, he had a man. He had a man he could see and lean on.

This new alliance between Sigerson and Mihilanus gave Sigerson a strength he was not accustomed to. It enabled him to move among his fellows at Cambridge and even to visit Ottoline on the island with a knowledge that he was not alone. The partnership between him and the dead man was perfect: it could neither be altered nor interrupted. It was, by its very nature, indestructible. Dead, Mihilanus would not change. Dead, Mihilanus was perfect. Yet this death Sigerson did not identify with the death-colour but with the life-colours. And so, eventually, he saw himself not as a man with cancer within but as a man lifelike within and hampered on the surface by a skin of herpes or acne or Dry Scalp – hampered, in fact, by himself, when within he and Mihilanus were very vivacious and would continue to be so, Mihilanus being dead.

As his obsession with Mihilanus grew, he came to feel that it was Mihilanus, and not himself, who was the nucleus of his being. He came to depend on the idea that if he could seek out Mihilanus' final resolution to the paradox of Coimheadach and individual humanity, he would find his own resolution. He saw his inability to realize his humanity – as a layer of malfunction, as O o Dry Scalp, which prevented the consummation of his absorption of Mihilanus within himself and therefore of his acquisition of his own realization.

Ambivalently he came that summer to Coimheadach both to consume Mihilanus and to rasp off the Dry Scalp. It was only after he had arrived, to find Ottoline in the chapter stroking the leather column in the chimney in the dusty, unlit corner where she sat, grinning, stroking, that he had realized that he did not know whether he had to find Mihilanus in order to scrape off the acne or herpes or whether he had to lose it first in order to achieve Mihilanus. But he did know that he was afraid of exposing an entirely unscaled, newborn pink skin to Ottoline. And that was when he became really afraid, for Ottoline was Coimheadach, and Coimheadach was Ottoline.

Sigerson had often read how, in war, men lifted the finger nails off their prisoners to make them talk. He carried in his head a picture of his whole being emerged in just that mass of agonized, screaming exposure to the dank air of Coimheadach, and he turned from the sight in horror, knowing that he could not bear it. In turning from it he knew that he also turned from Mihilanus and another, less distinct picture he had of a Sigerson without dandruff or herpes or acne or Dry Scalp, moving without the distinction of disease among the fellows whose acceptance was as warm and enfolding as a well-bound bandage. And Mihilanus was not among those fellows, for Mihilanus was dead whereas Geoffrey Cudleigh and Mary-Rose Deckle were alive. He stood as if in a cage of thorns and all about him coloured birds wheeled and spirit birds cawed.

Awakening, Sigerson O'Treann remained for some time very close to sleep. Uninformed by the wakened state his self hesitated in some remote place, cold and colourless, which was intrinsically uncertain, as is a desert edge, a shingle bank or a fen; some remote, marginal habitat into which he had just come or from which he must immediately go. This peripheral zone in which he lingered trembled slightly as if to the sound of unheard drums, hoofs or waterfalls; a sensation which withdrew from him as he emerged towards the edge of the unstable state into an awareness of acute loneliness.

D., Geoffrey and Mihilanus, whose presence had been as interior and pervasive as the vibration, had either gone on and left him here, or else had remained while he, alone, had come on through this shifting place where shallow-rooting herbs flushed in blossom and withered, and insidious, proliferating grasses massed and crumbled beneath his tread.

His involvement in some vivid mystery, some immediacy, wavered and dissipated in vapours and eddies so implacable and orthodox that its passing ebbed in his arteries as part of the process by which dying is determined. So he passed on into wakefulness with the same organic despair and ease of all hopefulness, and the sharp sound he now made had the same unforgiving pitch as the sound of an infant born not in a bedchamber but in a hospital theatre.

In his solitary bed in Coimheadach Abbey Sigerson lay just beyond the reach of the glazed, sea-reflecting sun. He looked straight out of the place where he had been into the shape of the tense lines of the Directoire bed. Beyond the formal verticals of the bed-post, a city-like design of glass panels shimmered in the light. Behind the light lay row upon row of his books; austere, punitive volumes which he did not ever use, held back by the octagonal casements and miniature brass locks of the Sheraton bookcase. In the uncertain brilliance of the sunshine the austerity of the case and of its contents seemed to point the finger at his reluctant return from the fictitious night – seemed to settle itself more squarely before him – gangster steadying the feet for the fight. Braced, trenchant, the carving table which he used as a desk, the little *belle-époque* chairs on which he threw his clothes, the *chaise-longue* on which he rested his weak back, his own room stood ready for him. Waiting. After the vivid, absent hours in another place, the knives were out again at home in his own back alley.

Sigerson the Treacherous, cornered in his tenement, had his back against the Directoire wall. Coimheadach had him. Coimheadach came at him softly, outstretched around him as if for an embrace, but at each side of him was a knife. There was no one in sight; D., Mihilanus, Geoffrey were not here in this alley among the high, scarred buildings which did not trouble to open their blind windows or their maimed doors to watch. Coimheadach crept in. Somewhere a scavenging dog gave a high howl and somewhere corrugated iron clattered. It was dim out of the sunlight. Sigerson waited, with nowhere to run. Helplessness loosened his hands and his bowels; the footsteps of Coimheadach echoed sharply on the dark flagstones, whack, whack ...

'God, what a noise that woman makes —'

Ottoline malingered in the bed. At her feet and behind her pillows the wrought iron framed her little body in a crazed case of metal vines and convulvuli run amok in a seed bed of betel-dreams. On either side of her the bed stretched out to her west and east, comfortless, hard and without depth. When Pinell had been married to her she had been restricted to one side of it, but after he was eaten she couched herself in the very centre so that the tray of coffee, the whippets, the tattered thrillers and the bakelite wireless sprawled across the suggestion of matrimony and eradicated it as the hollows in the very centre grew deeper with time passing. Lying centrally like this Ottoline was equidistant from the four daughters who stood one at each corner whenever she occupied the double bed. They were attentive as only a hunter can be attentive through long nights; without strain. The daughters were there now, the Daughters of Morning, the Names of morning. They never matured, they would never develop into women, she thought sulkily. Coarse, raw, they remained as when they were first made-up, whereas she grew older and more careless. One morning they would get her or she would no longer see if they were there, but they would stand at her wake, one at each corner, burning like bier-candles: Los Millāres, and Coimheadach, Auschwitz and Liverpool.

Ottoline did not make any great distinction between bier candles, the angels at the four corners of her childhood bed and the Daughters of Morning. Nor did she make any distinction between the support and the threat which her daughters offered her. The older and madder she became the more devious such distinction seemed to her to be, so that by now she merely lay among them, cradled in their statuesque statements as she had once cradled them and her other, unnamed daughter, whom she had left in Nazareth House. It was as if, having held them all to her breast, having given them all suck, they had imbibed from her strictures' limiting factors, which bound them all back to her. None of Ottoline's daughters would ever come to her entirely strangely, would ever be totally alien. The stamp of her nipple was marked on their lips as a scar. The Daughters of Morning held her in their midst and held her jealously so that their own threat, stamped with Ottoline's mark, was at the same time her safeguard against the unknown Names of madness. She trusted them, knowing that at the end they, and only they, would get her.

Ottoline Atlantica reached up behind her head and her fists closed about the tracery work. The bed had been made in Spain for the Great Exhibition and brought to Coimheadach as a wedding present for her grandmother. It was of painted iron, twisted and convoluted into impossible mazes of vine leaves and suckers. The curtains which hung on either side were no part of the original design but had been set there by Pinell when he had expressed a right to sleep in it with her. He had begged Ottoline to curtain the appalling windows which humiliated the gaunt room so that it lay exposed, saturated with the everlasting sky and the forever sea, but she had refused, standing naked by each of the lights in turn. There she laughed and, turning her body not to the bed but to the moon and the seal's rocks, would stand there, night after night in the early stage of their marriage, between the grey, strict stones and the brittle little stars and the smouldering fire which her woman had blackened over with fresh turfs for the night.

Fed by repetition Pinell's jealousy had mounted as he cowered in the impossible bed so set about with metal creepers and fever-ridden vines that instead of the stateliness of fruition it suggested only the wild virulence of sterile weeds. There he watched his ungentle woman turn her body to the stone windows and the Atlantic. And he would turn away, not because he was prudish in the sight of her shamelessness but because he was afraid of something he could not clearly see. In a world all made of stone and metal, a world shaded in night-tones of blue and black and white, of marine shadows and lunar shadows, it seemed that Ottoline exposed herself not of her own volition but in answer to some call. As if something was outside the circumference of their mutual identity, on the very edge of the night. And when Ottoline stretched out her narrow hands to the mullions and her finger-tips began the rhythmic caress on the grey stone smoothed by centuries of touch, Pinell would close his eyes, afraid of that which was on the other side of the casement, out of his sight. Afraid in case he might one night see and identify.

When his degradation had become almost complete he had caused the curtains to be hung about the very bed itself, and he would draw them tight shut, forcing Ottoline, in one final, desperate attempt to drown the sea and the sky, into the black enclosure, as into a lined coffin. The scream of the rings on the rail at night were to her the same as the shriek of a closing lid and she would lie, sweating, her eyes wide and blinded by the darkness, cut off from the air, the sky, Coimheadach. She would lie, sweating, waiting for the nails to be driven in, bang, bang, bang.

Sometime in that darkness the Daughters of Morning had developed in her; Sigerson had been conceived; foetuses matured towards parturition.

'Through the long night watches
May thine angels spread
Their white wings above me,
Watching round my bed,'

she murmured foolishly around the cheap little cigarette in her mouth, considering her daughters, her Names of morning, while about her long lips curled a caress for the one most like her, Coimheadach, whose features were her own and behind whom this morning sang in the windows far beyond the foot of the bed.

Each window of Ottoline's room was structured with three lights; severe, grooved only once, very tall and very straight. Not drawn by the mason's hand out of stone but emanating directly out of the morning. So precise a right angle, so exact a parallel between column and column, that the window sprang from the inhumanity of the light it framed; of the light, engendered by the light to give form and substance to a sky so withdrawn in its infancy that there was neither colour nor texture but only light. Whatever hand had made this window had died of it; it had left no maker's signal in its lines. There was no mediator here; no man looked out through the window at the sea or at the sky, or sheltered from either behind it;

or drew shutters across it, or opened shutters from it. For eight hundred years there had been nothing here but the direct relationship of the light and the stone. The faces that had shadowed the glass momentarily from within had peered, and the eyes had closed – or slept or died, what matter. They had been transient. So it was with all the windows of Coimheadach. Neither creator, observer nor sufferer was involved in the relationship between the morning and the three lights of the windows.

The controlled light of this morning passed through onto Ottoline. She lay in it, no longer assaulted but rather alienated, the object of an action committed from which the agent had passed on. The angle of the embrasure included her in the light, but the angle was part of the formality of the window; her inclusion was incidental so that momentarily she existed as beast do, tight-bonded and self-structured, lacking that capacity for obligation which is the end-product of imagination and ignorant of interdependence with their own kind. Beast and gods and Ottoline Atlantica merged in Ottoline's mind, and she bellowed raucously for her servant to come to her with coffee, sprawled across her bed, posturing as her own disgraceful god made up of inferior materials – a cue for laughter.

'Aelebel!' she screamed, 'Aelebel!'

Coimheadach – Ottoline Atlantica hit out ineffectively at the ash-smears on the pillow and shouted the name around the libidinous curtaining. Not Coimheadach her brother, whom she strained against, groin to groin in the interlocked fight of her existence, did she shout to, nor to Coimheadach the old mother from whom it all emanated and of whom Ottoline never thought as she never thought about God or the colour of her own bones, but to Coimheadach the Daughter who led the old women with the potato knives and who walked with a pointed cattle goad behind them all. (Of her fifth daughter, the silky-haired one whom she had left at Nazareth House on the mainland, Ottoline did not think, now, very often, for of all her daughters this one was perhaps the least real to her.)

Ottoline lay among her daughters, awry in her head, and made no attempt to particularize the beings by her bed, being aware of them only pictorially, in a banal way – as they might be illustrations in a storybook, standing in their girlish shifts with their arms crossed over their breasts. After a while she turned away from the Daughters, especially the one in Nazareth House, and shouted until she heard the whack of Aelebel's tread on the stone flags. Then she began to talk aloud to herself and to Aelebel, seeing no difference between the idea of Aelebel which she was addressing and the physical thing which was struggling towards her but was not yet present.

'Oooooh, here you come. How you do whack at the stairs ... almost you might hate them. I would, bringing me coffee every morning. But I don't have to, and maybe you don't know you have to. Maybe it's so natural, like me cementing, that you don't see that it's a "have to", a chore, an imposition on you. So old and fat, whack, whack. Fourteen stone, and pounds of silver perched halfway up it, to be lugged up the stone treads not as a "have to" but like living at all, like getting dressed; we don't have to dress but none of us would not. I can't see Sigerson and I breakfasting naked together, and you dropping your tits in the devilled kidneys. ... Morning hath broken, Aelebel.'

'So's the separator,' said Aelebel.

'Damn. Why?'

'Why what? What d'you want for breakfast?'

'Devilled kidneys.'

'You can have an egg.'

'I had an egg yesterday.'

'Well, didn't do you any harm, did it? You can have another, so.'

'Won't.'

'Well, you won't get anything else.'

'I never have.'

'Never done you any harm. What are you complaining about?'

'The separator.'

'Bust.'

Ottoline pulled a face and asked suddenly, 'Hi, how old am I?'

'Fifty-three. Your birthday's in seven weeks and four days.'

'I don't want to know that, I want to know about the separator.'

'I can't tell you. You'll have to get up and come and see for yourself.'

'Go and tell Sigerson. Tell him to do something about it.'

'Like what?'

'Like whatever you do to broken separators. Like, like MEND it!'

'How?'

'*I* don't know. How would I know?'

'Well, he won't.'

'He ought to.'

'Why? You don't. Why should he?'

'Because he isn't me – isn't any of mine. That's why. And you bloody well know it, you stinking, black –' Ottoline looked wildly up at Aelebel and then said ' – child,' without surprise. Then she said, 'Sigerson's not my child – he's not, he's not – he's not, he's not – until Aelebel thumped the tray on her legs and said, 'You don't want to be thinking like that first thing in the morning. It'll end up with you hollering in the toilet. I know.'

'I hate it now it's been done up. I won't cry there – I'll cry somewhere else. Remind me to cement that drain, will you? Where are the cigarettes? Pour the coffee, lots of milk. Might as well enjoy the cream since the separator's bust.' She wiped her nose on the napkin.

'Bust AFTER this lot. You've got no more cream than usual,' Aelebel said.

'O, get out! GET OUT.'

'Told you it would end badly. ...'

'GET OUT. ...'

When Aelebel had gone, slamming the door behind her with all the force of her fourteen stone, Ottoline sat still in the wild, wide bed of betel-dreams and continued to talk to whoever was there. She said, 'O, hell and damnation – I want to be a person in a book. Here, one of you, come on and put me in – I'm terrific. I'm all made-up ready for you, come along and put me in – terrific, and a cue for laughter. You don't have to do a thing except cut out the bits that hurt so, because they don't matter to your story. O, do come and cut them out – someone –'

Down in the foul kitchens across the courtyard Aelebel stood in the dairy doorway, a monolith, her little eyes gazing at the separator. She did not blink. So hard and black a thing broken down! So smooth a black, so thick in all its parts, like a tree in a picture-book, or a penis or an anvil, and yet no cream out of it. Wonder, a wonder where the thick, spotted cream went? No cream for Ottoline today – no nourishment, no seed, no sperm. Nothing today for Ottoline who wanted the yellow fatty cream from the shiny spout and could not see that today someone else wanted it – would never see ... the bitch. The broken separator kept the cream back in itself, in its secret parts, this morning. Would she come, howling, and suck it out of the smooth, cool spout as she had once sucked from Aelebel's mammy's dugs – first, before Aelebel? God rest the mother of the bitch that she tired of her and gave her over to Mammy to be a little sucking-sister – hanging one from each tit with herself, like bonhams on the great clean apron. God rest Ottoline's mammy that she gave her to her, so, to lie on the patterned woollen blanket with her, wrap her, love her, croon to her and warm her so, down here in the sty, piggy-kiddies side by side all those years in the reeking kitchen. 'Ottoline – Ottoline Atlantica, my love, my bitch – ' She crooned the name as she remembered Ottoline's lovely man crooning it. 'Ottoline Atlantica' he had called her; his love, his bitch; lovely man that he was that summer so long ago.

O, she had told her it would end badly, that idyll of her loving; end in screaming for the cream she wanted out of him when he, too, had broken down and left her dry. Upstairs, across the dusty courtyard, she could hear Ottoline crying in the toilet; tearless cries because the salt had got in where her lovely man had torn her open. No more closing with her now on the knitted woollens; on the green and blue and red and yellow ribbing blankets in the light from the stove to hush her and rest, rest Ottoline Atlantica. Heavily, lumbering, Aelebel turned towards the sound and stood like a mother without hands who would pet and cosset her fretting child; this way, helpless. Then she screamed across the court at the other windows. 'Let her alone, up there, you clumsy bastard! Can you not tell the noise of your mother from the bloody toilet?'

Then she screamed down the telephone to Mame to get Rory

back with the old cow that he should come and mend the separator so that Ottoline might have cream, and she went to the graveyard beyond the eastern range and ran at the red hens out there in the dust, screaming at them for having little combs on them like a cockerel! Apeing the rooster, little red bitches strutting like little red babbies with a scarlet prick on them no bigger than a coxcomb and no more remark on it.

'I'm going to put Emerson, Boyd, Popplethwaite and Burbage up in St Ursula's Baun on the top of the hill,' Ottoline said to Sigerson. She was leaning her elbows on the sideboard, ignoring its obvious emptiness, and staring moodily out of the window of the refectory at the great court beyond. Behind her Sigerson slithered his napkin ring up and down the stained damask roll, as if uncertain of the appropriateness of taking any further action with it. He smothered a belch and watched his mother's shadow darken the dusty surface of the table. Here and there the shadow deepened to the verge of reflection in circular patches where dishes had stood for some time before being cleared away.

'There should be good feed up there, still,' Ottoline said remorselessly, sprawling across the cherrywood and eyeing the yellow stalks, dead feathers, dust-baths and rotten granite chips in the courtyard. The ground of the great court was as sterile as a cenotaph. She gazed at it through the bright lights of the refectory window. Diverted eddies from the onshore morning breeze trickled the dust about the corners of the gatehouse where the carriages now rotted and Father Gilles had died. On the top of Slieve Coimheadach there would be green grass even now for the four beast.

'You won't alarm them, Sigerson, will you?'

'For God's sake, how would I ever alarm them?' he said to her back.

These were the first words they had exchanged since she had come in for breakfast, scattering cigarette ash all over the breadboard.

'They aren't used to you,' she said pettishly. 'They might become alarmed if you suddenly popped over the bank reciting. Or quoting. They are not accustomed to your manner of speech –'

'My dear woman, be your age. How likely do you think it that I – I – will go leaping about on prehistoric earthworks playing cowboys or declaiming the York Cycle, and terrifying four – was it four? – interbred, large-horned, throwback male cattle? How likely?'

'Sigerson, who were you talking to last night in the slype?'

'I was not talking to anyone in the slype. That was not what we were discussing.'

We weren't discussing anything, she said in her head, staring at the empty sideboard. We never do. We talk around each other a little, now and again on a fine morning. We exchange some remarks, and some of them bear some slight relevance to what the other has said beforehand. But we have never discussed anything. What is there to discuss? I think it's a little impertinent to suggest that we should do so now. I think it sounds like an invasion. I think it's something I will not do. What a pompous man he is. Interbred, indeed –

'You know nothing about genetics, Sigerson. My cattle have to be interbred. Selection it's called. Selective breeding. It's great fun. You spot a trait and – POUNCE – onto the next generation it goes, reinforced, reinstated, redirected from emergent to explicit! I'm thinking of writing a short paper on the matter. You know all about how to publish articles, don't you? – all those historical things you are always telling me to read – I should love to appear in print. ... The Pouncing Gene, by OttoLINE –'

'Oh, heavens, you're not really going to?'

'Yes, yes. The Pouncing Gene by –'

'OTTOLINE, for heaven's sake, that's a Sheraton you are jumping up and down on. Stop it at once!'

'Or The Bouncing Gene by – no, that would imply a skipped generation, and I only got that once on the frontal bone by Boyd out of Flopsy. Funny looking calf, that, wasn't it? Do you remember?'

'What did you do – let it go?' he said uninterestedly.

'GO? Go where? Where should it go? No. I shot it. With the .22 on the edge of the cliff. The carcass fell over. I had planned to have some of it for dinner. To test out one or two theories I have about differentials in taste between entire and castrate flesh and so on, but alas —'

'Do you mind waiting until I've finished my bacon? Incidentally, who is this morning's rasher?'

'Bought. Purchased. At vast cost to the exchequer. I say, Sigerson —'

'I know. You are poor again. I can give you five hundred. I had intended to, even if you hadn't mentioned it. You ought to have let me be generous, Ottoline. You have never let me be generous. You always demand so that I can never give. What were YOU crying about in the bathroom this morning?'

'I wasn't crying. That was the new cistern. It sobs behind the fuchsia tree.'

'O, Ottoline. Why don't you tell me? You never tell me anything. Your only confidante is that dreadful woman. Why don't you talk to me? I could help you, you are my mother after all. I know —'

'You know nothing. And if that description applied to my Aelebel, I'll thank you to keep a civil tongue in your head.'

'So you were crying! And you do confide in her! Heavens, how awful. ...'

Ottoline put one leg down to the floor so that she could stamp.

'O God, O Montreal! Sigerson, I've a big notice up, here, on my breast. Can't you read, don? It says "POISON LAND. Trespassers will be prosecuted." And in very tiny print underneath it says — oh bugger, what does it matter what it says? I don't care. I don't care why I don't care. I just don't want to know. You may want to know, of course, but you'll not be told. The more one tells, the more there is to talk about, and the more there is to talk about the more there is waiting to be told. And I'm not telling. Not — mark this, Sigerson, set it down for your annotated Characteristics of a Living Person that you will never write — not that there is much to tell. Even at an extreme of optimism, nothing at all. Ottoline Atlantica has nothing to say. Like the sea. How they do write books and poems and make music of the sea! And what does it say? Nothing at all. It moves and heaves and sounds come from it, but it never had anything to say. All the vowels and all the consonants it has stumbled on since the first distillation of waters moved, and it has never said anything with any one of them. That is a great marvel.'

Then Ottoline cocked her head on one side and said directly to him, 'What were you talking about in the slype last night, Sigerson? What did you have to say, in the slype? What words did you make, what tales did you tell in the slype last night?'

'I tell you, I wasn't talking to anyone in the slype last night.'

'But you were there. I heard you. I do, after all, know the sound of your voice.'

'I wandered, last night. Inevitably I passed through the slype. Frequently when I walk I talk to myself. Especially when I am writing. I like to hear the sound of the words. Geoffrey Cudleigh has a tape-recorder. He "writes" into that.'

'And were you writing last night, in the slype?'

'I cannot remember. It sounds, doesn't it, as if I was?'

'It sounded like a conversation.'

'Who else did you hear? You must have heard more, your room is directly over the slype—'

'If I'd heard the other person I would not be asking you who it was, would I?'

'Why are you asking me, anyway?'

'Because I want to know.'

'Why do you want to know? You don't usually want to know things like this. You generally display the greatest disinterest in all my affairs that is conceivably consistent with good manners. Sometimes it doesn't even reach that standard, and now you are obsessed with the idea that I hold secret conversations in the slype at one a.m.'

'There you are. You did. Otherwise you wouldn't have known it was at one a.m. It was exactly one a.m.'

'It's a figure of speech.'

'It's the time that that nice young man starts the tunes on the wireless that go on in such melancholy fashion. Do you know, he goes on until three? Imagine it, three a.m.'

'It's extraordinary the way you listen to pop music at ungodly hours of the night. I have never understood it. You, of all people! Like a housewife!'

'But my dear, I AM a housewife!'

'Not noticeably, Ottoline. And certainly not at one a.m., or whenever it was. I doubt if you know what a duster looks like.'

'Vomit-yellow. I'm too busy earning our livelihood and doing the outdoor work to waste my time flapping about with a scarf tied behind my cranium and a bunch of dyed turkey feathers, whisking ash off one pettish looking shepherdess onto her boyfriend in blue. Blee-uw! Ugh.'

'Ottoline, she isn't like that.'

'Who? What are you talking about? What a PERSONAL person you are, Sigerson. It's vulgar.'

'Heavens! It's not as vulgar as making ridiculous remarks about the only beautiful young woman within a hundred miles of this crumbling – structure! And talking about vulgarity, what on earth are you wearing? What IS it?'

'I don't know. It was on a cushion in the cat's cupboard. Pretty, isn't it?'

'Very. On a chair back. It IS a chair back, you know. Not a waistcoat.'

'It's a tabard. I unpicked this bit here so that I could get in.'

'Heavens, Ottoline, don't you care what you look like? You look extraordinary. You always do. Why don't you dress like other people? In CLOTHES? Fancy coming down to breakfast in a chair back and a pair of seal rivlines! With jodhpurs!'

'The stockings are the ones your father wore to play hockey for his college.'

'O, him.'

'Ugly, aren't they? They won't wear out. I shall give them away. As dusters!'

'Well, would you mind doing it quickly, because we have a visitor coming today.'

'Hell and damnation. We have?'

'Ottoline, I told you. I told you in the drawing-room and I told you in the garden.'

'Damn and blast. Who?'

'Do sit down, I'm getting vertigo trying to keep you in sight. You're like a restless jester. Where are the eggs? I can't sit here all day. Where are they? What is Aelebel doing to the eggs?'

'Rhode-Islands've strayed. I thought I heard her yelling at them when I came down.'

'She won't catch them by yelling at them. They'll only run away, won't they? Shall I wait for my eggs or go? Is it worth waiting, Ottoline?'

'I don't know. It depends on where they have gone to. It could be six weeks before we find them –'

'Why aren't they kept in the hen house?'

'They got out. They lifted the wire with their wings and crawled out from under. Clever of them, wasn't it?'

'When?'

'One a.m. Perhaps you met them in the slype?'

'Well, I didn't. Someone must mend the hen-run, then. We can't have this every morning.'

'We've had it every morning for seven months, and no one has complained yet. I'll do it next time I have some nails. The hammer is lost, too. That's the third one. I think Aelebel takes them to beat her meat.'

'BEAT her MEAT? Ottoline, wherever did you learn an expression like that? Heavens, o Lord God, what DO you mean? Aelebel? With a hammer?'

'You are supposed to use a wooden one with conical projections, but I've only seen them in picture-books. My cattle are a bit tough, I'm afraid. We need a hammer.'

'O, my God, O, heavens.'

'My dear, what are you fussing about? One always beats meat out before grilling it. It breaks the fibres and releases the juices. The meat from my cattle has the most fruity juices but tends to toughness. Do sit up, dear. Have you a weakness?'

'Yes. It's brought on by conversations like this.'

'Really, Sigerson, you are squeamish. You always were.'

'Yes, I know. I'm sorry, Ottoline. To get back to this girl – and please don't let's have grill tonight – I don't know when she's coming, but it is today sometime.'

'What's she coming for?'

'I'm not very sure. Something to do with her thesis. It's on St Cyril, but quite what aspect I don't really know. She isn't one of my own students; she's Geoffrey's.'

'Is she dining with us?'

'She can scarcely eat in the cave! I thought she could sleep in the *farmery*. It's quite dry in the summer, and the eighth cell has a big table she can work at, and a lovely view.'

'Of the sea?'

'Yes. What do you mean, Ottoline, of the sea? The eighth cell has had a view of the sea since 1157, yet you sound surprised.'

'It's just that the sea is not often lovely.'

'Oh, come. When she arrives, perhaps you could send a message? I am having coffee with Mary-Rose Deckle and then I shall be down by the cave, bird-spotting.'

'BIRD-SPOTTING? You! You don't know a turkey from a tern.'

'I intend to learn.'

'You'll find turkeys behind the bothy. Don't alarm them. ...'

'I will not be looking at turkeys. I hate the things.'

'That was what I thought. I thought it sounded odd, looking at turkeys. ...'

'I never said I was going to look at turkeys. You said that. I'm actually going to look at the wild birds. The sea birds.'

'Very relaxing. I am going to cement the drain. I think we will have to abandon our eggs. Would you like some mince-pie?'

'Not for breakfast, thank you.'

It is as if we come to this particular part of the coast. Here there is deep water which runs right up to a ridge of white-spined rock where one of old Mame's family once set great iron rings in the cracks for tying up the boats. Behind the ridge there is a platform of flea-bitten grey rock going back quite a way, littered with old crab pots shaped like pillaged huts, dented blue and orange diesel cans, rusty anchor spears and the empty eyes and claws of shelled things. Father Gilles of Savigny, the founding abbot, had a flight of steps cut into the cliff which rises from the back of the platform, and it was up these that he led the column of monks who had watched Mihilanus set out in the black boat when Mihilanus finally went away. Once someone tried to build a shelter on the platform but it fell down, having no foundations, and only lines of loose boulders and the occasional living sod which has survived from the roof are left. It is as if we all come here, filtering out of the cliff and along the platform in a restless, changing group; edging among the old tyres with their frayed ropes, the jerrycans and torn red lobster pots. It is as if a sort of concourse were held here, perpetually, but shifting and without sequence. It is always cold here, among the pallid limpets and the carmine sea-anemones. It is never silent, nor ever still. The sea and the wind come between us and our faces, tugging and misplacing all the time.

The things we say and do here are very private and not consecutive. Actions and narratives are always unstable, for we come and go and return and find others, and some the same; the Concourse is never totally different, never quite the same. And it never ends. At all times, coming here, it is to the Concourse that we come. At sea-level, it continues below the life of all the rest of the island. All the living of Coimheadach rests on it; it is the substratum, and to it we have always to come down. In a way it is everlasting peace, having no consequence, no development, no product. When we leave the Concourse, separately in our own time, we come away always a little less quick.

It is difficult to be clear as to what extent any of this actually happens, or ever did. The only way to express it is to begin as I have done: 'It is as if. ...' This affirms that there is certainly something, but something other than that which is subsequently described — something with an alternative structure. I am not suggesting that Ottoline or I, or Sigerson, or anyone else, actually goes and sits on these particularly dank rocks and hears voices. Or that we imagine that the influences of our ancestors, or the reflections of their actions, are perpetually re-enacted on some ghostly or spiritual plane for our edification. Indeed, no! Still less do I suggest that there is a presiding genius who would inform us were we to listen. It is more difficult than that. It is, perhaps, because this west-facing shelf has nowhere to look to except the sea (where occasional seal pass like warders between us and any horizon) that there is no centre of focus except the rock beneath our buttocks. Our hot, personal gases and wastes sludge down onto it, but the chill of those rocks creeps up the gut from below into the profoundest convolutions of the bowel; seeps up the great column of the spine to the very base of the brain until the mind is resting on granite – directly on the mica, felspar and quartz. And that cold contact is my story.

In touch with my rock-world, with my personal Earth, my congenital substratum, I lose my vision. I am chilled into acknowledging that my prime need is to warm my nates; I have an immediate desire to expel hot air or steamy piss. Sometimes I do, and I am not offended for it is not personal. Nothing is personal except the granite in the base of my brain, and its route there – the cold contact of mind and rock which creates this liaison between conscious intellect and unconscious matter which I have called The Concourse. For the rock in my brain is rock upon which all of us have pissed, watched seal, prayed, fished, murdered, slept. Fragments of all I have ever heard or seen or read or experienced of Coimheadach saturate the rock which fingers the base of my mind. I would say I am the Concourse, but only consequentially and incompletely. Ottoline, too, is part of the Concourse, and it is in her, or is her, relative to my receptiveness to Concourse.

But because this liaison is only imagined – I do not really go about with a hunk of felspar in my cranium or up my arse any more than I keep fairies at the bottom of the cliffs – its validity is open to question and its claim to reality is a supplication. It is because I am so aware of this supplicatory position in which I, as narrator, exist and in which I, as myself, exist when I consider myself, that I feel this need to acquire and display so many facts; geological, topographical, historical. The facts are important for three reasons: first, because they may help to convince you that I am serious – that I am modern and real and have researched my subject; second, because they convince me. They all hang together and make a logical sequence, a pattern, a credible environment which I find very significant in my own life. So far out here to the west, so unimportant and uninvolved as Coimheadach is, it is sometimes difficult to believe that I am as real, as important, as the people who live in, say, Shankhill, or Shapwick. But when I think of myself as an animal fact of the same weight as all the other facts I know about Coimheadach, I can control this feeling better and give more credence to my aches. Third, the facts are important because they are facts. They are what Coimheadach is.

When I come to this particular part of the coast and sit upon the white vein of quartz which runs to the edge of the deep water I cannot unlearn the facts any more than I can disremember my father's face or the interval between Gilles' steps in the cliff. All these facts are facts; are this place; are me; are Coimheadach. I am composed of them; they are synthesized by being known by me. Ottoline, who is me, too, is also composed of them, as they are of her in her knowledge of them. They are as important as the names of our ancestors, for they are our ancestors, our lineage, in the same degree. Thick with the nitrogenous blood of my fathers the thin soil of my island is devoured by my mother's children, and there is not depth enough now to bury our dead —

II

GO THROUGH the morning like a liturgy swung up from the sea. How Ottoline could have shot the grey seal bull when his head was swinging up the wind, looking for the gun whose existence was known in his guts, in his head, in the massive brain that held nothing but the knowing of the gun and what it was for. From where would it come? From when did he remember it? Would he recognize the bullet when it got him in the throat or would he be Ottoline by then? Ottoline Atlantica, a woman who would kill and then be made safe again, back in her sealskin slippers padding about the passages and the muddy coloured flagstones, peacefully, with her head up. Ottoline Atlantica in the morning, when the sun wandered up the sky, pretending he had nowhere to go and no reason for getting there.

Is this the way of it, then? In which Mary-Rose Deckle dolled up in her red nail varnish to meet Sigerson for coffee. In which Mary-Rose and Sigerson heard a gun fire (only once – she's a great shot, she could shoot the angels off of a pinhead, could Ottoline Atlantica. It wasn't for nothing he called her that) and in which the Girl with the Birdcage paid one hundred and five pence to the auntie of Rory who was up with the cattle when he was rung for to mend the separator, and began her journey that ended in the eighth cell overlooking the Atlantic, having come between the carven gate-posts of that place and one of them lost altogether, which is a great mystery.

But it is not like that. There is first the morning. The fineness of it and the newness, although it is no more original than the Second morning and every one that has come up since. Then there are the mornings of them all. The morning of Ottoline, who cried in the *necessarium* and pretended to her son that it was the flush in the fuchsia tree that grows up beneath that window, spreadeagled on the wall and pernickety with thick pre-Raphaelite colours like the interior of Castell Coch or Moroccan red wine in a coarse bottle. Ottoline's morning fraught with hazard, from the grinning griffons clinging to her clavicles. Where they came from nobody knew, least of all Ottoline herself, and what dissipated them was unpredictable. They had nothing at all to do with her, being older than the time when she was, being something she was born to and had endured without comment or complaint since the mornings when Aelebel had plaited her hair and tied the chequered ribbons in granny knots that would stay done up throughout the tugging, chewing, twitching forenoons of infancy. They were a deformity of her loveliness, for she was lovely and had always been so. She moved in the surety of her loveliness, not entirely aware of it but not ignorant; certain, as a man with two legs is certain that he will always walk. But her gait was somewhere halted; it was not obvious, not immediately perceptible, but the weight of the mornings could on occasion be seen to be heavy on her shoulders. It was a flaw in her, a fault in the mantle that covered her, through which unbegotten distresses emerged, making a threshold across which she knew it was best not to continue. So she never asked questions about it, never gave it her full attention, never really gave it any expression other than weeping through it, because the things that lay on the other side of the threshold were not to do with her but to do with something common to her tribe. To investigate would be to scythe down the isolation that was Ottoline Atlantica's identity.

Ottoline had no sense of self-destruction; like the morning she went on, and it was a progress without definition. Ottoline was alone at morning-time, as she was alone at night, and at tea or dinner-time. Ottoline was never in company, could never be seen to be with anyone. Mortals came and went beside her, conversed with her, moved with and about her, but no one impinged on Ottoline. No matter how intimate the impression, there was no intimacy. No contact. No witness. She had no friend, no confidant, no measure, no availability. Except Aelebel. Ottoline behaved as if Aelebel were an extension of herself and had no separate existence whatever. Ottoline had never been without Aelebel, or without one of her eyes or a limb. Since the days when she had been wet-nursed on one breast while Aelebel sucked the other, Ottoline had been complete. She had no need of assurance, no need of conflict, no need at all.

When she went inside to fetch the rifle she told no one what she was doing. If they had asked she would have told, for she had no need of much secrecy either. She went alone to the rocks to hunt her bull seal. The urge to hunt, to kill, to spill the silken blood, was a thing proper to her alone. The slaughter would have relieved her, like Confession or sex, and she desired it this way. The seal's dying was as full in her as it would be in the seal. When the skin was cured – in the old way, with bracken from the mountain, and urine – she would make new rivlins and wear him beneath her feet, and she would make a jacket and wear him on her back. Since the seal was too far out at sea she loosed off a single shot in the outer court, a shot that richocheted off a piece of drainpipe already punctured with innumerable round pepperings, and whined into the dust in the corner of the yard. Inside she cleaned the rifle and then took the pointing trowel from between two nails in the passage where it hung and went out alone into the great court to mend the drain. It flowed out at the roots of the fuchsia tree that climbed about the pillars of the door into the refectory. The roots had dug down and circumnavigated the outflow, hitching it up so that it cracked, and the odours struggled with the still red perfume of the little flowers. Ottoline, who had no idea of sanitation, was not unduly put out by the odour. She sniffed at it, curled her nostrils and set about mixing the cement. The flow tide crept up the rocks towards the seal's haul-out. The sun shone on Ottoline, the grey seal, the pampas-grass in the avenue, the sea, the great cattle on the hill.

Mary-Rose Deckle peered through the looking-glass as if she would like to see something altogether out the other side of it. She was one of those women who are not vain but who know well how to generate vanity and use it. She could put vanity on at will, acquire it for an occasion, believe in it for a short time and then discard it as irrelevant when the necessity was past. It did not affect her, did not make her vain, in fact, but lent her the grace of vanity at times when she needed such grace. Mary-Rose did this with other emotions as well: with jealousy, courage and confidence, and neither did they make any alteration in her, except in the beholding of them by the person for whom they were donned. For Mary-Rose herself they were no more an integral part than a new gown, or a suitable gown. Mary-Rose wore Coimheadach in this sense, too. The skeletal pillarations of the abbey, the tremendous significance of the pineapple-topped gates and their everlasting mysteries, the rose garden full of musks and ramblers that filled the interior of the church itself, the dark slype that went from cloister court to graveyard beneath the room where Ottoline was, even the granite welled out upon the clays and shales of the plain – all these and the blank blank sea were for Mary-Rose Deckle a habitat in a frame; a defined, selected area in which to exist, now, by choice. Choosing, she peered through her mirror, considering which of her many women, which were all hers, was most apt for this morning.

Mary-Rose had no trouble with her mornings. She made her choice at last and thereafter was swift. Garments, cosmetics, appertainances appropriate to the woman of the morning were to hand in known places. Mary-Rose never rummaged. She had no need to. There was, in her house, in her life, within her, only Mary-Rose. Since her divorce from Fergus there was no one with whose pleas or laxative powders her tears and eye-shadow could become entangled. Things were now simple, defined. There was no allowance in Mary-Rose for anyone other than Mary-Rose, or Mary-Rose's apprehensions of another. Her life was condensed. She had never killed, beast or man, nor had death caused. She liked to do one thing at a time. A single shot startled her as she zipped up her denims and she paused, arrested, her hands on her belly, her legs straddled, her dark face turned to the ogee window of her bedroom, reflected in the mirror, and that was the woman she was, and that was her morning. A rifle shot, and the wary, defensive posture of the animal, not in danger but aware of its existence.

Mary-Rose straightened, thinking of crows and rats in the farm up at the abbey. She twitched at the feather duster on its hook, and a spider scurried sideways towards the fireplace. The duster was made of dyed turkey feathers, orange, emerald and maroon, the native stripes showing sulkily below the new colorations as it does in a child's Red Indian head-dress. She did not take it down for there were no fires in this weather, no turf-ash to veil the delicate chinas and glasses amongst which she lived, and she closed the door of her comfortable, carpeted bedroom and moved silently across the comfortable, carpeted landing. The house was cool and smelt faintly of the stringent white-spirit she used to clean her paint brushes.

These are some of the mornings there were. Mary-Rose Deckle's and Ottoline's, Sigerson's and Aelebel's and the bull seal's, and for that matter his cow's, and that of the interbred cattle up in the Baun, and the Girl with the Birdcage; Rory and his auntie and the gulls who had to fly away when Sigerson clattered onto the cliffs, they all had mornings, too. The same morning and all separate and only touching at marginal points. Like Sigerson meeting Mary-Rose for coffee. That was a very marginal event. They sat opposite each other in deck-chairs in the sun, watching Ottoline cursing the cement, and discussed bird life, of which Mary-Rose had nearly no knowledge and Sigerson none at all. Sigerson was aware of Mary-Rose's ignorance because he had a mind trained to spot prevarication and evasion and so he was a trifle disappointed. Mary-Rose was unaware of his acuteness and talked a lot. But Sigerson was not hurt by the ignorance, only a little put out. To him it only meant that he had to take a little more trouble with something than he had allowed for; a little more time to be spent, more reading to be done. But it wasn't serious, and his project was one which, if it proved tedious, he could easily abandon without any sense of failure or loss. It was a marginal point. It was debatable whether a knowledge of the contemporary bird life in the immediate vicinity of St Cyril's eighth-century hermitage would greatly increase Sigerson's perspicacity over the tales told in St Ursula's *Life* or elucidate any significant points in *Rehemagnus Report* – an ill-preserved manuscript which had recently been turned up during the sale of an ancient private library. The *Report* had, however, given authenticity to the dim old mystic, St Cyril, whose mournful life had, apparently, been spent peering myopically at the piteously few wild flowers to be found on the island, taming sea gulls and receiving the abuse of the virulent and better-known St Ursula, who had hectored her meek flock of nuns into early and atrocious self-destruction on the site where later Mihilanus had built Coimheadach Abbey.

It was none of it of much worth in a morning that went on, not going anywhere. So Sigerson went down to the cliffs, and Mary-Rose left her deck-chair and strode over to the place where Ottoline was working and sat on the steps with her back against the warm stone that Abbot Gilles and Mihilanus had caused to be carved about the door into the refectory for their monks. Ottoline sang as she worked, a harsh, bitter-sweet tune that set the ears ringing slightly, the words of which were apparently nonsense:

> 'O, the lion in the fuchsia went roar, roar, roar,
> As he swiped at his Mammy with his paw, paw, paw;
> The lion in the fuchsia went roar, roar, ROAR,
>   O, hodie!'

The first thing of note about the morning was its fineness. It had a lavish quality, like a *Te Deum* in full choir or a documentary film about whiskey. It stood still over the sea and the mountains waiting to be expressed in some medium, slightly zany, slightly psychological. The Girl with the Birdcage noted it with pleasure. She put down the birdcage on the side of the road and mussed the brown hanks of her hair to let the air in. The air was sharp and unsheltered. Some of it came from the North Pole and some from Boston. She found it exciting and wondered if there were whales out in the sea. The people of the house had no doubt much experience with whales and other sea mammals which she had not. Like the jennet. It had not yet occurred to her to worry about the jennet, although it perplexed her slightly that she had not been offered a lift in it instead of being expected to walk five miles with her birdcage and briefcase when the jennet only took her suitcase. Perhaps it was a short-wheel-base jennet and already carrying something else. Oatflour or goats or a travelling library.

The second thing of note about the morning was its newness. It gave an impression of achievement; of having done its very Atlantic stuff and now sitting back on itself watching with complacency. The morning watched attentively while the Girl with the Birdcage turned in between the high gates, stepping carefully over the quarter-circle of runner set down in the earth and gravel for the wheel on the bottom of the gate to grind closely through. One of the gates had got lost and, although it was nine feet high and twelve wide and made entirely of highly wrought iron, it had never been found. It was a great mystery. The other had given up closing because of the plantain that grew in the dust in the runner and because there was no point in having only one of the pair closed when the other was altogether lost. For that matter there was no point in any of it for the gate stood alone across the track which ran from inland straight over the runners and up the hill to the gatehouse without interruption and without being set in any indication of wall or boundary of any sort. Behind, the grass ran up, and before it ran on. So why this tremendous gate across the track? It was a great mystery. The new bright morning arched itself unconcernedly over the omissions and pampas-grass, and the Girl with the Birdcage made steady progress up the hill.

From the top of the seven steps that led up to the frater Ottoline could see the Girl. She interrupted her singing to look down at Mary-Rose Deckle, who was squatting below her, leaning her back against the warm stones,

'Oy, oy.'

'Something happening?' Mary-Rose asked, faintly excited by Ottoline's tone.

'Worse. Someone coming.'

'Who?'

'I've forgotten.' Ottoline put the pointing trowel in the fuchsia and folded her arms behind her back. That way her breasts stood out like a girl's and so did the tapestried Follies on her tabard.

'How can you have forgotten? No one has come yet. Is it the

name that you have forgotten?"

'No. I don't know her name. I haven't been honoured with that little detail.'

Mary-Rose assessed the tone afresh. 'A friend of Sigerson's,' she decided.

'I understood that he didn't actually like her. No, not a friend.'

Mary-Rose clasped her hands above her knees and picked at the threads in the denim. She hung her head so that the long black curtains of hair slithered over her cheekbones and jaw, and she contracted herself and her speculations into the area confined by it and the blue denim. After a lull in which she thought about Fergus and the clear, definitive mornings since she had divorced him, and about the clear definitive mornings of Coimheadach, she felt the calf of Ottoline's leg stir and tighten near her head. She parted her hair with her pointed fingers and looked out.

The Girl with the Birdcage had arrived at the bottom of the steps. One of the Girl's most obvious features was the extreme redness of her cheeks. After her walk up the hill they were scarlet. This coloration, offset by her machine-washed white shirt and the strident blue of the sky behind her, reminded Mary-Rose of a rude rhyme. She looked at the red-white-and-blue so vulgarly splotched before her upon the definitive morning, and cackled out of her bow mouth, stretching her long neck like a pullet in the dew. The morning sat idly about them, not going on any.

Mary-Rose said, 'This is Ottoline.' She imagined herself as she was; sitting at Ottoline's feet, her pointed face rarely beautiful in the sun, curtains of hair like blinkers on either side, captured back behind the long pointed hands, the artist's hands, with blood-red nails, long and pointed, and the long red mouth opening and shutting in the feminine face of herself, saying eliptic, puzzling things. She stretched out a leg in the blue jeans, so that its slimness and elegance in the overworked cotton might show. She saw herself a phenomenon in the lazy-days on the steps of the secularized Cistercian abbey. She was pleased with the image she made. 'I am Mary-Rose Deckle.'

In the picture in Mary-Rose's mind the Girl with the Birdcage stood unsure on the fawn beneath the grey stone of the step. The elegant woman in faded denims looked like an acolyte – an intermediary – a *miquelet* on the return road, dusty with conquests brushed off the Great Angel. A degree of awe was proper to her apprehension. The closeness of her circumstance to the other woman on the steps hedged her about with thorns of austerity and significance. Her posture was curtailed, retracted, vital. Little lightnings of possibility flickered in the black almond-shaped eyes.

'Little bitch strutting like a red babby with a scarlet prick no bigger than a coxcomb and no more remark on it, little red bitch; little red BITCH ... .' screamed Aelebel from the coops behind the *farmery*.

'Little red bitches –' called the strident voice, so far away, not getting anywhere, not going on any, for the recalcitrant hen was hiding behind the gravestone of Brother Thomas where she had laid two small eggs since last Saturday, and not a speck of blood in either, poor fowl, though she could not peck it open and find THAT out.

The *miquelet* sighed. Mary-Rose looked out of her almond-shaped black eyes. The Girl with the Birdcage was blushing. The extreme redness was acknowledged by the blush. It deepened. The Girl acquired a dimension. She could be sought out and hurt by the extreme redness. Mary-Rose noted the acknowledgement of hurt but did not really observe herself noticing it. It went down into her mind where things thus noted lived. It was a region Mary-Rose was unaware of. But every so often things welled up from it, like the granite of the mountain, welled and surged, and could not be contained, and these things were flung along the surface of her living.

The fearful personal insult ground down the Girl with the Birdcage. The voice from beyond the range shouted on at her in the fineness of the morning. It was incomprehensible, illogical, appalling and inevitable. She set down her birdcage and put her hands over her ears, where the balance was that had brought her upright between the derelict gate-posts which demarcated nothing to the foot of the steps where the insult hounded about the foolish morning. She tottered and teetered in her idea of the morning and lost her verticality altogether.

'I'm looking for Dr Sigerson O'T –' she squealed.

Ottoline sat on the central of the three milk churns. It was cold, small, and would probably give her piles.

Aelebel said, 'Get down off of that, now; it'll do you harm.'

'Won't,' said Ottoline, brushing her rivlins to and fro across the metal, making a sound like one she had heard on her late-night jazz programme. She had come in the hope of tossing the butter, but there was a hiatus in the dairy due to the defect in the separator. Aelebel had unscrewed the upper mouthpiece that should deliver the cream into the smaller vat, and was peering into the hole as if she expected to find something comprehensible within. Since she could not see what she had found she unscrewed another bolt and dropped it on the floor. It rolled into the grate beneath the stone sink where it would be found five months later by a ginger tom with no name.

'Well, Aelebel, what do you think?'

'O, you. Look, YOU, if God were my witness I couldn't more sincerely be waiting for you to shut up. You can't mend it; Rory's old roan is at the bull, a sight too early, in my opinion, old red bitch that she is, and he can't mend it. Stop yabbering.'

'But was there actually anyone there? Was he talking to himself? I mean, Aelebel, who could have been there? He's my son. ....'

'He ain't. Come off it. He's no more your son than Rory is!'

'Yes. I know. But all the same he IS.'

'Not to you.'

'No, but really, Aelebel —'

'Don't Aelebel me. He ain't your son. Not to you. Who else can he be your son to? So give over, get on with something.'

'Do you think he thinks of himself as my son, perhaps? Is that who he's My Son to?'

'That's in his mind, where it belongs and where it's staying. You'll get piles sitting on them things. Get down.'

'Won't. But looked at it from his point of view —'

'That's his worry.'

'Not going to help, are you?'

'Look, You, you don't care a fig for him. All you care about is him being your son. And him being Pinell's son. And you wondering how you're going to get out of that fact of life, which you won't. Fancying yourself setting after him up there in the hills or on the shore with a gun in your hand, are you? The way you set like a dog for the nuns with the girl-child –'

'I had to –' Ottoline said softly, dreamily, as if she had often said it before. 'I had to –'

'I know, I know, You!' Aelebel's voice rose into a high ululation. 'I know you, and I know what you are, and one day how it is this way, you'll wake up and find your trigger finger broke off and in the pot with your fine bits of beef for our dinner. ...'

'STOP!' Ottoline screamed suddenly. 'Stop your filthy wicked tongue before I tear it out for the bloody gulls! It's not me that's mad – it's you, you Black! It's you with your endless black talk and your endless suggestions. I don't want to shoot him, he's my son!'

'And Pinell's,' whispered the other woman, placidly gazing at the machine, talking now as if only of facts; not strident, just ordinary facts. 'And what happened to him? He got ate. And you chose him. ...'

'No I didn't! I didn't! I didn't!' Ottoline drummed her soft heels on the empty cans in frenzy. 'I didn't choose him, I accepted him! It's different, you fool. I accepted him and then he went away, that's all.'

'And left Mr Sigerson behind, in you, You!'

'O, Footboard –'

'Don't you be telling me all that again, You, do you hear? I do most honestly NOT want to hear about your bedding –'

Suddenly Ottoline sat upright, properly, and looked at Aelebel, properly, to impart news. 'Did I tell you? He's going to give us five hundred pounds. We can get a gramophone and some records and a new gutter for the Abbot's range –'

'And a new separator, damn you, why didn't you tell me before? Will you go and telephone someone to come and mend this great black BITCH. ...!'

Aelebel withdrew from the separator like a gynaecologist, covered in slime and rancid grease, and folding her red arms across her bosom lifted her right foot and kicked with all the strength of her enormous frame at the black enamelled machine. Somewhere a washer tinkled sadly on to the flags. Ottoline shuddered. 'My God, I hope you never kick me –' she said softly.

Aelebel flung back her head and roared, the laughs erupting from the great thick neck in breakers as high as a man. 'Ho, ho ho! Ho, ho, ho!' bellowed Aelebel in the dairy long after Ottoline had crept away.

The sunlight flowed in through the arched window, set low in the wall, and wrought curious colours on the flagstones with which they were faced. Greens and ochres crept out of the muddy grey, and orange tones like lichens, sphagnum stalks and feathers emerged and paused, as if at the threshold of a transfiguration. Beneath the sink, where footsteps had worn deep hollows into the stone, the sun caught on a harder, slightly glossy pattern. It was uneven, black shiny dots and sub-rectangles, glowing over a small area. Remotely it made the shape of the body of a fish. The sun struck a shine out of each fossil scale and the curved, smooth line of the obscure fin. The head was lost under the wall, the tail was not apparent, but the body, the centre-piece, was there. The sun brought it out, gave it substance, called it up out of the stone and the shadow. It lay placidly in the light, not far from Aelebel's foot.

There were other things in the room, in the stone, beetle's wing-cases, snail shells, fragments of eye and spine and the shapes of fern-like plants and curved, minute claws. A blue-bottle wandered carefully across the top of the tilted cupboard where the jugs and tubs for the milk, cream, butter-milk and butters were stored. The door of the cupboard gaped open. A spider had made a web and the beginning of a nest in the corner. It was red, and its body glowed in the light. The bluebottle was high above the spider; emerald, aquamarine, lapis and periodot exploded out of its wings and back as he walked in the sun. In miniature, fragmented and slightly dimmed, emerald, aquamarine, lapis and periodot glittered on the worn edges of the fishes scales, refracted and reflected on the edge of their raised surfaces.

Aelebel stood in the centre of the room, halfway between the fish and the bluebottle. Her fuzzy hair and the gaps of pink scalp stood before the light like a veil or a filigreed wimple. The heat brought up the veins to the surface of her skin, and traceries of scarlet, crimson, mauve and blue lay over her flesh, over her square, laughing face, and her oblong arms and legs. Her laughter filled the room, echoing off the insects, plants and fish which surrounded her, off the greens and oranges and blues and the sheens, lustres and matts of the planes.

When she had ceased laughing she left the room abruptly, and soon after the sun passed the window and rested outside, making long, tricky shadows on the gravel of the yard. When the sun had left the room the colours withdrew back into the stones and into the bodies of the creatures that were still alive. To the next person to enter the dairy it was grey. All over, it was grey.

In the eighth cell the Girl with the Birdcage sat at her table and drew pin-men on the blotter. The Girl always drew pin-men because she was not able to draw people any other way and she liked drawing people. She seldom, even doodling, represented anything else. She pin-manned an Ottoline, very little with spiky legs and five methodical fingers on each stiff arm-stroke. The Ottoline was little and angular. She made a big, curvilinear Sigerson, who stooped slightly as he walked, a habit acquired in adolescence from continually having to stoop as he wandered about the abbey, having grown taller than the height estimated for by Mihilanus when he had the doors built. She put some specs on the Sigerson and got the perspective twisted so that he looked as if he were holding a primitive gun to each temple. When she remembered the screech of the woman chasing the Rhode-Island Red in the graveyard behind the *farmery*, the wild squeakings, imprecations, squeals, yells and harsh shrieks that were all uttered on the same high scraping note so that it had at times been impossible to tell which had been the dementia of the errant Rhode-Island and which the ecstasy of the galloping huntress, the Girl let a large, ungainly drop fall onto the blotter, splat into an uncouth shape and lie, coarse, unformed and black, beside the spiky people.

The room was in deep shade because the only window faced due north, and although it was of astonishing proportions, so large that she could have walked out of any of the three arched lights, it only permitted a slant of sun to enter at morning and evening in the summer. Thus it was very cool and without any glare. An ideal place for paper-work. It was one of the cells into which the *farmery*, originally one great open hall, had subsequently been divided, so that ailing monks could lie in peace and be restored to function in privacy. It had no fireplace, and the streaks of fungi, weed and moss which drivelled from the sill suggested that it be uninhabitable in winter. Across the ceiling ran one of the ribs of the vaulting of the original hall. Because it had no relevance to the shape or size of the later cell it ran diagonally and apparently randomly from a third of the way along one wall, at a curious angle, and vanished two thirds of the way across the wall at right-angles to the first, and not quite at ceiling level. Because it was elegant, severe and smooth, and so much more purposeful than the later walls, it contrived to make the cell look as if it were lop-sided and unsymmetrical, whereas in fact it was completely cubic, and the rib was the irregular feature. The Girl thought it must have had sinister effects on any monk with a temperature over the regulation 98.4°.

There was a giant bed with a black iron head and foot, at least five feet high, and elaborately gated and jointed with arthritic knobs and gilded baubles. One of these, at the head end, was loose, and the sharp metal unfurling from around the iron ball it was supposed to cover. It struck out like a razor blade at the point where one, reading in bed, would rest the back of the scalp. The Girl had immediately wound elastoplast around it. The bed had curious sheets with a glassy, unwelcoming glaze upon them; surprisingly, when touched, they turned out to be thin and limp, like a rag. It had taken the Girl some minutes to realise that it was very old, very fine linen. The Girl had never slept in linen sheets, and the material surprised her by its floppy texture and chilling shine. On the corner of the pillowcase, also made of the fine linen, was an indistinct pattern, which, when inspected, revealed itself as a bishop's mitre, appliquéd. Having a persistent nature, which fact stood her in good stead upon most occasions, the Girl had untucked each corner of the bed and examined the corners of the two sheets. On one corner of each sheet was the mitre, appliquéd. Each mitre was slightly variant. The Girl wondered if these had been made by a seamstress, a maid with neat fingers, or some Renoir child with straw hat and plaits learning her skills in a bare schoolroom. Without, no doubt, a fireplace. The Girl had not yet seen a fireplace anywhere in the abbey and had a relief so great that it almost provoked nausea that she had not opted to come in the Christmas vac.

She leaned her elbows on the table and stared out of the window into the monks' graveyard. Somewhere out there, amongst the tilting stones and suggestive bulges in the grass, the founding abbot, Gilles, was buried. Behind it and directly opposite her was the east end of the church beyond the transept. Its beauty astonished her. More accurately, her appreciation of its beauty astonished her. She admired architecture but seldom for its own sake. The Girl dragged information out of stone, like unlikely blood. Shapes, forms, structures spoke to the Girl from buildings; ornaments shouted at her; sites produced an acute, observant look in her eye. But the information so granted was not of a pleasurable kind. It was accurate, academic information, supplying dated events and likelihoods; information about economics, laws, systems. Data.

The east end of Coimheadach Abbey was dilapidated and spare, the great east window above the altar being round the corner from where the Girl was looking at it. It was also apparently roofless and ended at the string course. Thus it presented a pure rectangle of stone and one impeccable buttress directly opposite her. Through the single-arched window which punctuated the façade, the leaves and three blooms of a crimson rambling rose silhouetted themselves against the sunlight which passed over her head but filled the interior of the open church. It was the astonishing colour of the roses which roused the Girl's admiration. In another climate or another district subtle ivories and peach, rubies or old golds would have been trained up those walls. There was nothing subtle about these small, crimson heads. Feral, they slammed themselves upon perpetual grey.

To her left the south transept of the church linked itself over an arch beneath which ran the shadowy slype that joined the cloister garth to the graveyard to the east range. From her room she saw the east windows of Ottoline's quarters which had once been the monks' *dorter*, and the outside of the whole cloister. The cloister court lay beyond and was hidden, but she could see the crumbling tower of the gatehouse and the weather-cock that had been perched upon the remains of a fallen pinnacle rising up above the roof of the east range. She observed that there were, in fact, chimneys set in this roof. They were empty of smoke, and their positioning did not indicate from whence they might proceed.

To her right there was a mysterious area where, despite no obvious demarcation, the curt grass of the graveyard changed abruptly to heather and shallow strips of lurid green and hunks of pale granite. The heather curved away and formed a horizon below which lay the sea. It was very blue. A light line betrayed where the sky ended and the water began. Just a line of light, indicative of a space.

Quite suddenly through the deep silence that lay over the pounding sensation of the sea came the sound of an exaggerated Cambridge accent yelling, 'You bugger ... you prescient bugger ... you bugger. ...'

Surprised, the Girl leaned forward to see what was going on. Her eyebrows moved up a little, and to her right the beady eye of the Rhode-Island Red popped out from behind Father Silas's footstone to assess the emergency. Father Silas, who had been prior when the cells were built in the farmery, had donated his illegible headstone to the construction of the eighteenth-century coach house in the outer court, beyond the cloisters. It was in order that her coach should have something to sweep through that Ottoline's great-great-grandmother from Barcelona had had the pineapple topped gate-posts erected and the wrought iron hung thereupon, one unit of which was lost, this being a great mystery.

III

O O DRY Scalp!

Now, how does a man with dry scalp come to terms with it? What does he DO?

Initially he is enraged and then he ought to come to terms with it. He ought to look in the mirror and say, 'O, o, Dry Scalp! Now where is that nice new tie I bought. ...?'

Lots of women have no horror at all of dry scalp. Women are not as squeamish as men. They accept things like dandruff and socks without the direct revulsion which men see no need to conceal.

Dry scalp spoils a man's beauty, and men have to be beautiful. Women do not have to be beautiful because they are, just as they are also revolting. Men are not beautiful and so have to become beautiful, and the dandruff spoils that.

There is no problem over how a woman can accept a man with dandruff. The problem is, how can a man with dandruff imagine that a woman can accept a man with dandruff?

Or with herpes?

Or with a job in Tampax?

What does he DO?

There are as many things to do as there are men to do them.

Sigerson O'Treann (he spelt it Ottraine in England) did not work for Tampax nor did he have dandruff. But he thought he did. He thought he had dandruff or acne or herpes or something like that all over him. Not in any literal sense, he only had to have a bath to observe that – and he was a pernickety man and had a lot of baths. But either just outside his skin or just inside it was this layer of disease.

He saw in his head a picture of himself. Not as he himself really imagined he was, but rather as if he were seeing it from Ottoline's eyes. The picture, immediately became ridiculous.

He told himself firmly that ridicule was only a nightmare, that there was no need to 'face up to it'; that it would never come and so there was no need to be realistic and forearm against it. He told himself clearly, 'One day I will invent some fluent verbage to cover any eventuality and learn it by rote. This isn't absurd, this is being sensitive. One must organize one's priorities. It's all very well swimming along through life with my eyes shut, imagining that everyone else is therefore blind. They may not be. It might be me that is blind, not seeing how much they can see, because I have my own, perfectly good eyes shut. I might need help. Sort of emotional spectacles. Cateract of the persona. But only one eye gone. The other is perfectly good; I'm sound in one eye. I glare, like Cyclops, at my mother. Ottoline. OTTOLINE. That's the direction from which the ridicule will come. Undisguised, unmisunderstood. OTTOLINE.

For myself, I think I can detect the first prickings of dandruff. There was a ludicrous advertisement in the Tube once; it said: O, o, DRY SCALP. It was of an Unloved Man. Then somehow, some day, Ottoline said it at dinner, looking at the crackling on the pork. She said, 'O o Dry Scalp,' just like that – not as a quotation, or a joke or anything. How like her. She just picked it up and warped it into one of her own comments. It's become a piece of her, now. A fact in her. Totally self-generating, that is what she is. And the thing was so pathetic; this nearly middle-aged, unloved man with dandruff – O o Dry scalp had turned into a comment on the meat course.

Carefully Sigerson had built up within himself a replacement for Ottoline. Dry Scalp was his defence policy against Ottoline; against his isolation from Ottoline and against his intimacy with her savage self-sufficiency. He came to realize that Ottoline, by her wild singularity, could, should she put her mind to it, force him to love her instead of hating her. Should she want to. He was unsure of her; he watched her like a cat, spitting at him, circling him, gravitating towards him and away from him, assessing whether she did want him to love her or whether his hate was less unwelcome. Lest she ever came to the decision that appalled him, the day when she would come to him with a white veil flung hastily over her tawdry compulsions and holding out that bloody hand for him to clasp, saying, 'Now, Sigerson, now love me. I command it,' he made sly provision, for he understood well enough that he would be unable to resist this tatty marriage of their bitternesses. So he had allowed the herpes to grow with him, a conscious decision akin to that taken by a girl who after careful thought decides against abortion. He thought that he could manage herpes better than he could manage his mother.

It was not long after this that his work had led him to find, amongst the haunted slim volumes of the Early Ecclesiastical Texts Society, the *Letters of Mihilanus*. Opening the quiet, brown book, translating in his literal, undynamic fashion from the sensuous Church Latin of the text, Sigerson O'Treann had discovered who it was that lived just inside, or just outside, the layer of herpes or acne.

Sigerson wound his arms about his head, crossing them over his forehead and locking his hands on their opposing shoulders. The ground beneath his body was hard and uneven with buried flags and disrupted surfaces that time had hitched awry and veiled, with thin earth, dust, sand and shadow where stringy grasses and intricate mosses could densify and submerge. The sun struck through the pillars and the two remaining arches of the clerestory and beat on his body with the rhythm of a heart; a drum; a blood-stream. He lay in a frame of shade formed in 1159 by Mihilanus, and he knew it. Directly above him the outside of the north wall ran straight across the sky where the string course below the clerestory remained firm even in those places where the arches themselves had vanished. It cut off the sky diagonally from in front to his left and across his eyes and vanished uniformly and predictably behind his interlocked arms. It, too, framed him. It cut him off from the sky in the west and the south. The invincible sun came through the columns and arches, devious between the stones. It ducked the string course and blasted in below it. Sigerson watched the blue blue sky. It had been blue like this since he had been lying there. Not sky-blue – as Ottoline would say, 'Blee-uw', like an insult – but hard, heraldic, militant. Sunset would not soften down through the spectrum tonight with turquoise, gold and tawny. It would pass straight into indigo from this crude intransigent cobalt. Lying so long, watching it, he began to see it wheel. Fearfully he eyed the rolling blue infinity, and beneath him the grass and moss began to well, thrusting him up from his right side, so that he was heaved, prostrate, towards the straight encroaching line of the hard string course ... The abbey surged up to the north and turned on its side. It rolled over onto Sigerson. ...

With a sudden cry he whipped round and flattened his face and chest into the lumpy earth. The giddiness passed. The motion drifted out to nothing. The solid earth lay still under the blue blue sky, and the framed sunlight pulsed in onto Sigerson. In the hot afternoon he shivered in his frame, and from a long way off the sound came of the Atlantic shivering on the rocks.

How Mihilanus had caused so strict and strong a structure to rise up over the sound of that perpetual grinding and erosion was in itself a miracle. The whole abbey was sodden with the sound of it. Every vacant space, every gap in the interior rubble in the walls, every space between façade or panel and the inner mortar, echoed and rumbled to the roar of the waves and the perpetual pawing of the breakers against the granite face that reared up out of it. It loosened the roots of the trees planted, and they died and shrivelled in the salt of it; it caused them to quake and to fall, and on all that hillside not one stood to survive to maturity and cast shade or shelter. Only the strong abbey did that. Only the strict, Cistercian abbey made patterns of shade to frame a man; like it might be the strict, straight bars of a cell that lay on the ground, or the retaining wall of Mountjoy or Fontrevault. It had always been so. Father Gilles and Mihilanus had made it to be so.

Tentatively Sigerson stretched out his right arm. Fully extended, the fingers came to the end of the shadow bar. Sigerson felt the chill after the hot, brittle grass in the sun. The physical affirmation of the fancy startled him. He stroked the perimeter, his hand moving to and fro across the cool and the heat. The movement was like a caress, and he turned his head to watch it. There was nothing beneath his hands but grass, each blade individually coloured, individually stemmed, individually erect. Homogeneity was a delusion of distance. He ran his hand up the stem of a blade, cutting it in half with his fingernail. It split and fanned sideways, unlike itself, but not beautiful. Bifurcated. Rent. Like a man must look to a salmon.

He raised his head and looked down at his legs. They lay splayed out in front of him, with obtruding sandals at ungainly angles, one at 80°, one at about 55°. They were not precise, not angled for purpose. He straightened them to 90° and looked at the upright toes of a corpse.

Into his mind floated a picture of the funerals at Coimheadach – the solemn walk, men first and the women behind them, the coffin and the laced priest before. He saw how at his own there would be only a few mourners; some tenants perhaps out of decorum, graft and curiosity, Mary-Rose Deckle out of inevitability. Geoffrey might cross over for friendship's sake. And Ottoline. There would be no one else. Like the man with Dry Scalp, he would look, mystified by his isolation, out of the wooden sides, up at the jaws and projecting nostrils of those above. O! How they would rock about, their noisy mouths shaking out the scorn and gaiety around him, their eyes wet with pity and hilarity, and, he smiled, not one of them as safe as he, in the centre of the laughter. O, it was all so harmless. So safely, correctly harmless. Safety, he thought. I know more about safety than the fire brigade.

The sun slithered away to the next column. It was not hot. He was not at all hot. Mary-Rose's room would still be in the sun. She would have sherry and books and that awesome, still home which was like Cambridge, or a place he needed, sometimes, to be in. He sat up and pushed his hair neatly over the back of his head. He rose clumsily to his feet, a picture of Mary-Rose in his mind, and was face to face with the stone. It was four inches from his eyes. It blotted out all else there might be.

'You bugger ... you prescient bugger ...' he yelled at Mihilanus, beating his hand at the cold, strict column, and his face twisted up like a fresh gargoyle.

'You bitch. ...' screamed Aelebel behind the south range.

IV

WHEN THE sky had gone from cobalt to indigo and vanished in the darkness that came up from the sea and out of the mountain and was harder than any mere absence of light, they gathered about the fireplace in the chapter as if it held a focus for them. The Girl with the Birdcage, being unused to Atlantic architecture, had interpreted the chimney place as an alcove or a small inner room. It was within it that they pressed. The mantel cut them off from the length of the room; Sigerson had had to stoop to pass beneath it. Within the chimney the flags were laid differently, in a transverse pattern, whereas across the remainder of the draughty floor they had their long axes up and down the room, drawing the eye along the major distance in great strides to where Ottoline sat. The chimney had been a concession made in times later than those of Gilles in whose day the only fire had been in the novices' warming-room, now the library.

Within the chimney the lamp was lit, but in the rest of the room the hard darkness hung on the stone walls and swung from the groined ceiling so that a tunnel of yellowish glow passed down the centre where the chimney lamp reached out. The dog grate was empty, its black grid rigid and uncompromising. On either side andirons crouched, wrought in the shape of stylized hounds. Their long noses hunted up the room, while from the chimney flue muffled snufflings and whines dissolved in the beat of the sea and the beat of the generator and at Ottoline's feet the two pale whippets quivered and moaned. When, periodically throughout the evening, she kicked their shoulders and flanks, they started and wept, and huddled closer to the iron hounds and to the sealskin rivlins that delivered the soft blows.

Ottoline stared up the room. She sat with the grate at her left, facing out of the chimney. Her eyes were blank, and to her breast she cossetted a glass of whiskey. The Girl, Sigerson and Mary-Rose Deckle sat politely on the wrecked sofa, fingering port glasses as a ship's lad might stroke the anchor in his nightmares. Boredom had shut them into their own thoughts; port had darkened their complexions and sombered their minds.

Mary-Rose had drawn her feet up beneath her and sat like a brooding bird, her long face bent above the emerald shirt and the emerald trousers in which she was so brilliantly clothed. Lace ruffled about her neck; a bright pendant formed in the sign of a Capricorn swung from a black ribbon onto her bosom; her wrists lay brown and slim like a designer's dream within the silver bracelets, and a diamond quivered from the deep shadows of her clasped fingers. All around her the sea air mellowed into the perfume of sandalwood, an aromatic oasis in the saline night.

Ottoline stared vacantly into the gloom which she was pleased, when in company, to designate 'drawing-room'. She was quivering within. As tense as the whippets she started and bolted inside at every turn, every sigh, from around her. The confusion around her was a double thing but so finely interlocked and involved in her that she could not respond separately to either part alone. Unaccustomed to being in physical contact with others of her kind, she was acutely aware of Mary-Rose Deckle, the Girl and Sigerson with that heightened perception felt by very solitary, or very old, people.

Sigerson, watching her for the first signs of tongues of illusory illumination like flames made of tinfoil and lit by a thousand watts to start about her silver hair, said, 'And how are the cattle today, Ottoline?'

Sensing patronage, mistaking despair for denigration, the warning lights switched on and off jerkily about Ottoline. Red, orange and mauve, they flashed and sparked radiating attracting charges from skin to thought and back again through the great flesh. Alone within the positives she replied, 'Peaceful! They are too peaceful. They must be fierce. They are without any incentive to ferocity or curiosity, mollycoddled up there on grass rich with the dung of history.'

'My mother,' said Sigerson, turning politely to the Girl, 'breeds back to what she thinks prehistoric cattle looked like before they were domesticated. The question that is exercising me is what she will do with the herd once she has achieved it.'

Great noises vibrated in Ottoline, metallic like brass bands and clangorous electronics, heating up the charges about her, becoming dangerous, giving off vapours of maña and seething ice, gyrating up from the cold flags to the silver visage paled in their obscurity. Did she not see them every night? Did she not know how they were, the moon lying at rest upon its back, couched individually in each pair of embracing horns; knee deep in swirling mists they waded from the drowned estuaries into her rest, with each certain stride more enormous, more menacing, more beautiful? All the sin in Ottoline leaned up from within her towards the swinging dewlaps looming over her, for behind them lay her self, her abilities, her dream, hidden by the bulk and beauty of the nightherds that rode her.

Laughing up at the sharp encroaching hoofs she shouted to her son, 'I'll tease them. I'll taunt and seduce them and watch them charge!'

Not knowing her lascivious desire for penetration by the pointed hoof, the immaculate pain of the dreamer dying in the dream, so like his own and so obscured by his own flesh from entering hers, Sigerson saw only the bloodied mother and the bliss of the other side where ridicule had a gravestone engraved 'Sigerson can RIP. Here lies Ottoline.'

Into the floating, discrete visions beating at the chimney wall the Girl said, disbelief raising her voice to reach the sane man from her world over the head of the shouting little woman with the whiskey glass, 'Why?'

Even Mary-Rose turned up out of her maunderings amongst the

grooved necks of embraced men and the perfumes of Arabia and tip-tilted her lashes at the stranger whose child-like let-off bolted through the fragile dreams drifting up the chimney. 'To create fantastical *trouvailles* in Sigerson's dusty skull,' she said crossly.

'It would be better to make them a little less fantastical and a bit clearer,' said the Girl sharply. 'That's why I am here.'

Ottoline twitched slightly and stretched out her hand in a convulsive gesture to the black leather column that stood on the table by her chair. 'Why have you come?' she said. 'What is your name? What are you doing in my house?'

The Girl looked across at her from under the heavy cap of hair and said clearly, 'My name is Dorothy Lambert. I have introduced myself three times already. I am here because Dr Ottraine gave me permission to come.' She stared boldly at Ottoline.

In the chimney there was a moment of silence. The wind sputtered a little eddy of turf ash across the hearth. Ottoline's fingers tightened about the leather and began to move slowly up and down, up and down its length below the white tip-ring. 'And?' she said.

'And I am writing a thesis – a sort of paper, you know – about elements of continuity which are found in the siting of monastic foundations. Now, for instance, here,' she clasped her hands and leaned forward in an effort to make herself clear to the two older women, 'here we have a foundation in a site which catchment analysis indicates is devoid of resources. This is very interesting. The founding abbot –'

'Gilles,' Ottoline said loudly.

' – yes – why did he choose to come here, of all places?'

Mary-Rose settled into the broken spring of the sofa and watched Sigerson, a slight smile as of conspiracy hardening her softly made-up lips. On the other side of the Girl Sigerson smoothed down his dry hair with a rapid, slick jerk of the wrist. He did not look at anyone.

'The island is a non-place,' the Girl went on, quieter now. 'It had no future then, it has none now. No way. So why come here unless there is some non-material reason. Now the only reason that has emerged so far is that the island is the traditional home of Little St

Ursula the Very Much Lesser and St Cyril of Coimheadach. And they were a way-out couple, they were wild men!'

Up and down went Ottoline's fingers on the leather.

'She was as crazy as, and he was a dim old father-figure who wouldn't accept the new dating of Easter! Whether or not the pagans – your ancestors, Madame Ottraine? –'

Ottoline acknowledged the compliments with a nod. 'O'Treann,' she corrected.

' – really lopped her hand off for baptizing their chief's son –'

'No!' cried Mary-Rose suddenly. 'How awful! Ottoline, dear, did they really?'

Ottoline ignored her. 'They did,' she said to the Girl.

The Girl laughed. 'Now you see it, now you don't,' she said cryptically. 'Well, there's no proof. ...'

'Perhaps you would like to look for it?' Ottoline suggested magnanimously.

'O, I don't think it's the sort of thing which proof is relevant to –'

'I meant the hand,' Ottoline said. 'They burnt the rest of her – she was a very bad thing for the island. She didn't manage her stock very well. Now I –'

'I mean!' said the Girl, looking hard at Ottoline.

'What do you mean?'

'The sort of proof I am looking for is hard. Hard, heavy stuff. I want to look at the manuscripts which belong to this place and which have never been published. Dr Cudleigh says they exist and that you have them. He is Dr Ottraine's friend. I am his student. It is time we saw all that material – more writings of Mihilanus the architect, perhaps even the drawings; the bills, receipts, perhaps even some correspondence about the erection and organisation of the abbey. They may not exist any more – your ancestors may have burnt them, too – but we want to look at the papers, to find out just what is there. They might go to a museum – they might be valuable –' she bribed.

'Heavens, I didn't know about any of this! Ottoline, are you really sitting on priceless old manuscripts and secret documents?'

'I am sitting,' said Ottoline loftily, 'among my own possessions.'

Sigerson said, 'Including Gilles and the saints and the fossils and the exclusive copyright on all thoughts or emotions engendered by this damn oblique place. You know, Ottoline, you can't slap a preservation order on curiosity!'

'A man's tenure of his place is brief,' Ottoline said, staring down the chapter, past the whaling harpoons and the gazing armadillo, 'but while it continues it is absolute. My fathers, myself, my sons ... Gilles. ...' Her voice died out in a whisper.

Very faintly, on the sea wind, the cruising seal could be heard moaning. For a moment they all heard it, and the hounding of the draught in the flue. The Girl looked quickly at Sigerson and then to Mary-Rose, who was leaning forward, her breasts pressing against her knees, her long neck stretched out at Ottoline and her almond eyes slit almost as narrow as a conventual grille.

Breathlessly Mary-Rose said, 'Why, Ottoline, you talk as if you were one of them – the same as them –'

After Ottoline's rhythmic intonation and the Girl's anxious tones, Mary-Rose's flat and nasal voice was as taut as an E-string.

Ignoring the others, Ottoline looked into the narrow eyes. 'Can you draw me? Can you paint me? Me, Ottoline Atlantica? Can you draw me?'

'I've tried –'

'But can you do it?'

Ottoline suddenly hurled herself at the back of her chair as if she would have it for another spine. She dragged at her Woodbine and glared at Mary-Rose.

'Look, darling, you know I can't because you always behave like a – oh, I don't know, but not like I want to paint you. You know that!'

Ottoline laughed coarsely. 'No,' she shouted, 'I don't behave like you want to paint me. Try me like this, eh?' She picked up the iron mounted column and stuck it on her lap, cackling round her cigarette.

'Gracious, Ottoline – we have a visitor – Ottoline, I implore you –'

'Sit down, Sigerson, you silly girl,' she yelled, grabbing the tangled fairy lights and draping them round the leather stick. 'Let's have the lights up – switch me on, Sigerson – switch me on –' She belched and reached for the switch herself. Yellow and green and red and blue bulbs glowed and illuminated her body. 'Try this, eh? Eh?'

Mary-Rose said, 'O, Christ, you make me feel sick –'

Ottoline shrieked with delight. 'Know what it is, Girl?'

'Ottoline, I beg of you –'

'It's the stuffed cock of an –'

The lights fused.

'Damn,' said Ottoline, ' – an ostrich.' In the dark they heard the thump of the ornament being set back on the table. 'A bloody ostrich.'

In the dark the moans of the dogs and the bull seal were clearer.

'Follow that!' said the Girl. She was laughing.

The faint glow of moonlight and ash-light accumulated in the chimney. The deeper darkness which was Ottoline moved and crossed the red smudge on the hearth. She said in a matter-of-fact voice, 'My husband, Pinell, you know, brought it back from one of his travels. I don't know what he wanted it for. He studied natives and so on.'

'He did!' said the Girl. It was not a question.

'Natives. Yes,' Ottoline's voice receded down the chapter. Her shadow moved across the tapestries and the dusty glass over the primrose jabot. Reaching the door she hurled it open and screamed out into the courtyard, 'Aelebel! Aele-bloody-bel!' at the top of her voice.

'Natives!' squealed the Girl, gasping with laughter.

Mary-Rose said, 'O, do stop it,' furiously.

The cockroaches, thinking it was safe, began to scrape on the stones under the sofa. Ottoline yelled again.

Sigerson said, 'I'm sorry –'

Mary-Rose said, 'Sigerson, do stop her. It's awfully bad for her, all this hysteria –'

'I say, gracious, o, don't cry, Mary-Rose, please, it doesn't mean a thing –'

'Of course,' called Ottoline from the door, 'they ate him in the end.'

'O, of course, Madame Ottraine –'

'O'Treann –'

Mary-Rose screamed. 'There's something in the sofa!'

Across the court lights moved suddenly. They all turned towards the window and watched breathlessly as Aelebel crossed the dirt yard clutching an armful of lit candles and walking sideways like a feeding crab on a dark shore. With her great bulk she shielded them from the gusting wind and in answer they flickered and streaked across the undersides of her flesh, highlighting her features in a style forgotten in an age of artificial light. Entering the chapter at the farthest point from them she seemed to bring in with her more darkness than her candles could dispel.

'Natives!' whispered the Girl, clutching her glass.

Over by the door Aelebel held a candle up to Ottoline's face. 'You should be in bed, so,' she said. 'It's too late for games.'

But after she had gone, leaving a cluster of light on the floor of the chimney, they all lingered on, settling around the warm flames as if pressed together by some element beyond them in the long space of the chapter and outside in the sea-reeking night.

Suddenly, into the candle-light and the muted howling of distant winds, the Girl said, 'Why? Why do you do it, Madame Ottraine?'

They all looked at her in surprise. Her voice was that of the university where Sigerson came from. He used to come from Coimheadach; now he came, definitively, from some other place. The alliance between him and the Girl became apparent and strong. It made a hard frontier within the chimney. Both the older women were aware of it.

Mary-Rose looked at Ottoline for confirmation. Ottoline sat alone on the right of the chimney, outside any alliance, that of the flesh which had tangentially formed in Mary-Rose's words with Sigerson or that of implication which the Girl's voice had just made substantial. Mary-Rose, sited outside this, saw herself also as alone and not in contact, even implicitly, with Ottoline in this, because there was never any contact between Ottoline and anyone else. To Mary-Rose this made her less isolated than she was herself, because Ottoline, so pure was her habit, was unaware of solitude whereas to

Mary-Rose it was a state or condition peculiar in its quality. It was this purity that placed Mary-Rose in an acolyte's posture before Ottoline.

Unexpectedly the Girl continued, acting on them like a preyer; harrying them out into the open so that she could look at them, examine them for her own ends. Or so it seemed to Mary-Rose. The Girl became a sudden source of danger against which they were all unforewarned.

The Girl was looking at Ottoline intensely, 'Why do you breed primitive cattle?' she asked. 'Why not cattle for meat or milk? Why not in the direct line of the economic trend? You don't milk yours or eat them —'

'We do. We had a bit of one for dinner.'

Sigerson asked, 'Had it — had it been, you know — BEATEN?'

'Thoroughly.'

'O heavens. Ottoline, I asked you —'

'You didn't know. You gobbled it. I saw you. Tasty, wasn't it? Rich?'

'Pungent,' said Mary-Rose, wanting peppermints suddenly, or milk.

'What sort of beating?' asked the Girl, sounding as if she regretted the necessity for the question but had to have the answer. Flagellation? Perversion? Cruelty to Animals? Would there be an RSPCA out HERE?

Ottoline said briefly, 'Before cooking. I breed them to be muscular.' She rolled the *r* at the end of the word, like a pantomime warlock or one of Sigerson's erstwhile villains. Her eyes flashed. 'MusculaRRR!' she repeated with delight.

'O heavens —' Sigerson said faintly.

Mary-Rose laughed. The Girl looked satisfied. There seemed to be no immediate need for subversive action against the stock breeders. She relaxed a little, yet somewhere a naughty disappointment unsettled her. Ottoline was watching her, the violet eyes shining in victory. The Girl felt the night that sauntered up from the flagstones cold around her legs. Little hairs stood erect upon them and tickled. The warmth of the port and the coffee was dead in her. There had been no invitation in the cool sensation of the novel linen, appliquéd with distant mitres. Bishops might sleep cosily in them, wrapped in the feather bed of the Dove, but she judged no eiderdowns of heavenly direction would cuddle her tonight. She had not seen the cattle but imagined a vast herd, small and black, standing in the eternal sea wind above the cliffs. The chill of their artificial existence gnawed at her toes, cramped in the open sandals. She wriggled them to bring warmth back.

'And do you milk them, too?' she inquired, politeness so apparent that answer became stigmatized.

Ottoline said sourly, 'No milk out of them. Only little dribbles. And no cream on it. They're not for milk.' Unexpectedly, she amplified, 'I have other stock. Beef cattle and milch cows. Pigs, too, and sheep and goats. But I have no heart in them. Like you said, they are not in the direct line.'

'But surely —'

'They're boring. They moo and baa, and none of them has ever tried to run away. I've never even seen them swim. Now Popplethwaite's grand-dam swam from Coimheadach to Cnoc Skerrie one evening. I don't know why. Perhaps a fly got at her, but it was a strong sight. The horns nearly got her down, the weight of them on a body not yet perfect to carry them, but she beached like a dream. We went after her in the boats. It was a rare sight, all of us in the boats, streaming out across the water after the beast with ropes as if we were after whale or drowned sailors. ...'

Withdrawn in the memory, her hand held her chin and she stared up the chapter where the old faults were entangled behind the swinging silks.

Sigerson thought: The inadequacy of the description! The bloody animal running away in the only direction left from that woman, straight out to sea! She only hit Cnoc Skerrie because it was in the way and she was in too much of a blind panic to see the damn rocks ... and Ottoline hounding her by boat with a lasso in her hand like a cowboy, standing in the boat, rocking it and whooping ... from the nursery window where I had bronchitis and was indoors, watching it all, horror that the old cow might drown herself; either old cow, Ottoline or the other. Muddled up in the fever and the fear of Coimheadach without Ottoline to hold up the crumbly walls ... out on the wicked sea, dancing in the yellow evening light, and Rory's father ducking the lasso and bellowing for her to keep quiet, clearly heard across the water and the slashing waves and the Ottoline who might die under them and vanish for ever, letting the abbey fall down onto my bed and break me bone by bone, mercilessly, and the death of the cow coming up behind her through the yellow-green sea, and the merciless rage and grief that would come up from Ottoline with the drowned spume and bubbles of the death and be revealed to me, scene after scene, breaking me down, bone by bone, mercilessly. ...

And Mary-Rose thought: ... like a Lascaux painting! The actuality of it! The primitive hunt out to sea, towards those frantic, pointed rocks, like a cathedral city, so sharp, and every CREVASSE WHITE WITH A DROWNED LIMB, AND GREEN WITH SEA CABBAGE! Straight and pale as the hunters who are never shown, an essence of hunting, a distillation of the arrow in the prow of the first black boat! No need to portray her, the image leaping up out of the association of the silver ripples and the white, straight limb-bones in the grey rocks ... the arrows of speed leaping back where the black boats darted over the shimmering sea ... would she have shot it if it had seemed to drown? Would she have come up out of the sea, red and streeling, tiny on the beach, the sea-wind in her hair, blood stroking her frail arms and slender shoulders, steaming in the sunlight on the shore ... like today, after she had shot something in the yard ... and I missed it. ...

'It must have been exciting,' said the Girl politely.

'Ugh,' said Sigerson, remembering. 'It was dreadful.'

Ottoline amplified. 'She was called Sugar-Puff. She had a tendency to get blown at the same time as Sigerson had a passion for eating breakfast out of a packet.'

'It's better than trying to get it out of a hen with persecution mania.'

'No, no, dear. You have an awful tendency to anthropomorphize these fowl. The hen does not have persecution mania. She is merely persecuted. She tries to escape. It is only natural.'

'I heartily concur!' said Sigerson with feeling. 'If I were chased before breakfast by Aelebel screaming that I was a little red BITCH

75

I would try and escape, too.'

'Incidentally –' cried the Girl, loudly,

'Incidentally –' continued Sigerson, firmly.

They paused and looked at each other. They both smiled courteously.

'I don't take morning tea,' said the Girl.

'Nor do I,' said Sigerson.

She was a bit madder than usual that night. She knew it. She could feel the distance of madness between her still-actual hands and the tiredness in her head. Between her action and her endurance of action. It was the flaw that showed in her features, the flaw that enraged Mary-Rose. It was a great silent space in her. Nothing that stretched across that space now could be a whole thing, only two broken ends tied together. At the moment she could do nothing about it, had no desire to knot up ends or over-reach her meagre power pulling at the two sides of the space. That could be left. In the meantime she must rest.

She was an old woman – how old? They suggested that she was very, very old indeed. Then no wonder she was going in the head. Ursula, of course, she had been gone in the head, too, but differently. Ursula had been red-mad; vicious lascivious activity. But Ursula had been young and stupid, had got herself talked about and burnt and made a legend of. She was older than that, and not stupid; only gone in the head when she had worked too hard.

She had outlived Ursula because she ate her own cattle and protected her house from the bull seals who took her mackerel. Except for Ursula's hand – the petrified hand that had held the goad and the child. The hand irritated Ottoline, who didn't believe in it, because it kept Ursula hanging around with dim old Cyril in tow.

Even the boat that served the island was called the *St Ursula*, and now, just when she was tired and mad, they wanted to write books about it and tell tales. It was true that her Lovely Man had written a book about it, but he had told no tales in it. She had seen it, a little pamphlet sold in the ticket office to strangers, and no name to it, his or hers, and none of their poems in it or the tunes he had played on his fiddle, dancing on the rocks, or in the yard or among the calves or the curraghs; no word of the terns that had baited him and stolen his corned-beef sandwich on Cnoc Sligeach, or the French letters they had made so roughly out of the dead cow's udder. No name for her, or for his daughter.

Ottoline Atlantica swayed with her remembering, brushing her cheek against the stone and the tales he had spun, surely untrue, of the strange creatures who had fed on the strange plants from which it came, all that grey stone. She had forgotten the names of the creatures but not the laughter in his imagining. She had forgotten the dates and the names and the familiars, but she remembered the tilt of his head against a flank in the dairy, and a year later she had bitten from his daughter's hands little half moons of nail nourished by the milk of that cow and she had swallowed them.

What could she do, now? What could she suffer, now?

Whether to be agent or patient?

An enormous inertia broke in her, widening, widening the great space till it was almost impossible to see from one side to the other.

Ottoline Atlantica stood by the window, dozing on her feet.

In his bed Sigerson lay still. His arms were folded above his head upon the pillow. His face was turned to one side. His eyes were open and he breathed through his mouth. His torso was spread prone, but from the hips down his legs were curled up slightly to the left side. He was very still. The red blanket that had covered his bed since boyhood was crumpled, and hillocks of frozen action ran athwart his form. His eyes were swollen, and dark rings of uneven flesh curled beneath them. The small ears were reddened where he had tossed his head, and a fleck of spittle ran from the right corner of his mouth. He was aware of it and blotted it irritably in the pillow.

His mind was totally confused. Sleep was creeping up him, numbing his limbs, so softening his internal processes that a minimal nausea touched his stomach but not his consciousness. His weight dragged his spine down through his body into the bed. His warmth cuddled him.

In his folded hands, which were at the same time above his head and in the very pit of his being, just above the tainted stomach, he held a glass island. The island was so small that he had been able to swallow it easily, with his hands about it and the sea which swept its shore. His secretions warmed it to his own exact temperature so that his awareness of it there in him was not sensational but rather comfortable. He had been lying around his glass island for some time, he could not tell for how long. It may have been an hour, or it may have been since he was about eight. There had been no discontinuity in his awareness of the island, and so there was no way of measuring the time elapsed. The shores of the island were crusted with spray and spume, ground and opaque, but the centre was totally lucid, and enclosed within its depths like coloured feuillettes in a paperweight, magnified into a still, coloured brilliance which no air could tarnish nor mockery displace, lay a hand. Sigerson reached down into the glass, and his own hand, as he did so, became minimized and brilliant, until, straining to meet the awaiting fingers, both became of the same substance and the same dimensions.

The fingers did not quite meet

A residual sourness of the hatred against Ottoline.

The fingers did not quite meet

Sigerson moved his head on the pillow, restlessly from side to side. His hair was damp and rough against his forehead and made minute sounds on the linen. He relaxed his neck and made his right shoulder more comfortable. He flowed around the island, circling it like a hawk, slowly coming down to settle.

Still the fingers did not quite meet.

Ottoline. Warily, he lifted his head. The room was dark. There were no clocks, no rustling curtains, no tapping twigs upon the pane. Four hundred feet down the sea murmured and splashed upon the ebb and a seal barked, a high raucous note in the dark not unlike his own voice. A bull seal, mourning on the ebb against the bitter blubber loneliness wedged in the fissures with the barnacles and the limpets and the salt.

Ottoline

The feuillette fingers were long and narrow with the sculptured appearance that lack of flesh donates to all thin hands. Deep hollows lay between the knuckles and the ligaments, and pale veins swam beneath the skin. Upon one finger a garnet ring set in yellow gold showed a space between metal and flesh. The gem was fractionally crooked. He yearned to set it straight.

But he could not reach the finger, the fourth of the left hand.

Sigerson unclasped his hands and passed the palms over his spiky hair. The shape of his skull started out beneath them. He clutched at the hard bone, cradling it in his own embrace. He pressed the muscular heels into his eyes, until sparks of colour and light ran about the line between sight and thought and transfixed him. He jerked his head away and turned on his back.

Oh God, I hate you. WHY, Ottoline, why? Why? Why?

There was no answer to this question. There had never been any possible answer to it. Ottoline was impervious to questioning. In any case, he never asked her, only himself.

Sigerson lay in the dark, and the perfect prison contained him.

She was capable of every degree of murder. She was small and black, like her peasant and her own mind. She was as mean as the saints, as harsh as they, as faultless in her impeccable surety.

She was a murderer. A line of deaths stood at her hand; some real, some not so real. Like the seal and the hunted cattle, or his father and the mythical lover of her girlhood. What had she done to him? Driven him over the cliffs or sent him mad or taken away his dreams? 'He who stealeth dreams is accursed.' Certainly she had killed him. He had heard how she had killed his father.

Sigerson twitched in the bed. His legs bolted under him. He sat up and could not see. When he lit the candle the room cowered under the light. It wavered in the ceiling and along the bookcases, it deepened the carpet, it flowered in the still ink-stand like the jet flowerets of death in the glass domes. ...

He walked over to his desk. The information on it was false. It was only relevant to Ottoline. It belonged to Ottoline. He hitched his pyjamas and sniffed. He might have been crying.

Where he stood now, looking out over the ruins of the west range Mihilanus must have stood looking, too, at the west range rising inexorably from the builder's rubble. The sea whispered and wapped at the rocks, dashed with starlight, scoured by the everlasting whining wind from the west. The ceiling that Mihilanus had built gripped the vacancy above his head. God help the poor lost devil writhing in the eternal perdition of choice, have mercy on his soul. More mercy than Coimheadach would ever show.

Poor Mihilanus! Sigerson stared grimly at the typed sheets and shivered in his striped pyjamas. O o Dry Scalp. How much of Sigerson was there, glaring out of the type, grey with a dying ribbon, posing itself as History, whatever that might be; and as Mihilanus, whoever he was. Scorched soul indeed! This was the mechanic of civilisation; these scorched souls were the ones that made the wheels go round, as the saying went, and it was the historians, as Sigerson knew as well as any other, who directed the wheels. For there is no more hindsight than foresight.

He could not see Mihilanus in any other setting than that of the prison/sanctuary which he, Sigerson, had made of Mihilanus' abbey. Clamped inexorably in Grace, trapped flailing like a moth under a sieve in the benefaction of sanctity, as he Sigerson thrashed under the protection and custody of Ottoline within the same walls. As far as Gilles had ordained that those walls should rise to entrap Mihilanus, so did Ottoline support them now, both to enfold him and to crash down upon him. His hatred of Ottoline was partly based on his own awareness that once he lost her, whether physically, as he had feared as a boy, or emotionally by ceasing to hate her, the greater share of his portion of human response would be amputated. So it was that on nights like these, perched among the barbarous walls, redolent with extinction and failure, he would whip up his fury and his fear, twisting Ottoline around him like a dying man cowering in the warmth of his own shroud.

Images of death came easily to Sigerson. His infancy had been passed among the harmless fossils whose living descendants paralysed him with fear – spiders made his spine crawl, lobsters made him retch and sweat, the great, ponderous clawing dangers in the rough featureless shells, studded with sea minutiae, alien, meaningless and terrible. Thrashing fish in the casies whose convulsions flung them witless against the dry heather creels, small birds trapped in unpredictable violent spasms in the dark ceilings, sudden frogs and toads, hideous beyond nightmare – all these things had streaked the years with episodes of horror, and only among the traceries in the walls, the safely dead, the harmless, predictably silent dead, had been an assured safety from the sudden terrors.

Sigerson embraced history as a schoolboy with a passion and a single-mindedness that had eventually made a scholar out of him and which kept him safely out of the reach of the wayward living.

But Ottoline. He had to have Ottoline. He had to have her. Ottoline was his humanity. He knew this. His passion for Ottoline was too old, too bitter, to die out. Ottoline's ferocity, Ottoline's meanness, Ottoline's blind savagery, were the same as the vrump of the lobster's claws. Ottoline was alive. Ottoline was real. Her blind selfishness made her unpredictable to him, and because unpredictable, therefore overwhelmingly, gloriously alive. Not all Sigerson's dead men had always been dead. They had, after all, suffered humanity, and for their sakes Sigerson suffered Ottoline.

He clutched Ottoline in the name of reality. She was at once the most intimate and the most terrible reality of all, a totally human idea at whose poisonous dugs he had dredged his life. He often dreamed that he had grown premature teeth to bite them off with. He was ashamed of this. But still the sour milk he had imbibed had been blood hot, and he used the ferocity of his attachment to her to keep him warm in the cold, dark world he had bolted into and which, at times, numbed and tugged like the ebbing tide on the rocks below. At night, during nights like this, Sigerson was afraid. Only Ottoline stood between him and the waste infinity of unreality.

Ottoline, OTTOLINE, Ottoline. ...

Thinking of her suddenly, actually, asleep in her great four-poster as she must be, in the curtained, bedraggled sluttishness of her bedroom life which had so alarmed and repelled him as a child, he felt cold and immeasurably lonely. She had come between him and the hermitage of his mind; she stood like a taunting militant outside the cave of his rest. He had nowhere to retire to. It was cold, outside. ... Carefully he bent and put on his bedroom slippers. They were brown check, and each slipper had a little brown bobble sewn on the top. The bobbles dotted and wobbled as he walked down the great flagged stair and out of the main door. Across the garth he could see a light in the kitchen window. It was golden and like something out of a child's Christmas. He stopped on the gravel and stared at it. The tall windows, crossed with stone traceries, were as pure in form as when Mihilanus had designed them. Darkness took away the chips and cracks, the straggly fuchsia, the ill-fitting glass. He stood at the window of a world which was his own, in which he was as familiar as any man who by right had walked towards it for six hundred years. His mind filled with sudden love; sudden identity with the candle light and the stone, with the high silhouette of the roof above and the wide, star-blessed sky. The sea murmured and sang, the wind whispered among the stones; the air was warm, idle, at rest. Certain of his welcome he moved to the door of his home. He had been away, he had spent a prodigal youth six centuries long — home was within reach of his hand raised to the latch.

There were tears on his cheeks when he entered the room, a tall man with dry hair, adrift on a dream. ...

'Good evening,' he said ludicrously.

The black peasant looked up at him calmly. As if expecting him, as he was, out of his dreams, she half-rose and settled back in her chair.

Sigerson moved towards her, holding out his hands as if she might take them in hers. 'Help me. ...' he said, so softly that she did not appear to hear.

He crossed to the fireplace and crouched at her feet. He shivered in his pyjamas and huddled into his own arms. The warm air of outside that had embraced him momentarily was gone, and the heat from the smouldering turf was chill in contrast. The glow and flames nagged at the turf, exposing shreds and stems of heather and moss, minutiae of ancient footprints that had once crushed it, the cast of resting bodies that once slept on its gentle surface. Shadows of clouds and birds settled in the white flaky ash; reflections which had gleamed on pools glowed in the fire's heart and the heat of old hearts drifted out into the night on its perfume. Dead, dead for five millennia. So much time drifted into the chimney. Time without scale, without inheritance. Time unacknowledged.

Aelebel said, 'Mr Sigerson?'

'It's all right, Aelebel. I'm awake. I'm not sleep-walking. I saw the light, and I came in. I thought it might have been someone else. ...'

'Your mother is in bed. ... There is no one else of yours out now.'

'Of mine? What do you mean, of mine?'

Aelebel shrugged. Her flat face expressed disinterest in his question. In her hands she held a long spurtle with which she was stirring something odorous and meaty in the pot, a riveted cauldron affair which sat on tripod legs over the fire. Sigerson remembered the bran mashes for his mother's horses being stirred in that pot, suffusing the house with the heavy, costive stench of hot stout, eggs and boiling bran. He remembered, too, standing eternally at the Chapter windows waiting for her to come back, in case she did not come back, his eyes huge with freedom and his knees weak with the horror of what he desired and did not desire. ... Honour thy Father and Mother that thy days may be long ... and the sudden death, always always in the grey sea among the cold fossil fishes and the wrack and the everlasting wind that lurked behind the walls of his dreams, the immutable answer as consecutive as butterfly to chrysalis and as beautiful in its simplicity. It seemed to him suddenly as if Aelebel held all those past dreams in her rough hands, as lightly as the spurtle. The hands were plump, not with fat but with age and old muscle. The nails were flecked with white as if too much had been given out of the body, as a pregnant girl's nails fleck and streak with lack as the voracious foetus grows. What foetus gnawed at Aelebel? The idea made him shudder, and he stooped so that the nausea on his face might be hidden. But Aelebel was looking in the cauldron. She was dealing with his old dreams dexterously, stirring and weaving them into eddies of pungent steam about his nostrils, mingling them with his present fears and his sleep-craving eyes.

'For heaven's sake,' he said irritably, 'what's in that Iron Age relic?'

'Bones.'

'Bones, bones? Goodness, what for?'

'Your mother wants them. She boils the flesh off of the old cattle and takes the clean bones away. I wouldn't know what for. The hens eat the pickings.'

'She takes the bones? Ottoline goes off with bundles of bones? What does she do with them?'

'I tell you, I don't know.'

Aelebel didn't look at him. Her face was bent over the crass iron pot. Sweat ran in little trickles down her creased, shiny brow. It fell into the pot, to seethe and bubble in the geysers of memory. The balding eyebrows failed to entrap the drops, and their passage over Aelebel's eyelids made her blink as if she had a twitch. The turf fire etched out her features, such as they were, making hooks of the small, pointed nose, the spade-like chin, the flat cheekbones and flat brows. Her straggly hair, half-brown still, half-grey, twisted about her ears and neck as if tortured by fire into that shape. Burned out girders and scorched curling papers hovered in the tormented screws.

It came into his mind that anyone else, from outside Coimheadach, would see them as a conversation piece – witch and client – and he wanted to laugh, suddenly. How would they appear to Geoffrey, with his mania for comfort; Geoffrey who would not know how to light a Tilly-lamp, much less be induced to do so; Geoffrey with his collection of eighteenth-century toy musical boxes whose rooms were a moving spindle of chimes and fairy tunes, for ever mobile, for ever exquisite, eternally fatuous. Geoffrey who complained so petulantly that Sigerson should work in such barbarous times, who moved behind his golden velvet curtains and his elegant phrases, hidden in a toy world of embroidered waistcoats and Chinese innuendo.

When they spent an evening together it was always in Geoffrey's rooms, for he could not bear to be exposed to the discomforts of Sigerson's moulting chairs and popping gas fire. Moreover, whilst Sigerson always had plenty of reputable alcohol from the college cellar he had nothing much in the way of an aesthetic treat to drink it out of, and this Geoffrey resented. His ring, he claimed, looked like a Woolworth's display upon Sigerson's modern glass, whereas upon his own very fine London cut it appeared to be what in fact it was, a thing of brilliant worth.

Sigerson indulged Geoffrey's luxury without demur, for in his eyes there was one thing which saved Geoffrey from ridicule. One evening when they were going to the theatre together, Sigerson had been with Geoffrey when he had retired to the bedroom to change his tie, and Sigerson, glancing through the open door, had seen beside Geoffrey's bed a large low table, spread with meticulously deployed toy soldiers. Curiosity had brought him into the room, and Geoffrey, watching him through the mirror had said laconically, 'Malplaquet. Battle of.' Nonetheless, Geoffrey had coloured slightly under Sigerson's smile. 'I play with them,' he had said lightly.

Sigerson questioned this, 'Play?'

Geoffrey's throat had moved, either under the question or the exquisite nature of the flowing knot.

'I replay the great battles, with toy soldiers.' He had stopped and looked at Sigerson, anticipating the mockery which was not there. Reassured, he said, 'At first it was a game; megalomania or something turned into harmless Children's Hour incidents before sleeping. Then I thought if I studied carefully like a military historian would study all the emergencies, all the shocks and contingencies of that calibre of battle, the happy jettisoning of life after life, of limbs, precedents and plans, I might come nearer to understanding how the men's minds worked. By their reactions, you know? When the same men who fought were also politicians, it seemed like a revealing bit of pop psychology.'

'And does it work?'

'I don't think so! I've never held a gun in my life; Pay Corps in Wiltshire was the full extent of my Army years. It doesn't mean a thing to me, all this blood and guts. Even in play time.'

He dismissed the subject lightly, but on the next occasion when Sigerson had caught a glimpse of the bedside table the soldiers were in different order. Geoffrey, seeing him look, had said gently, 'It's a harmless fantasy. We all have fantasies, don't we, Sigerson?'

And Sigerson had felt himself silently looking at Geoffrey like a dumb, brown ox. He had said nothing. He felt nothing. He thought of Mihilanus and said nothing.

Aelebel's murmured words about someone 'of his own' had automatically called Geoffrey up in his mind, and Geoffrey's imagined reaction to the pretty piece entitled Witch and Client.

Geoffrey in the room with them made Sigerson nervous and sceptical at the same time. He had a highly developed sense of the ridiculous which he used like a flagellant's cat-o'-nine-tails, and he drew on it now to save more serious embarrassments from becoming conscious. He did not want to consider how much he desired to put his head on Aelebel's smelly apron and be stroked like a little boy. So he scrambled to his feet and prepared to seat himself augustly by the fire to draw a curtain over the sentimental picture, but could find nothing better than an old three-legged milking stool. Its total height was about forty centimetres.

'Goodness, do you have enough furniture in here? Would you like me to find you another comfortable chair, or a sofa?'

Aelebel indicated the enormous hooded seat within which even her amplitude was housed with facility, and at the same time she conveyed to Sigerson the impression that any one else in her kitchen was adequately provided for by the stool, hierarchies of some significance thus being unmistakably expressed. It was some years since Sigerson had sat at the feet of Gamaliel, and when he had that Personage had not stunk of bones with an undertow of herring guts. He positioned himself carefully, drawing the gaping fly in his pyjamas studiously between his crossed thighs. Aelebel sniggered. Sigerson retracted with a scalding blush and glared at her. ...

'Would you ever be imagining that this wee bone would be the tail of that great beast Rabellay — seems almost rude to it, don't it, Mr Sigerson?'

'Rabelais? O, o most absurd, was it really? What happened to him?' Sigerson felt the crimson withdraw down his throat like hot water streaming off after a shower. He shivered again.

'Your mother shot him up in Ursula's Baun a week or so ago. He'd lost interest, and she has a better bull in Popplethwaite, she says.'

Aelebel held up the boiled caudal vertebra of the great bull and looked at it. Sigerson fleshed it and saw the tuft of coarse hair; felt the whip of it and the lash of the ligaments as taut as piano wires. The bone encircled the point of the spurtle; drops splatted back into the pot, from its intricate striations. Sigerson knew that he would never partake of oxtail soup again.

'Where did she shoot it?' he asked anxiously.

'In the Baun, I said.'

'No, no, where in the animal?'

Aelebel stooped and grunted. From the dusty hearth she picked up a misshapen glob of dull metal and held it out to him. It was flattened at one end as is the world.

'Fell out with the brains,' said she laconically.

Sigerson looked at the metal world that had dropped out of the bull's brain. He said, 'My mother kills a great many things. ...'

Aelebel dropped the bone back into the pot. It vanished beneath the scum and breaking bubbles.

Sigerson took the bullet from her and put it in his pocket. 'Why does she kill so much?' he asked. The tone of his voice had changed from the dreamy introspection of his remark into a sudden, conscious questioning.

Aelebel noted the change, and her eyes dropped so that she did not look at him again. 'A woman who has not killed is dangerous. That is what your mother says.'

Sigerson tried to find comfort on the low stool. He failed. His buttocks were either the wrong size or the wrong shape. 'Do you believe that, too?' he asked curiously, giving up the battle.

Aelebel sniggered again. 'That is what SHE says.'

Sigerson looked at her curiously. As always he was at a disadvantage with Aelebel because he firmly believed that she meant more than she ever said.

His disadvantage was enhanced by his position on the low stool. He swayed about to prove that he was not affected by the suggestive differentials in the seating arrangements and said mildly, 'Honestly, Aelebel. My mother does kill a lot. Most women don't go round shooting things, cattle, seal, whatever it may be. Or hunting them, do they?'

'You must think then what would be after happening in her if she didn't go out killing, now and again.'

'What on earth do you mean? How could that endanger her? She's in much more danger from one of those warped old blunderbusses back-firing in her face.'

'She uses a .22 and she cleans it herself.'

'Exactly. You've seen things after my mother has cleaned them. That's exactly what I mean.'

'Have you ever shot with her gun, Mr Sigerson?'

'Well, no, of course not. I don't shoot.'

'You can't shoot, Mr Sigerson. Not don't – can't. Who else will put down her old bulls for her – you? Who else'll cull them seals off her herring ground and her mackerel runs – you?'

'Well, I mean ... some men could be got, surely, to – er – to deal with these things?'

'What man?'

'Well, Rory?'

'Rory? RORY? She'd put a bullet on a nail in a tree while Rory was still wondering where the trunk was!'

'But this is scarcely the point, Aelebel. It worries me that she should have to be involved in all this violence and blood-shedding. Damn it, my mother is in her early fifties – she will have to accept sooner or later that she won't be able to go prancing over the rocks pot-shotting at seals or tearing over the bog after those whippets chasing hares, let alone imagining that she is going to turn herself into some sort of Lusitanian toreador teasing wild cattle up there in the Baun; it's absurd. It's worse than that, it's bloody dangerous.'

'It is that.' Aelebel stirred the pot reflectively.

'Can you say anything to her? Would she listen to you?'

'She would.'

'Well, will you try and stop all this bloodletting? Say something to her. Please.'

He no longer felt like putting his head on her apron. He had talked himself into a different mood. The idea now repelled him. Aelebel stank of gutted fish and flesh. He stood up and looked down at her. He could feel his height and his masculinity in the slow room. It was a room in which dominance could easily be achieved. Its space and echoes, its shadows and stark lines, were created for the preservation of dominance.

'No,' said Aelebel.

'Oh,' said Sigerson. Dominance had indeed been achieved, topsy-turvy, like. 'Oh.' Lamely he asked, 'Why not?' and his voice had a surprised naïvety that infuriated him.

'Because it would not be right.'

'But you just said it's dangerous – you agreed with me!'

Sigerson's voice rose impotently, and his ears burnt with the sound of it. It was, he felt, like fighting against a machine. It produced the same unreasoning rage that he experienced when his typewriter ribbon broke or when his electric razor inexplicably failed to start. There was nothing one could do, one's hands, fingers, were inadequate to make any sense out of the stupidity of disfunction; there was no alternative but to hit or smash, destroy the thing that ought to function and would not, yet was too inanimate to have obligation. Thus, Aelebel. The obtuseness of her was a violence against his reason, his humanity. He clenched his fists in an urge to do violence in return.

'Look,' he said with consummate patience, 'we agree that Ottoline ought not to behave as she does. We agree that she would listen to you if you spoke to her, and yet you say you will not do so. Now, Aelebel, why not?'

Two little black eyes looked at Sigerson. They looked straight out of the pit at him. They looked up out of the sty, out of the encrusted stupidity and grossness of animal existence. They looked out of the huts and hovels and shacks and shanties, out of bushes concealing excrement and old age. The two little black eyes looked, and Sigerson read no message in them. Suddenly afraid, surprised by his illiteracy, he backed away.

'Well, I shall,' he shouted defiantly.

Ottoline continued to stand by the window. The chapter-room behind her held her there, pinned to its windows. She did not wish to be anywhere else and knew at the same time that she would not be able to be anywhere else. She rested in her tiredness, unwilling to fight it, content to lie in it, inert, insufficient. The room would support her until she was vigorous again. She was a woman, suddenly, again, with five daughters – they weighed on her, and their absence was intolerable. They grew up some days out of the mornings into evenings that became like this one; where were they, her terrible daughters, Los Millāres and Coimheadach, Auschwitz and Liverpool, and her other girl, her girl in Nazareth House?

Aggression had been committed, once, when she took her there, over the sea, over the rim of that world which was Coimheadach the Place. She had travelled with the child, had left it in anonymity, had sought asylum and given his child away out there, given her Lovely Man's child away. She did not want the child back, but now, suddenly, she wanted the act of donation back. She wanted the enormity of the action, the sensual ecstasy of doing that terrible thing again. To feel her hands coming up out of her mind as the drowned children's hands floating up to the surface to become explicit, familiar, actualized as her own hands, aching in joints and the deep ligaments to hold the flesh of that daughter and feel it pass in its soft woollens out of those hands which had supported it for so long. As the room supported her now, resting in it. It was as if she must do something, or suffer something, of such enormity that the old action, thirty years passed now, need no longer be the consummation of her body. The hands which had become her own pulled and poked at the stonework. It was true, every joint did ache, the hands had worked all day. Yet of all of her they were the only physical members to be still restless.

What can I do? What can I suffer?

The Daughters of Morning were all round her; she looked at them warily, as if something might come from them, but they were passive, not even waiting; just passive, overgrown girls who lived with her and thought that they would turn into angels when she died. She was impatient with them but too tired to dismiss them. They were there.

It had been a spring day when she had brought the child. The institution stood high on a hill, and in front of it field grass had been cut by scythe into a rude lawn which ran, naked of flowers or paths or bowers, to the hedge which bordered the road. The drive was of pale gravel, sunk deep between the high turfs of the field grass, and curved so that immediately in the centre of the grass, before the centre of the building, there was place for the tall, white flagpole. That day the yellow and white flag of the Pope fluttered from the mast, pale in the pale, spring sunlight. The building itself was of the faintest yellow, bleached by wind and purity, and all its windows were very strict. No curtains fluttered, no swifts or martins swept about the lintels. The wind from the east was chill and dry, singing in the wires of the flagpole and whipping the new long leaves of the ash saplings. All over the prickly grass girls walked in threes, not touching each other, side by side. Their green gingham dresses and identical cardigans were beaded about with the heavy black of the nuns. Ottoline stood in the drive. No sound of laughter disturbed her.

She had no pity for the child in her arms, wrapped up in Aelebel's crazy crochet in multi-coloured wools; emerald, scarlet, yellow. The child did not know, would never know. The child was more in her head than in her arms, as if it had been born not down between her bloody legs but inward, into her spine. Three girls, passing slowly, anti-clockwise about the flagstaff, did not look at her as their shoes crackled in the chopped stems. Their voices were dry, like the east wind. In front of her the building stood tall to the sky, and there was no cloud in the sky, nor any warmth. Ottoline's shadow began to move evenly over the cut grass stalks and in her head she began to shout 'Coimheadach – Coimheadach –' until the noise cracked in her throat and in her hands. Her fingers screwed into the greasy wool of her own sheep as if by digging into it she could grip the stench and the oils and the heather stems which had been washed out of it in the iron vats. 'Coimheadach,' she shouted in her belly, her shadow moving faster before the wind, hurrying to get to the high, alien door in the high, pale façade. She held the child tight against her chest as if it were a shield against the moment when she would cast it aside and stand naked in Nazareth House.

The child mewed at her and she did not hear it. Nazareth House rose high, sheering against the sky.

Her asylum; not the child's, hers.

'Asylum –' she shouted, reaching out for the door.

Gilles structured me. Bless him, curse him and ignore him. Gilles is my father. I love your face, Father, hanging from my gutters; your invectives aflow with mosses in the rains. I love your face, Father. I love your open lips, Father, spitting blessings on my lips. How long is it, Father, since your lips were kissed? With a ladder I could climb up to you and lay mine upon yours in the rain, drinking what you discard. I could stand on the rung at the top and reach up, Father, to your cold lips. Would your old effluvia bless me, Father? The dead feathers, the grit from between the tiles, the single flakes of liverwort and rust that block my drains; the solitary crow that died beneath my chimney, the tern that dropped its dirt upon my roof, are they your blessings, Father?

You have no need of blessing.

What's that you say? No need? I, Ottoline, Ottoline Atlantica, outside the need for blessing? What punishment is this, Father?

FATHER ...?

Father, every night I watch the moon and stars curl round the corners of the walls to touch your hands and kiss your lips; is that the cold kiss you want, only that? Father, listen, listen to me, did you know that those stars have gone out? That they went out before you came? THAT THEY WERE NEVER THERE in your sight? That it was a mockery of starlight that illuminated your praying hands, pointed in the shape of the arches you made Mihilanus build for a choir to praise God in. Didn't you know, Father? They'd GONE OUT THEN? They fell into a black hole, a space, and whipped into nothing, torn, twisted, the multiluminous points wrenched off them and the body, quartered, drawn, hurled, disintegrating and screaming in its gyre, down into the black holes of nowhere? Your star went to hell, Father, like the disentangled body shared out along the four ways of a crossroads. There was nothing there to kiss you, Father; there is nothing there. Now do you want my kisses? Shall I fetch a ladder? Shall I run in the dark to the toolshed and drag it across the garth, and set it up against the severe wall and climb up to it, climb to the top rung and kiss you, father?

What need is there for kissing?

Need, need, need ... there is no need. Needing is delusion, like the stars that show you it is night. But want. I, I Ottoline, I know this. Father, do you want my kiss?

FATHER?

Listen, Father, you bore a son in me, and made him a eunuch. Is this your blessing? Let's not get confused. You got a son. Your son was dangerous. Did you castrate me, me Ottoline, because of the danger that is in me? Revert me to womankind, which is only a synonym for the smile a male sees on the face of the angels. Is that what you want? To make my bared teeth the smile of an archangel? Father, there is no archangel. They went out in sequence, Gabriel, Raphael, Azrael, Michael. Then the star was torn apart at the crossroads. They ran up the ladder to the gibbet in the dark, took it down and divided it up for burial so that the parts could never join again at the Resurrection. What's that you sing? Ave, Eva, Hallelujah? What's that Ave mean?

Ave, Eva, Hallelujah –
up the leg of her drawers, like I said, the castration that your fine fingers made upon my birthday. Wicked Father! Father, listen, father, when you made Mihilanus put down those fierce lines on the hill, as bare under the sun as the lion's jawbone, you made the pattern of my bone. You structured me out of right-angle and rib, groin, arch and above, the light clerestory. Out of granite. Out of vision, out of meanness and stricture and rule. That you set Mihilanus to make, I am. And that was a hard thing, a male thing. A thing full of desire and without wisdom or guidance, like all male things. A thing at which stones can be thrown, but which the waves will break. And then, Father, you set me down between the low tide and the high tide, for the waves.

Why, Father?
Why, Father?
Why, Father?

Was I too strong, too glorious, or not glorious enough? Was I insufficient that I could not stand in the inter-tidal regions unassaulted? Yet I am still here. The abbey is still here. I am not alone, not disgraced, not bowed. Yet I am defeated. In some way I have been defeated. I have been castrated – but what have I lost?

How the night wind does stir in the potted palm. The scratchy sound of its fronds is like the people, all the people, scratching to get in. Scratching at Ottoline. Let it bloom, monstrous waxen blossoms, carmine, peach and ivory in the stillness of my room. Let it put out giant petals, cold to the touch, curved symmetrically about anthers as rigid as a wand. Let the draughts die, and the flower sit, and the turf ash drift about it. Let it be rare, and isolated and dangerous.

Rare, isolated and dangerous.

Then it would be like me, Ottoline, a male flower without pollen. It would be me. The male flower of a potted palm.

Was that it, Father? Was it the pollen that you cut off on my birthday? The dusting of others or of myself upon others that makes me one with them? Because I am not one with any. Rare and isolated; and being rare and isolated, dangerous. The one who stands outside the herd. The cripple, or the wayward. The rare, male blossom.

Is that why, Father?

Am I a rogue beast? Am I outside the humanity and the existence of the people? Is this what I am, or what you have made me?

It's what I am, you say? Your son, yes, yes, like your abbey, like your mean, inhuman Rule – rogue living, rogue existence in a world of people, you set eunuchs' and angels' minds spinning wheels of prayer that could not keep a pauper warm when the north winds come down from the ice with the green falcon spread on the blast. Ha, Father, we were glorious, your abbey and I, and we smile like angels! But we never warmed a breast. Abraham took the sharp knife to Isaac, but he never had to use it. Where was your god on my birthday that he couldn't find a ram to toss down into a thicket? Perhaps because we have no thickets – just the sea and the rocks and the heather and the sky – and in the middle of it all the rogue blossom, carmine, rose and mother-of-pearl, as still and cold as porcelain.

Well, Father, maybe my kisses are not to be desired. Do I forgive you, or do you forgive me?

I Ottoline, Ottoline Atlantica, what need have I for blessing or forgiveness?

V

DOROTHY LAMBERT, for she was alone, stood at the centre of chaos. In her youth she had possessed a grandfather, who had retired to a bungalow at Chichester where he had grown Christopher Stone, the Peace Rose, Mrs Sam McReedy and Weichsel's Orange Star. Dorothy disliked going to visit him because of the antimacassars which his housekeeper draped about the uneasy chairs and because of the way her father spoke to him as if he were a retired joke taken out at Christmas time for tradition's sake. Grandpa had smelt of Bass and coarse tobacco and he sang songs about when the Bloody War was Over and Patsy Fagan and Holy Moses, to none of which her mother would let her listen. He had a tick in his upper lip contracted by having anticipated Going Over the Top for too long. The roses in the clayey garden and the Roses of Picardy had been for Dorothy inextricably intermingled, petal for petal, in her memories of Grandpa's wheezy whistles and the January pruning and the pale, cold skies of suburban Sussex. To her a rose garden was an evocation of the bungalow estate life; the Retired-Behind-the-Net-Curtain life; the life that was studded with strange names like Mons, Allenby, Sassoon and Madame Lonlong; an alien, discarded life, invalidated by her father's friends in the Duke of York and her mother's in Wilberforce Close; by Worrels and Vera Lynn and by the Dam Busters and Don Bradman. Grandpa had finally dwindled away and waited a long time, and they all waited with him, to Go Over the Top; when finally he did he had become so meagre, what with 'South Pacific' and 'Dare to be Free' and the coming of nylon, that he simply slithered down the other side and they barely noticed.

So Dorothy stood in the middle of chaos, because all about her were Mrs Sam McReedy and Weichsel's Orange Star and the bloody Christopher Stone, and others like cabbages and some severe as kings; complicated, rambling, unpruned roses with mad, tasteless colours and spendthrift odours hurled away on the west wind. The violent crimson of the rambler was an offence against all gardening; a hue so crude and congested in the vulgar clusters that they were more reminiscent of hat décor than of any living thing, just such hats as came to the surface at the Lord Mayor's Show and on postcards sold in Scarborough. Indeed so crude and earthy were these stumbling horticultural experiments that they bore no kinship whatever with Madame Lonlong or Grandpa, let alone with the new, thornless, scentless artifacts of the great nurseries and cultivators, which gave such grace and form to the quietly fertilised beds in Wilberforce Close.

Dorothy stood in, approximately, the aisle of the abbey church. The crimson profusion which had so stirred her admiration from the window of the eighth cell now revealed its luxury in full sunlight all over the south wall. To her left, with a lack of imagination quite staggering in its magnitude, a similar glaring white rambler flung theatrical bouquets against the shadows on the north side. The aisle, and indeed the whole nave, surged and swayed with beds of reeking roses; mostly musks, but with a leavening of floribunda, they clamoured and exuded and exulted beneath the swinging sky, streaked with white clouds and screaming gulls, wastrel of rose, rose, rose crammed like the brilliant miscellany of a child's toybox into the confines of Gilles's austere church. The chaos of the ragged stones; of the missing courses, the lost lights and tumbled groins; of the chips at the feet of the pillars; of the ferns ravishing the joints and the moss sealing the torn bondings; the chaos of the high racing sky, careless of cloud, of sun, of dawn or darkness; the chaos of the prodigal roses feet deep in manure and effluvium with blood-red thorns and congested buds curtailed for lack of space in which to blossom; the chaos of expended force, up from the débris hurled upon the ground and down from the mighty stones flung up against the sky, all these focused on Dorothy Lambert as if she were their natural centre. So strong was her feeling of centrality that she condensed herself, as if for defensive action against her oppressors. She drew her arms into her sides, clutching the long stick tight against her chest and straddling her feet slightly like a flyweight boxer, her chin pointing east towards the blank wall over which no rose ran and behind which sheltered the evidence of Mihilanus's disaffection.

'The lion in the fuchsia went roar, ROAR, ROAR, ROAR
And he swiped at his Mammy with his paw, paw, paw –'

'O, God –' Dorothy said aloud, wheeling half-right and definitely fewtering her spear. 'O my God.'

Down the night-stair which debouched over the end of the crimson Souvenir of Scarborough came Ottoline. Or pranced, or even, remotely, danced Ottoline. Her silver hair flew about her, her violet eyes flashed in the sun, her mouth sang irrelevantly and she carried a weapon. The west wind hurtled through the west door, scattering salt, sea rumblings and nightmare about an already nightmarish experience. Clad in a black fisherman's jersey and a pair of heavy hunting boots into the polished tops of which were tucked white cricket flannels, Ottoline seemed oblivious of her combative appearance, or perhaps not quite, for she too carried a long stick, lightly grasped in the right hand, butt behind her and head lowered, slightly athwart the body, pointing directly at Dorothy towards whom she advanced with a mincing gait.

'Saw you prodding me musks,' she announced ingenuously. 'Brought this just in case.'

The tip of the long stave came to rest remarkably close to Dorothy's bowels. Pins and needles scuttered up and down her back from neck to bottom as she wondered just what case she might inadvertently present that would necessitate the use of so obsolete and invincible a weapon. The head was fitted with an iron point some seven inches long, and the end gleamed dully in the swift sun.

Behind the point a sharp hook projected backwards and then out in a graceful curve; it, too, gleamed at the needle tip.

Ottoline eyed Dorothy.

Dorothy rested the end of her bamboo cane on the ground, the top pointing to the sky in a gesture of respectful truce. Ottoline's stave did not waver. Dorothy said, hopefully, 'Good afternoon, Madame Ottraine.'

'O'Treann,' said Ottoline, inserting a slither into the vowels which immediately rendered the name totally unpronounceable to those born east of Coimheadach by even one mile.

'Yes,' said Dorothy evenly, not rising to the bait. She had a hallucinatory second in which she saw herself and Madame Ottraine facing each other among the roses in the ruined abbey, armed with spears, intent on disembowelling and framed by a greatly be-cherubed proscenium arch. Hysteria mounted up her throat. She thought how to escape from this entertainment. Ottoline with a prong six feet long aiming at her liver was not entertaining.

'I am looking for bones,' she informed Ottoline.

Ottoline looked amused. 'You'll find them easier in the graveyard,' she remarked, 'or my bedroom. What sort of bones would you be requiring?'

'Er, human ones,' said the Girl, falling into the manner adopted by Sigerson.

Ottoline was having the same effect on her as she had on him. The Girl heard herself become pretentious and unreal in the way he did, although never at Cambridge. She had heard it frequently in the last few days. She, for example, was not accustomed to hearing herself asking for human bones in someone else's rose garden. Her conversational facility deserted her; she could find no way of returning in time or context to the identity acknowledged by New Hall or Wilberforce Close. She glared at the weapon and the farce in which it entangled her. Then she elaborated, in the hope that it might distract the aggressor, 'I am searching for signs of building, floors and so on, under your rosebeds. Most particularly for graves.'

Ottoline refused to be distracted. Smiling wickedly she said, 'The nave was paved. If you strike through the manure firmly, thus –' and she jabbed with the spear (the Girl refused to retreat. Ottoline's eyebrows twitched in acknowledgement) '– you will strike the flagstones. Flagstones. Not bones.'

'I was unaware of the flagging,' the Girl said with hauteur. 'I had hoped to find the traces of the graves of the Dark Age inhabitants.' She detected a phraseology worthy of her thesis, and bridled. The Redness began ... she was aware of it among the crimson roses.

Ottoline tossed her silver head. 'Oh, them,' she said scornfully. 'Are you ashamed of them?'

'No!'

Ottoline lowered her spear and grinned. 'I am,' she said confidentially. 'Awfully coarse people – always quarrelling and indignant about something. Indignation is awfully coarse, isn't it?'

'NO! I mean, no, not particularly, is it?'

Ottoline grinned again. The Redness grew worse. The roses incarnadined, the sun flashed. The butt of the spear rested among the Mrs Sam McReedy. The point glistened. Ottoline leaned affectionately against it, like a shepherd.

'My son tells me about those people,' she said. 'In fact he INSISTS about them. He doesn't think they're coarse, now.'

'No,' said the Girl, faintly. Determination not to watch the spear eradicated all other emotions. She had not yet adjusted to the change of weapon.

'It is lamentable how the most intelligent looking people find relief amongst the crudest surroundings,' Ottoline said imperviously. 'Now take these Celtic geezers, for example –'

'Celtic what?'

'Geezers – people, you know?'

'I don't know.'

'No need to be humble –'

'I'm not!'

'Just as I was saying – but these early saints you and my son plague, what were they? No, I'll tell you – they were mystical *nouveaux riches*. What could be cruder than that? And every time they were accused of it, they became indignant, like Tudor earls or that man Mellors, you know who I mean?'

'Lady Chatterly's lover? That one?' the Girl said, astonished.

'Was he really? Yes, I fancy Sigerson did have something

interesting to say about him apart from the indignation – I can't remember the story but I recollect the impression well enough. Well, that's the way of these Celts, as I see it. Not that their displays of mystical luxury are particularly Celtic; it's more that a novel form of self-indulgence came their way and they made a great deal of capital out of it. Which is, of course an excellent thing to do. I often wish I had done it myself, although not in such an immaterial way, but then, you see, Girl, they went too far, on and on almost into respectable times, squandering it on more self-indulgences. Very vulgar, all these cheap tours around the Continent, being Celtic in perfectly civilized places and so overdoing it that they muddled the local peasantry. And, of course, the height of extravagance, they died in the throes of it, knowing perfectly well that they were saints. They never died until they WERE saints. So exaggerated, I always think. It reeks of pink chandeliers and power.'

The Girl looked upon her hostess aghast. 'Power?' she queried, determined not to be ground down among the pale rose roots with the grubs and the cattle dung, to be flattened against the impenetrable slabs of the aisle beneath her intelligence.

Ottoline poked at the ground, as if she, too, were aware of the slabs as the basis of their argument. 'Power,' Ottoline repeated like a liturgy. 'Power has never been practical out here,' she said, looking up at the sky.

The Girl looked with her. Apart from the fact that there was rather a lot of it, she could discern no such omnipotent direction in its aspect.

Ottoline said patiently, 'It carries the salt. From the ocean. It lays it on the land. The trees die of it. It is like a bitter poison to them. Do you not see? We have no trees. They have all died. Without the trees we have no soil. Have you not noticed that we have no soil? What there once was the wind took and strewed it in more happy places. And what was left the rain wept on and washed down into the sea. The sea. ... My roses are growing in dung. There is no soil in the abbey.'

'Then,' said the Girl, perceiving chasms of allusion and significance opening beneath her stained footwear, 'what do your cattle feed on?'

'Grass,' said Ottoline laconically. She was losing interest. The Girl was stupid. 'Down by the estuary, where the clays are, there is grass down there, and some soil. Full of minerals and lively elements. The cattle feed on that. In the summer I put them up in the Baun on the hilltop. There is grass there, God knows why. If you enjoy barbarism you should go up. As well as my cattle you will find earthworks. God knows why,' she repeated.

'What sort of date?' the Girl asked. She clung to practicalities, she was only a research student.

Under the high sky Ottoline's voice had become singsong, almost as if she were chanting of the soils and the wicked land where she lived. God knows why, God knows why, went the chant, the up and down rhythm without let or expression like a long tale told so often that the meaning of it had no sense in it left. Have you not noticed that we have no soil? Have you not noticed that we have no soil? Do you not see? We have no trees? My roses are growing in dung. ...

Ottoline moved her spear a fraction to one side so that the Girl might see the whole of her, standing among the roses. That the Girl might see how slight a thing she was, and that her hair was made of metal, wrought out of the mountain's foot, and her eyes of shadows mauve on the north face of the Slieve, mauve in the troughs between the green crests. That she was as transparent as the water, as bitter, as senseless, as inevitable; that the shape of her flowed in the garden, distorted, wavering and reflecting, and that the mountain stood upside down in her body, and the walls topsyturvy in her hands. Through the reflections and the ripples of her the spine, opaque but seldom straight, ran at the base of the pool, where the strength of the land was; not of destructible calcium, but a garland of carved blossoms uncurled and laid out beneath her, petal for petal, mercilessly, carved artifactually from a pale substance as accurate as silver, as cold as porcelain, carmine, ivory and peach. I Ottoline, Ottoline Atlantica. ...

Behind the Girl Sigerson came through the floribunda roses, looking at his mother baiting the Girl, and his lips twisted in recognition. 'What on earth is that for?' he asked her crossly, pointing his long finger at the spear.

'I thought,' said Ottoline 'that it might be of assistance. It's sharp, much sharper than bamboo.'

'But what IS it?' he insisted, stooping to examine the long weapon. His face wore the anxious expression of a man who wished he had his spectacles on. He touched the glittering tip with a shy finger. 'Goodness, it's like a razor!' He raised his eyes. Because of his stooping they were on a level with his mother's mouth; only inches from her cruel, smiling lips.

'It's a cattle goad,' said Ottoline.

The Girl began to laugh. Dorothy Lambert threw back her hanks of hair and opened her mouth and laughed. She laughed directly at the excruciating, massed roses fawning like a thick-skinned puppy upon the sunlight; she laughed in the face of the sly woman in her ridiculous garments and her wild grey hair streeling in the wind. She laughed at the *nouveaux riches* saints and the anxious intelligent eyes of Dr Ottraine peering nervously at his mother in the absurd garden; at the cattle goad and the bamboo and dung heap on which she stood, crowing, like a little red BITCH in the gaudy sun.

'God, I shall feel like Little St Ursula!' she laughed, wiping her eyes. 'Plunging around with a cattle goad! I didn't know such things existed still – I thought they died out when the lowing herds finally got home!'

'They're still around here,' Sigerson said sarcastically.

'I suppose you've got the temperament,' Ottoline snapped. Nastily she said, 'See if you can prang her through the heart, then we'd all believe she had one. Sigerson, don't gape – it's ill-mannered.'

Sigerson made a startled little noise and then shut his mouth. The Girl took the proffered goad and masterfully restrained herself from pointing the end at Ottoline's liver. Ottoline eyed the Girl to see if she would point it at her liver. When the Girl merely clasped the thing and put its butt firmly on the manure, Ottoline laughed. It had an old fashioned, raucous sound, like the wartime slang.

Sigerson said solemnly, 'You could kill someone with that. You could really.'

'Yes,' said the Girl, still laughing.

'I know,' said Ottoline, laughing. Then she said, 'There's guinea fowl for dinner, Sigerson. Don't be nervous. And do remove that bolting look you have acquired lately.' She strode through the roses, calling back over her shoulder, 'I'm glad I was useful —' with a somewhat conceited air as she vanished through the lacuna in the west wall.

Sigerson found that both he and the Girl were looking after her. 'WAS she useful?' he inquired with interest.

The Girl looked doubtfully at the weapon in her right hand. She thought there might be considerable defence potential in the arcane tool. 'I think she may have been,' she said uncertainly.

Sigerson watched her in dismay as she began to pass her hands down her thighs over the soft flowery wool of the unsuitable skirt. The hands caressed the stuff or else cleaned themselves upon it, as if the enthusiasm for work or the prospect of earnestness required physical expression which was yet inhibited. Dorothy flushed slightly, from a strange extrovert intention too profound to be concealed. Sigerson prodded hopelessly at a bunch of chickweed and tried not to look at her. It was his earnest desire that she remove herself just as soon as possible, not only from the abbey church but from Coimheadach itself.

'I have a terrier mentality,' the Girl said lightly, 'at least, that's what Dr Cudleigh calls it. I have always been a great admirer of your work and of your systematic approach. It is completely exciting for me to be here and to see you at the grass roots of your discipline.'

'My God,' said Sigerson miserably. He passed his hands over his hair. Behind him he was aware that it stuck out like a signpost saying This Way He Is Not Going. He wondered if this completely appalling Girl was aware of Geoffrey's frenetic abhorrence of all canine creatures, epitomized by the littler, barkier sort. 'Does he refer to me as a terrier, too?' he asked timorously.

'Not to me!'

Geoffrey no doubt had some fancier, more ironic pet name for his intimate friend. ... Be that as it may, he was not going to be cajoled into discussing his systems or his grass roots or his disciplines with anyone, let alone with a Girl with a birdcage. It occurred to him that Ottoline would call it vulgar, and rightly so. As if his systematic approach were anything but habit and a fear of computers, or his grass roots nourished on any succulent other than dung and ash. Neither subject was a suitable conversation piece. He felt the heaviness of solemnity stealing up in him and fought it off deliberately.

'Well, let's continue with what we think you are doing, shall we, and see where we land up – perhaps in the sainted laps of the Ursuline feminists themselves,' he said, wagging his eyebrows to convey levity and a change of subject.

Dorothy was puzzled. She had expected him to show interest, concern, even appreciation of her remark. His dark, somewhat twisted face had suggested to her that he might be one who would be willing to talk in personal, immediate terms. His blank rebuttal of her enthusiasm in itself did not contradict this but added a challenge to her, in that he was evidently neither willing to help nor easy to approach. She watched curiously his return to the frivolous level which he occasionally displayed at work, the reason for which she had not yet been provoked to investigate, while he ground his mother's cattle goad down onto the impervious slabs with an excess of strength which indicated nervous irritability rather than academic inquiry or horticultural enthusiasm.

Dorothy took a firm stance beside Sigerson and drove her bamboo sternly into the manure.

After Ottoline had left her son and the Girl setting-to at each other in the rose garden, she was filled with a sense of impatience. This penetrated her stride, which was never graceful and was now lengthened into the ugly, hip-swinging gait of tremendous length but moderate pace which distinguishes the hillman from the lowlander. Each leg swung before the other in that disconnected movement which car manufacturers refer to as independent suspension, so that all hillocks, tussocks, unanticipated rises and unevenesses in the stony surface were absorbed by the ilium and the whole frame above moved without let or hitch.

In a drawing-room such a stride is ungainly and irritating to the beholder – many times Mary-Rose had been frustrated in her attempts to find a word for the sensation which Ottoline's indoor movements provoked in her. She would have had the slight silver heroine of her Atlantic days move with the grace of a greyhound or of Madame Pompadour. Mary-Rose would have had Ottoline an epitome of unconscious beauty, which was reasonably successful as long as the older woman stayed still, but as soon as she moved her prowling wench-gait destroyed the image and upset Mary-Rose. Even a minor operation like the pouring of whiskey upset her; Ottoline would clutch the decanter about the neck with the veins and muscles of her hand bulging like a wrestler's fist, as if the bottle or decanter were of abnormal weight and equipped with the power to fly from the smallness of Ottoline at the slightest opportunity. So she would seize it tremendously, and Mary-Rose's illusions would refract and scatter in the planes of the cut glass.

It was with this appearance of tremendousness that Ottoline now mounted out of the abbey enclosure and emerged onto the heather above. Trails of grass sank low beneath the brown dry stalks, spotted with sheep droppings and pocked by glittering granite. The heather was tall, high enough to brush with a rasping whisper against the tops of the leather hunting boots which were of such a height that Ottoline was seldom scratched by the sharp twigs or the thorns of the gorse. Which was why she wore them so often. She did not like having her legs torn and scratched. Because she was equipped to do so Ottoline ignored the rabbit and sheep trails and moved directly uphill.

Above the boot tops she was exposed to infinity. Tied tight below by the stalks and twigs she emerged at knee height, an attached emanation, rising directly from its element into the vacancy of the sea winds and the sky that went on until it appeared again as itself having surrounded the world out of which Ottoline Atlantica grew. Reflections of clouds whipped in the heather and lashed past her as blocks and shapes of distinguishing colour; where, as an artist would render them in solid paint, in colours which the finger nail can chip and the magnifying glass reveal as striae, grooves and rills, Ottoline glided through them unaffected and unaffecting, neither subject nor agent, like a summer shower.

The world wheeled off to the west where a long arm of wet darkness covered the blue, as if the mountains and the sea suffered some craving to meet under the shelter of the cloud. Ottoline glanced at it, but its presence was a nullity to her. Clouds were the ceiling; clouds had always been the ceiling, as rain had made immaterial walls. She no more resented either than Sigerson resented the brown stripes on his wall paper in Cambridge. The natural coloration of the limit of her horizon was grey. She accepted weather as a boundary as Sigerson accepted that rooms had walls.

One of Ottoline's limits was the sea. It was a source of constant tragedy to her that she had been forced by her governess to learn what lay on the other side of it. She had a wooden globe in her schoolroom and had spent years resenting America. It shut in the Atlantic with a patchwork quilt of fat names with Os in them: Boston, New York, Baltimore; round, closed Os which would never open and which entrapped her great Atlantic. She still rather resented it and glancing at it now felt a rage that a time had passed when she could have recognized it for what it was, a thing boundless and invincible, unknown, uncaring, blind and forever. She would have had herself dismissed, like Gildas, for whom she had some sly liking which she never acknowledged to Sigerson, in a boat to go forever to wherever forever was or was not. So, too, she yearned in her guts for the countless who had embarked along her coast, the known coast which stretched up and down the known world, trusting that beyond there would be Somewhere and who had never found anywhere at all. They were moulded in her bones, those old men, who had set out in the long black boats, not knowing that here was the end of creation, and had found out at a distance so great that it was beyond hope and beyond despair and beyond existence.

Ottoline would have preferred that time to have encompassed her, so that she too might know the vision and the despair that lay over a sea which had no further shore, and over which, riding the millennia and the waves together, the long black boats still travelled, west of west as their cargo of bones sifted in the gunwales and settled among the creels. But Baltimore bounded her. Nova Scotia grounded her. She ran aground on time, on history, on acknowledged facts which she was powerless to disbelieve. What was the use of not believing in Baltimore? It was there. It had been founded, built, and its photograph appeared in the *National Geographic*. She could not but be cognisant of Baltimore. She resented the existence of Baltimore in her time, labelling it a spoor of time, a quirk, a malicious twist of history that there should be Baltimore on the other side of her Atlantic. For Ottoline was disrespectful of time. To her time was a characteristic of existence, not a basis for it. She had no sense of the past, just as she had no sense of other people, because she had none of herself, or of herself as a feature in time.

Ottoline was not one of the creatures of time so much as a creature of place, and her place, her land, was one with which temporality had never interfered, and only locality and place made manifestations. In this sense Gilles was indeed her father, and she knew him as such. Gilles had chosen Coimheadach, one promontory out of many. St Cyril of the Promontory was far from alone in his sanctity, far from idiosyncracy in the miracles of nature attendant upon the disposition of his mortal remains. Many a more forceful saint than Cyril might have lured Gilles; many a more charitable evangelist than Little St Ursula the Very Much Lesser. But it was not for charity nor for mystic power that Gilles had been searching, but for the Power of Place. And for this reason alone Coimheadach became his most elect Child of the Monastery, and to the power of the Child the father had bowed and in so doing had invested the Child with the insignia and the tools of authority. Thus far distant down the line, Ottoline, reared among the rigid lines and angles of Gilles' structure, was herself formally created out of the very dust of the soilless land, a new Eve as old as the first, but with no soil in her garden. Ave Eva. ...

Out of breath Ottoline arrived at the first bank of Ursula's Baun. The bank was more a terminological feature than a topographical one, being no more than a circular ring some eight or nine inches high and more easily discernible from a distance than at close inspection. This ring, now scarred into barrenness by the sharp hoofs of the sheep which ran on the hill, lay outside an inner ring of everlastingly fertile grass.

Ottoline had, at great labour, encircled this precious ring with a wire fence to keep the sheep off it and to keep her cattle on it. She 'had dragged bags of sand and cement up to it, heaving them into a pony cart and leading the unwilling animal through the heather, heaping imprecations upon his head and lashes upon his ribs whilst he yanked back under the impossible load with his mouth open in disbelief and the bit clattering about among his yellow teeth. Then she would jump into the cart upon delivery of the load and gallop him down the mountain, heedless of the brake, yelling like Boadicea and whirling her whip about his flattened ears, only to load him up and start off again. When she had begun cementing the posts to the bared rock surface she had been clumsy and the cement had dried out cracked and useless, or else she had made it so wet that instead of holding the posts in its tightening grip it had flowed slackly about their feet. But under the battening of the sun, the lash of the wind and her own self accusations she had mastered sufficient of the art to erect a substantial fence on the bank. Around this the sheep now circled endlessly, seeking entry to the lush growth within where the long-horned cattle browsed in superior content.

Captivated as much by her expertise as by the proximity of the great beast, Ottoline would come up to the Baun day after day, and sit, breathing heavily after the climb, with her back against one of the posts she had erected. She did this now, her booted legs stretched out before her, the post as strong as herself behind her and all the Atlantic stretching away to Baltimore before. After a moment, in which she recovered her breath and cursed her approaching old age, she rummaged in her pocket and withdrew a tin. It had a colourful representation of a yawl in foul weather upon its top, and beneath a little key. She inserted this with great concentration onto the metal tab upon the tin lid and began to turn, the ligaments in her right arm rolling beneath the fisherman's jersey sleeves. When a fraction of the tin lid was twisted away from its sealing an odour escaped into the air ... a warm, salty odour. Ottoline sniffed tremendously, and a smile spread across her long lips. Behind her in the sun the bulk of an enormous creature throbbed in the grass, vibrated in the earth beneath Ottoline as the beast crept closer. The tremor of cloven hoofs and the warm wet breath blotted out the sun. Contentedly, in his shade, Ottoline and

Popplethwaite ate soused herrings out of a tin.

While Ottoline sat by the Baun sternly ignoring Baltimore in her apprehension of the infinite distance stretched out in front of her, Sigerson was whipping himself into a rage in the abbey church. He had seen Ottoline emanate from the heather and begin her climb, and had watched her through a gap left by the second fall of a fifteenth-century Magdalen until she vanished over a false crest on the mountain-side. He assumed that she had gone to moon over her cows. The fact that the beast in the Baun were all male failed to affect Sigerson's thinking. To him a bovid was Cow, unless it personally impressed some other aspect of its gender upon him. He had been away for so much of the last ten years that he had lost touch with the individual development of the herd and could no longer assign a name to each individual as he had done as a boy. He did not view this lapse with any particular regret. On the contrary, if he considered it at all it was with relief that he had become sufficiently detached from his mother and her vagaries that he no longer knew nor cared which of her pets was which. He did not know which of the whippets was which either, but that was due to the fact that he had never been told, since Ottoline herself seemed not to distinguish them in any way and roared 'Dog!' or 'Whippet!' at the two indiscriminately. They were from the same litter and being highly bred had kennel names of such length, unsuitability and absurdity that Ottoline, out of sheer discouragement, had failed to rename them. These two were now nosing about the distrubances in the rosebeds, quivering and shaking with advanced neurosis to such an extent that one, which was visibly smaller and creamier than the other, seemed like to wobble right off its feet.

The Girl was regarding them with disfavour, and for once Sigerson felt himself in sympathy with her. Gloomily he said, 'Perhaps we could set them to work, to track down graves or something –'

The Girl grinned cheerfully. 'I don't think they would be much use,' she said.

Her voice sounded sufficiently different for Sigerson to look sharply at her when she bent again over her bamboo and he could peep without discovery. Her cheeks had pinkened somewhat under the freshening winds from the west, and her hair, usually so smooth and heavy that it sat upon her like a cap, was ruffled and tossed by the exercise. Her long skirt pulsed with the rhythm of her movements and the tug of the wind, and blew about her legs, subtle green and ochre, flowery, ornate and with that rather uninspired design which he knew was the height of present fashion. Above the skirt she wore a black jersey with elbow length sleeves and a low neck which revealed the top of her protruberant ribs but no bosom at all. This he found remotely disappointing and felt cheated by the pale knobs of the sternum and clavicle which were displayed in the racing sunlight. He had a sudden picture of lacy bra tops, or the lacy top of something, peeping out above the light wool, and how pleasant and exciting it would have been ... anything to enliven the drear abbey and the monotonous prodding in the manure to which he was devoting himself for no very good reason that he could see. But the Girl seemed in some way refreshed by the episode, as if the roughening of her exterior were causing coloration to spread over her attitudes in place of the stultified devotion which she usually presented to her academic superiors.

Under his look the Girl moved her head restlessly and her eyes met his. For a long moment she looked at him and then, without comment, without sign of what the look had conveyed to her, bent her face so that the brown hair collapsed again and obscured her from him. Sigerson swallowed tightly. Irritation mounted in his chest and darted into his face as long, rigid lines in the cheek muscles. He turned his back on her and in so doing turned it also to the wind which whipped up behind him, seizing the cloth of his trousers and shirt and impaling them upon him so that every line of his form was suddenly distinct and obvious, and he was acutely aware of every lineament of his body. He stood still for a second, appreciating the phenomenon and then he said some very rude words to himself. He added aloud, 'I'm afraid I'll have to leave you now. I have some things to see to this afternoon.' Without looking at the Girl he strode away from the garden through the west door, into the high sky and the buffeting gusts.

Sigerson had run away rather precipitously after the Look. Sigerson did not like Looks. They unnerved him. Infuriated, he glared at the outside of the walls within which the Girl, presumably, prodded on. What had she seen with the Look? His dislike? His unease? His acne or herpes? It was the coldness, the flatness of the look which riled him. There had been nothing in it to comprehend, nothing to judge or assess. In no way did it impinge on the established lack of relationship as a Look properly should. Yet it had enraged him, made him carnally sensate in a way he was unaccustomed to. It had had effect but solely on him. It was as if she had manoeuvred him into calling forth the Look so that of the two he was culpable of it, although she had perpetrated it.

'Culpable? Culpable?' he thought savagely. What had put that word into his mind? Of what was he culpable? Of receiving a Look? What was blameworthy about that? It was not as if he had been lasciviously peering at her, or even lasciviously imagining her – his thoughts had been centred on what she did not have, rather than on anything she might possess which he could be considered in some way blameworthy for speculating upon. He thought miserably of the long extension of time between the afternoon and the evening when he might reasonably expect a change of mood to relieve him.

Evenings at Coimheadach were undeniably different from the days there because of the quality of the withdrawing light and the privacy of identity permitted even in the chimney when Ottoline would retreat sleepily and well fed into a wrapping of incoherent daydreams and leave him alone, peacefully beside her, without jabbering and questioning and prying. Perhaps if he could encourage her to eat vast quantities of suet pudding or something for lunch the afternoons might be as somnolent, as private? Not that Ottoline ever took lunch that he knew of. Meals in the middle of the day had always been something which in childhood he had partaken of with whichever hired guardian happened to be *in situ* at the time, Nanny, then Governess, then Tutor, and finally he had eaten alone. Ottoline came and went, ate things out of a tin, snatched a biscuit or whiskey or the interminable coffee and cigarette and vanished. Politely he would eat his chicken and greens and then he, too, would go, somewhere, anywhere, to fill in the time. It did not occur to him that anyone who ate as much or as bizarrely as Ottoline did at breakfast almost certainly had no need for lunch, and he did not consider that her disregard of lunchtime gave her a liberty which his rumbling stomach and need for a break in his congested thinking denied to him.

Today he and the Girl had eaten chicken and greens politely together in the warming-room, as if he had grown into Tutor and she, in a weird way, into him, and the idea had so upset him that he had consumed jelly and custard without reflecting on what an unsuitable dish this was to offer a lecturer and a PhD research student. Perhaps, he thought, it was because of this distressing collation that he had been sufficiently distrait to leave his own work and join the Girl in her sterile game of Hunt the Saints in his mother's manure. He found that he had brought the goad with him when he had left so hastily. He flung it against the wall of the great court, which he was crossing. It hit a drainpipe, clanked and slithered into the dust. Eight feet of rusted and bullet-peppered drainpipe followed it.

'O heavens!' said Sigerson aloud, gazing at the jagged break above his head. 'She'll see it the minute she comes through – O Lord –'

Without reflection, Sigerson scuttled into the nearest doorway, and several minutes later, with a furtive glance around the court, he popped out again with a dilapidated piece of grey asbestos sheeting, torn in several places and unevenly spattered with orange lichen. This he hastily propped against the area down which the broken drainpipe should have run, picked up the latter and threw it through the doorway from which he had just re-emerged and jumped a good two feet from the ground in terror as the action was greeted by a howl of such agony and ferocity that the iron rang in echo. A black cat with red eyes and a stringy tail swept between his legs, shrieked again and disappeared beneath a water tank. Silence fell in the yard. The sky, which had been leaning down, watching the affray out of inquisitive pearly scurries of wind and cloud, retreated back to the heavens. The sun shone. Sigerson dusted his hands, looked quickly about him and slipped silently out of the yard.

Following Sigerson, the wind gusted into the abandoned court, took a tug at the asbestos and discarded it with a thump on the ground.

Sigerson went directly to Mary-Rose. He went without thinking, as if the avenue between the pampas-grasses and the space where once a wrought-iron gate, nine feet by twelve, had stood were the only way which he could take. He marched quickly and breathlessly, his eyebrows drawn down and his lips moving, but he was not thinking. Somewhere far off at the other side of him he was casting about looking for something. He felt disconnected, cut away, as if his emotions and his head had taken him over and he might at any moment lose consciousness of his feet and fall. If he did, he knew he would not have the incentive to rise. Dimly he was frightened, but there was not enough of his self-awareness operating to put the fear to any practical use, like walking slower or deliberately reciting a poem or a formula or a king list. The wind thrummed about his head, cushioning it on the outside from any sound or sight which might impinge on his outward frame. Had Ottoline at that moment chosen to shoot him at last, he would no doubt have been aware only of the wind getting inside him rather than of his life getting out.

Wrapped in the wind he strode past Aelebel who was clumping in the same direction with an empty creel upon her back. The wind that obliterated him left her untouched. She bent her flat head into it, cursing it as it smacked her face and insolently tweaked at her hair. Her black eyes flickered and grew small as Sigerson passed, and stayed like a pair of sights lined between his shoulder blades until she turned off towards the sea and he, continuing inland to the Grange, passed on down the hill.

At the top of the steps which led from the rough bog which lay between the avenue and the cliff and which gave access to the sea and the platform where the anchoring rings were set, Aelebel paused and turned. Far off to the left Sigerson dwindled away down the track. He grew smaller and smaller, and then there was only the bog, and the wind and the sound of the forever sea beneath. She stamped down the three hundred and five uneven steps until the spray sipped at her lips and there was only the wind and the sea and the living rock behind her, and then she sat on a crab creel and waited for the long black boat to come in. It would come in with the crabs in the withy creels, with the barnacled lobsters with pearls in their claws; come in with the metallic mackerel from the blind world below where the rowers were of the long black boats that had not come in any more. The long black boats for which we waited; are waiting. And she would cook the crabs and the lobsters in the iron pot; break the harsh unworldly shells with cold iron and feed the flesh to Ottoline. Feed her with the flesh of the sea, morsel by morsel; feed her; feed Ottoline, Ottoline Atlantica, my love, my bitch.

Mary-Rose opened the door of the Grange and let Sigerson in. He walked in with his hand to his brow as if he had been studying too hard, or walking in a gale. Mary-Rose smiled politely at him and peered past his shoulder to see if it was windy. The westerly onshore was rising to a steady thrum and it was beginning to skither with rain, but there was no hurricane, tornado or other supreme phenomenon such as would account for Sigerson's distrait appearance. She made shooing movements with her arms as if to hustle him out of whatever difficulty he had been in, and he complied, wandering into the drawing-room and plummeting into the depths of the one really comfortable chair. He had possessive feelings about the chair, because he had bought it.

When Ottoline had decided to amend her failing financial matters by letting the Grange, which Sigerson had always secretly wanted for himself, she had furnished it out of a catalogue. It had afforded her vast amusement to select furnishings in this way, and the resulting conglomerate was noticeable for its singularity and not for its comfort. Sigerson had interfered and purchased the one armchair, in which he was now sitting, and a bedside lamp.

For some reason Sigerson thought that Mary-Rose did not integrate ill in her bizarre surroundings. She herself had the studied casualness and superfluous luxury that went with orange cardboard coffee tables and lamps like electrocuted hedgehogs. He was accustomed to furnishings which led to this impression; he passed much of his time amongst Beardsley posters and thick plastic framed mirrors in primary colours, and he knew about women who stroked china figurines in the dog hours. It was not natural to him, but he could accept it. Which was more than he could do with a three-legged milking stool which had begun life as a three-legged milking stool.

Mary-Rose seated herself opposite him beside the fireplace, and the familiarity and normality of the action tugged at his heartstrings. He looked at her helplessly. 'Could you give me a cup of tea?' he asked wanly. 'Not coffee, or whiskey, or stout and pickled herrings – just a cup of Indian tea, with milk and sugar?'

Mary-Rose laughed. 'Having a bad time with your mother?' she said softly.

He laughed, too. 'O, Mary-Rose, she is AWFUL!' he said in despair. 'Do you know, I left her in the abbey – well, she left first actually – with an enormous weapon with two hooks on it like an impaling stake and it was a CATTLE GOAD. Honestly, she said it was. And she was prodding at that poor girl, Dorothy, as if she was going to run her through. Then she wandered off up to the Baun saying she was glad she had been useful! USEFUL!'

'Perhaps she thinks you don't like Dorothy. Is her name Dorothy? Ottoline always calls her Girl.'

'She's too lazy to learn her name. Yes, it's Dorothy. And she, well, she's bottom. All she wants out of life is a date.'

'A date? Which sort of date?'

'I don't think it matters.' He snorted miserably. 'And sweet you, you don't mind if I come and sit by your fire and complain? You aren't working?' he added anxiously.

Mary-Rose gestured at her bare arms and the blue smock. 'I've just stopped. I was on my way to the kitchen to make just that cup of tea. Why don't you light the fire while I put another cup on the tray. It's going to be a chilly evening.'

When she left Sigerson set about lighting the fire. He had Anglo-Saxon tendencies in the matter and so, he discovered, had Mary-Rose. He found a tidy basket of kindling, a neat pile of old papers – *Illustrated London Weekly*, which wouldn't burn, and some *Guardian*s, which would, a few *Statesman*s and a *Times Lit. Supp*. The feel and aspect of them soothed him. The layout, typography, format, fell to his hands like old caresses. Ottoline lit fires, when she did so at all instead of screaming at Aelebel, by waving a paraffin-saturated rag over a heap of turf, muttering, mouthing, blowing and blaspheming, as if fire lighting was a novel and complicated art acquired in the last two days of her existence with great difficulty. The way she did it, it was difficult. Mary-Rose's fire, on the other hand, lit aromatically and instantly. With a complacent smirk he sat back in his chair and watched the lively little flames spark and flirt about the wood chips. From the kitchen behind came an almost forgotten sound: the clatter of china. When Ottoline served tea it tended to clink in the fashion of glass ... O, Ottoline ...

Exasperation brought him to his feet and he went to the door and leaned against the jamb, watching Mary-Rose move around her domain. 'She knows nothing – NOTHING – of civilised comforts!' he expostulated loudly. 'O, gracious, let me carry the tray for you – heavens, is that all you've got in the way of a tray? Mary-Rose, you must complain. I can't let you be afflicted by Ottoline like this. Heavens, I'll bring one back next time I come.'

'But, honey, it is a tray. At least, now you mention it, I suppose it is. What else could it be? I think it's just very modern. Lots of things come in this blue plastic these days.' She looked doubtfully at it.

'Where did you find it?' he said.

'On a piece of white marble with a gilt palm leaf and three black legs.' Then she added carefully, 'In the bathroom.'

Perplexed, they looked at each other. He held out his hands dumbly for the object and carried it gently into the drawing-room. For lack of an alternative he put it on the floor. Since no other response was possible Sigerson and Mary-Rose both laughed again. Then she took the china off the tray and set it on the floor. She handed the plastic to Sigerson. He removed it from the room and returned without it. Facing each other they took tea. Each time Mary-Rose bent forward to pour, stir or offer, the top of her bra was visible through the opening in her smock. Sigerson rested his eyes upon it. Like a man with long sight after much reading, he rested his eyes on the unlimited vistas of the twist of black lace.

After a while he said, 'Don't you find it irritating?'

'Coimheadach?'

He did not reply but looked at her expectantly. This threw Mary-Rose into a dilemma. Inside her butterflies of uncertainty had their way. Cautiously she said, 'Not irritating, no.'

'What then?' he countered.

She hoped he would supply a description which she could take over and agree to, but he was obstinately silent. Mary-Rose remembered the moment of alliance between him and herself which had somehow failed to manifest itself in the chimney last night and said hastily, 'It makes me a bit aggressive!'

To her relief he snatched at this and said quickly, 'How much better. What an intelligent person you are! I get irritated and ruffled, and you merely become aggressive and so do something creative! Clever you. Does it make you paint better, do you think? Or do you just kick the – er – décor?'

'I wouldn't call that creative – more destructive!' Her smile encompassed him and drew his idea up to stature.

Gratefully he laughed with her. 'But really,' he insisted, 'does all this inadequacy stimulate you?'

Relieved to be able to answer honestly Mary-Rose said, 'O, yes. Definitely. And the loneliness, too. It's useful in a way. It's dreadfully hard to explain – I've never been good at explaining things in words, and I have no hope sitting opposite you: words are your business and you use them, well, like tools –'

She stopped and looked at him, almost as if she wanted him to do her explaining for her. He nodded, acknowledging both his ability and her weakness.

Slightly irritated by this bland assumption of an inadequacy which Mary-Rose felt that she alone had the right to indicate, she continued, 'I use paint in the same way – as a tool to say what I mean.' This set them on an even footing, and the conversation could now continue with equilibrium. 'You called Coimheadach an 'obliquity' last night. It annoyed me at the time, but I have thought about it and I think it's a perfect description, really. I mean, it is oblique to the way most people live, and made more so by your mother and her – well, her eccentricities. I don't want to be rude – I admire Ottoline enormously as you know – but it is all at a tangent, isn't it? To the style of life that you and I live normally?'

Somewhere in her long narrow eyes Sigerson saw a friendliness, an attachment to his life, a care, a concern. Suddenly it arose in the words 'You and I'. Desperate to foster it, to nurture, tend, feed it, he leaned forward in his chair, clutching his chest and gripping the sleeves of his shirt as if cold threatened him again. 'Yes?' he said anxiously.

'It's oblique to us,' said Mary-Rose quietly, rearing the delicate thing herself, 'but it has a basic straightness. I mean, Coimheadach is REAL. It's right down at the bottom of living, isn't it? All this concern for mere shelter from the weather – the enormous amount of energy Ottoline puts into things like keeping the gutters in place and the roof in repair –' (Sigerson had a spasm of guilt over the drainpipe in the yard and the eight feet of rusty sieve he had slung into the shed, but he ignored it.) '– and making herself shoes out of seal skin in the old pattern and so on. And eating her own stock – it's all, not primitive, but sort of precise. Do you know what I mean?'

Sigerson sensed in Mary-Rose a lack of attention, an inarticulateness, which was a characteristic, a sign of personality, which was the result of insufficient attention to subject. He thought that she described his mother as she would have liked Ottoline to be and that for some reason this was because she had not looked at Ottoline as she was. Whether this might be because she preferred to make of Ottoline something comparable to some dream of her own and therefore dared not inspect the actuality, or because close attention was a labour which she was either ill-prepared or ill-equipped to undertake, as yet he did not know. To test her in some way and to reassure himself he said, 'And do you not find our lives precise?'

Mary-Rose hesitated again. Very loudly she could have shouted 'O yes!' and meant it, glancing over her shoulder at the train of linked or arbitrary events which had culminated in her leaving her husband Fergus and directing herself to live in the place described in the advertisement as having 'unusual and primitive charm'. Equally well she could have cried 'O no!' looking at the nervous shape of a man fidgeting in her chair and hugging his body as if reluctant to let go of some unassailable reality. She floundered in her ambivalence and smoothed down the front of the blue and stained smock over her breasts. The gesture had an appealing self-consciousness for Sigerson, almost as if he had made her squirm, and yet it was so immediate of her to resort so simply to her own beauty as a defence that he caught his breath and leaned still further towards her so that she was forced to sit back in order to keep his apologetic eyes in focus.

'No,' she said at last, 'I cannot find anything very precise in my own life. But yours always looks, at least from the outside, as if you know where you are going. I mean, look at me, Sigerson! I just hang about in beautiful places waiting for something to hit me! And, of course, I should probably hate it if it did, because I am so distrait and vague that I would never be able to get up off my back once I was knocked down onto it. That's always been my trouble, you see. I suppose, really, that's why I am here. Thank heavens, at any rate, that Fergus is rich enough to pay me to stay away and indulge my faults, which is what alimony really is. Marvellous institution, divorce!' She gave a little laugh and turned her face away from him.

Uncertain whether to read bitterness or relief into the complicated sound, Sigerson said gently, 'My dear, I could always be found to give a helping hand.'

It was the sort of soft remark which made Sigerson so beloved by women. There was no insincerity in it, there could not be, but equally there was little likelihood that his strength would be sufficient to achieve anything much were he ever called upon to use it. Yet the manner of his speaking betrayed his care, his fondnesses, his appreciation of the littleness of insuperable individuality.

Mary-Rose responded by turning her long face to him again and rewarding him with a frown which tokened her earnestness. 'How nice you are, Sigerson,' she said. 'Niceness, as we know, is not in plentiful supply around here, is it? I suppose it's too human for Coimheadach. Not at all grand or elemental. I suppose anything here has to be either horrifying or magnificent to survive. Like your mother. Like Ottoline.'

'Terrible,' he agreed, slightly irritated that she should return to the subject of his mother. Again he thought he detected a lack of attention, this time to himself. 'You're very impressed by Ottoline, aren't you?' He made it sound slightly childish of her.

Mary-Rose said 'Yes!' with astonishing complacency. 'And so are you, you know!'

By the fireside Mary-Rose was exuding perfume in the dry warmth. It was not strong, yet it pervaded the room. It made of the room the possession of a woman; of the precious woman who baths delicately and is fragrant at all times. There was something touching about the scent. It was personal, a trail left by this sophisticated animal for him to track and pursue. In her sandals her feet were long and narrow, like the slot of a roe deer, and as aromatic. Like most women Mary-Rose did not easily change her scent. She had worn sandalwood for more years than she had spent at Coimheadach, so that the scent was for Sigerson entirely hers, retraceable through periods of acquaintanceship, running on into the time of companionship to come, laid instinctually and followed without premeditation. It intensified his self-consciousness as directly as the wind about his clothes had done in the church. But this time there was no tension, no lack of grace, no concern for culpability. Thus aggrandised he was able to answer what had sounded like an accusation with unwonted firmness.

'Yes,' he said, smiling at her dark, almond eyes and the smooth long hair which shone in the firelight and hid her neck from him. 'I am impressed by Ottoline in many ways. But she is not careful. What she personally is not concerned with she dismisses as a thing of no value in itself; and when this is applied to people it makes her a rather less admirable figure than you would have her. Don't be taken in by her, my dear; she is powerful enough, as you said, but she is totally immoral.'

'Do you not mean "amoral"?'

'No. I mean immoral. Ottoline knows very well what she is about. She has an acute understanding of people, and she uses them and plays with them as if they were toys. And this is what makes her immoral – she is well aware of it! If she were merely 'amoral' she would have no apprehension of the rights and wrongs of living within a given society. But she has. She is fully conscious of inflicting hurt or damage or benefit, but she only operates to please herself. Mary-Rose, I beg of you, don't let that 'niceness', that humanity we were talking of, be distorted by living close to Ottoline! She is the most totally self-centred being I have ever come across. I don't believe she was ever born, despite what Grandfather used to say about that! She is self-generating, self-propelling.'

Mary-Rose suddenly laughed. Her expression of slightly haughty superiority had not altered during his expostulations. It was obvious that his words struck her as wildly inaccurate. Somewhere he had been inadequate in seeing Ottoline through Mary-Rose's eyes and thus being able to explain to her the Ottoline which he saw himself.

'You do hate her!' she remarked, on the verge of being amused.

'Yes,' he said.

He did not want to discuss the matter further, he was choked with Ottoline. He had found a scent to follow which was not bovine. He did not want to be distracted from it. Ottoline had crowded out the scent, overlaid it, over-run his questing muzzle. Irritated afresh he looked up to the huge canvas which hung over the fireplace.

Mary-Rose followed his look, and then said softly, 'You've never liked it, have you?'

Sigerson hesitated. He had no desire to be rude, no desire to hurt her feelings.

She continued without waiting for his reply. 'I remember your watching me paint it. Do you? You liked it at first, and as it grew and grew and came closer to being finished you took against it and stopped watching. You wandered up and down, or talked about your history or the abbey or your friend – Geoffrey, isn't it? – and lost all interest in the picture. Why?'

'You remember all that? I would have thought you would have been too busy with the act of creation to observe my reactions.'

'Now, don't be sarcastic. That is unkind of you, and you know I rely on you to supply kindness. ...'

'My dear! It was an expression of conceit! How you do misinterpret me – I am flattered that you were aware of my hanging round watching, and that you remember so accurately!'

Mary-Rose's laugh took the malice out of their exchange, but her eyes glittered so that he was under no illusion that the conflict did not exist.

'You haven't answered me – why do you not like my picture?'

'When you began,' he said carefully, 'with bracken in the background, done in ink, so exact and so vast, the size of the first fronds, you remember how they filled the entire frame? I loved that. The colour was faint – it was like an oriental dream, and it had the precision of a dream, but very far off. It spoke to me. I wanted it then. I would have liked to possess it, to have it in front of me for rest, at all times. As you drew closer to the foreground and each advancing frond was the same size but harder in colour, it became impenetrable, and then, with final strokes – that terrible blood colour there on the left and the enormity of the individual pattern going back and back, each under-lying one as meticulous as the one in front and only the hue receding, with no dimension, no perspective – it turned into a nightmare. Now it gives me the shivers or makes me want to retire to the other side of the room."

He looked at her, embarrassed by the sudden explanation which flooded out of him. She was watching him, her eyes narrow and her mouth, darkened and formalized by lipstick, drawn and puckered with concentration.

'It was the first thing I did at Coimheadach. I have done very few real pictures, always the landscapes and the little minute designs of living things in the landscapes – partly for pin money, partly for – I don't know exactly. But that picture wasn't for sale, it was for me. It was how I felt about Coimheadach. The remorselessness of Nature, of uncontrollable expense, really. An extravagance of power coming up out of the very ground, on and on and on –'

'Why did you not do it in heather?'

'HEATHER? Why? What do you mean?' Mary-Rose looked at him blankly.

'Because Coimheadach is covered in heather, burdened down with it. That is what even the peat is, you know: decomposed, ancient heather. And there is hardly any bracken. ...'

'O,' said Mary-Rose, 'I didn't know that –'

VI

HOW IS IT possible for the slight person to feel so much? It was as much astonishment as agony that exhausted Sigerson. The summer, indeed his whole slight spring life up to the summer, was but a drawing up to this, a germination, a formation, a budding to this sudden blossom, this explosion of pain like the bursting of the first amazing flower. As poets compare bomb blasts, incredible wounds, flames and births to the violent flowers of high summer, so to Sigerson the catastrophe in his frame was at once wild beyond his knowledge, vast, yet meticulous, exquisite, perfect. It came from nowhere he could recognise, but had no derivation in him, no analogue of lesser dreams, of expectations or of fears. It came from places so far within that only their forbidding mouths in the narthex of his consciousness betrayed their profound existence, and the aspect of the entry was so appalling that even curiosity was not aroused. But the flowers that sprang forth from thence were as perfect and severe as those that bloom in any man; their exact formation aligned on abstract planes common to him amongst all, and therefore not blemished, not subformed, but mature, exact, entire. And around it formed Sigerson, as yet but a foetal cast of himself, blundering in possession of the blossom, inept, like a deformed child incapable of dealing with its disobedient limbs, crying out for the doctor to help him support the power of his humanity. Reeling in the spikes of rain that swept the hillside, blinded by them and by the inturning of his staring eyes, Sigerson crept up the side of Coimheadach carrying the flower.

Somewhere in that grey mass of stone, dead fish, fossils, flags and wind was his mother — a porcelain blossom as cold as death. Ivory, peach and carmine, growing directly out of the mountain up which he laboured.

Who gives flowers to their loved ones? Who can bear to give expression in so transient and rare a form to the blossoms that explode from within? Who would so symbolize, with things as perfect and as known, the whole reduction of the mass of man as a gift? Who can afford to look at flowers like this? Who can tread on them in the lane, pluck and then discard them by the road, knowing them to be the heart of any one particular? Who treads the petal? All the time, through time acknowledged and unacknowledged, the petal is trodden.

Below Sigerson, all the time the sea pawed at the feet of the mountain, its structureless noise swinging in his ears, a-CUSH-la, a-CUSH-la. ...

From the Grange Mary-Rose could hear it distantly; to the abbey where Ottoline sat immobile, somnolent, on a high, hardbacked chair it called from below; at Aelebel's feet it cast its cold petition where she sat stroking her life as it were Ottoline's cheek, Ottoline Atlantica, love, bitch.

a-CUSH-la.

The sad weather persisted throughout the evening. It surrounded Ottoline in her high conservatory and did not touch her. It poured and streamed over the glass roof built out over the annex to the night-stair, echoing the sound of Sigerson's murmurs and faint footsteps recurring in the moan in the fuchsia. It came down onto the abbey like a visitant, like a mask of God, a paraclete of withdrawal. It was double-edged and double-tongued like a criminal. It held itself over Coimheadach in the act of extinguishing it and all its inhabitants, at the same time revealing itself by the action as a physical, irrefutable instance. Like a murderer it had crept up behind the world; like a murderer it obliterated the world by the fact of its incarnation, of its arrival here, now.

It fed Sigerson with nutrients of despair; it provided him with external tears so that he need not busy his eyes. It removed Boston and not Boston from Ottoline so that she, too, was removed in it. In the Hebrides and St Kilda it raised threats and dangers, and down the Skerries the swells answered it from the depths of Rockall. The young man on the wireless spoke of it to the men out on the Icelandic Bank; the Old Cattle turned their fawn loins to it, and Gilles spat it out from the gutters on the cloister roof.

The betrayal was so strange. It was a betrayal and yet not like one. There was no way to make amends; no one to whom to turn to say, simply, 'I am sorry'. For the first time there was something he could not say to himself. There was something which defined Mihilanus in a way he had no presentiment of; as a thing so singularly precious that he doubted his capacity to contain it. And all because of a sweet smell, a perfume with a meaningless name which touched him on a plane to which Mihilanus had no access. There could be no competition, no adjustment, no jealousy. All the direct responses which arise when one man scents two hearths were denied to Sigerson, for there was only one hearth.

Which one?

And still it rained.

It rained for forty days and forty nights.

About the middle of the fortieth night Ottoline banged on his door. Sigerson raised his head stupidly from his hands — he had been suffering from insomnia and was not in bed. He turned up the collar of his maroon dressing-gown to ward off the cold that would come in with Ottoline and looked fixedly at the door. The door vibrated as Ottoline shook it.

If he did not open the door she would get in through it.

Ottoline put her head round the door. Seeing him sitting by the table, with his head in his hands, she said, 'Are you indisposed?'

'Yes,' he said furiously, 'I've got rabies — please, Ottoline, not now. ...'

'RABIES? Damn it to hell, what do you mean? Been bitten? Here, let's have a look at you —' She seized his shoulders and swung him round to face the light from the window. 'What do you mean?' she repeated.

Sigerson looked up at her. Her beautiful face was so small, so lovely. There was no concern in it at all. Outside it was raining.

'Your skin is like porcelain –' he said softly.

'SIGERSON! For God's sake, boy, what's the matter with you?'

Since she appeared angry rather than troubled, he blinked sleepily at her and lied again. He said he had been drinking. That the weather had got him down.

Ottoline giggled like a schoolgirl. 'Don't let Aelebel hear you say that, she'll tell you it's what it wants to do. Is there any more?'

'Any more of what?'

'Of whatever you've been drinking. Tell the truth, I've been to sleep myself. I could do with a drop invigorating before I face dinner – that damn Girl, Sigerson, when is she going? I always rather liked Geoffrey, why did he send her here? What have I done to him to deserve a Girl with a Birdcage? Aelebel tells me it's in her cell ... it's empty. Now a BIRD I could understand, it could feed with the Rhode-Islands –'

'No, Ottoline, I beg of you –'

'Do you think I should offer her some hen food? Which reminds me, it's guinea fowl for dinner – you always used to love it –'

'It's such a long time since I ATE guinea fowl; no one eats GUINEA fowl nowadays –'

'Rubbish – the poulterers sell them for three quid a bird in town. I read it in the *Farmer's Weekly* – now what's the matter?'

'It's bad for you to smoke so much – and I think you are going to drop ash on my carpet –'

'Your concern touches me. Worse, it irritates me.' Ottoline looked at him crossly.

He was unimpressed by her crossness: she had other emotions and reactions which were dangerous; this one was not. He struggled with his mood. She watched his struggle. For one who cried in a newly decorated lavatory she showed remarkably little understanding or sympathy. He had a feeling he was interrupting her in some way – that his mood, his unhappiness, was getting in her way. He pulled his dressing-gown closer round his shoulders so that he looked like a crow in a children's book: hunched, queerly coloured, significant rather than impressive.

'Why did you call me Sigerson?' he asked. He had often wanted to know.

'Because I wanted to,' she replied dismissively.

She was not attending. He wanted to teach her himself, but she was an intractable student and would not learn. ...

'Why did you ask?'

'Because I wanted to know,' he said, not concentrating any more.

'There you are, then.'

Such fatuosity threw him into a rage. Stiffly he said, 'Did you want something? Did you come here because you wanted something?'

Ottoline stamped down to the kitchen. There she found Aelebel holding a very large cabbage leaf in one hand and a piece of frayed white paper in the other.

'Here, You,' said Aelebel, 'where's my scissors?'

'I've just called Sigerson a toffee-nose so we may be only two to dinner. Here, have you anything to drink? I've perpetrated an enormity – Sigerson had but he wouldn't give me any ... trying to punish me, I expect.'

'What have you done this time? And go and get my scissors. You had it last to cut out pictures for your scrapbook ... it might be in your room – You're little, run up and fetch them –'

'No. Listen, I couldn't get him to concentrate on me. Hey, and he said he had RABIES. He couldn't have, could he?'

'Little RED BITCH! Bitten by the little red bitch! Go and ask him which one of the scarlet bitches bit him! Go on. You, do you hear me? If he's got rabies it's not from your dogs, and you'll satisfy yourself as to which of the bitches or no bitch it is that is biting him and driving him mad. He's on his way to madness, him and his rabies, I tell you, coming in my kitchen in the night and asking questions like a nosey priest about you and me, questioning me in the dark about Ottoline, my Ottoline. ... Here, You, get out and fetch my scissors. ...'

Aelebel clutched the cabbage leaf in her flat hand and wiped her face with it. The green passed across her features making a myth of her as her eyes returned again from behind the green leaf. They were brilliant and wide, refreshed by the stroking of the leaf. With its coolness still held across her coloured cheek she stared at Ottoline and began to laugh. Her noise came deep from beneath the depressed breasts, the ignored pendulous food source that had never given suck.

Ottoline strode down the dank, semi-subterranean kitchen, which stank of milk and breasts, rats and turf. The shadows strode about after her, rearing and pounding among the ribs and vaultings, leaping in the jerky flashes from the open fire, dancing dangerously amongst the pans and cans and platters and crocks on the stone dresser built in the thickness of the wall and the blackened shelves urging their coppery utility into the stark cave.

'He'll concentrate on me now, all right,' Ottoline said grimly. She sat on a sack in the corner of the room. Under her movement a thin trickle of pale meal and dark mouse droppings scattered onto the flagstones.

Aelebel twisted the ragged piece of paper about her finger like a jagged ring and watched Ottoline. Her pinafore was splattered with blood from the gutting of the guinea hen; red droplets and smears among the pernickety flowers, all daisies, all five-petalled, none real. In blue and yellow and mauve. The ribbons, washed and wrung into strings, disappeared into her. The flowery pinafore grew on her, not a garment, a super epidermis.

'I'll wring a gift from That One, if I have to draw him to get it out for you,' Aelebel said, watching.

Ottoline stroked the glossy leather of the high boot. It whispered like silk; the sound ran with the silky rain and the fine wind and clouds. The whispering of the rain and the sea, a-CUSH-la, a-CUSH-la, and the leather boots. She began to laugh. 'What would he have thought, if he could see us now? Two tatty old women, pecking at a boy like hens, cackle cackle, and not a drop of love to spill out to him? Would he have gone on loving us, Aelebel? Would he have come back to us – to two tatty old hens, scribbling and cackling and growing older and more ignorant with every turn of the tide – WOULD he?' The laugh swayed about, shortened, turned into a whimper. Nightfall reached down tentacles of shadow from the carved ceiling.

'Ah,' said Aelebel, 'he was a lovely man – a lovely man, he was, so. ...'

'A lovely man –' said Ottoline slowly.

Between the two women the unbasted guinea hen lay on the dish. Plucked, its skin was pale and dewy and wrinkled. They stared at the skin of the naked bird, soft as fleece. When their remembering coincided they looked up, and their eyes met – the brilliant crystal and the glittering mica.

'I MADE it!' Ottoline said indignantly, at dinner that night. 'I made it out of some writing paper, and as I couldn't find the scissors, I tore the pattern. I think it's very beautiful.'

She sat back in her high-backed chair and considered the little paper crown around the curtailed neck of the roast fowl. It had a sort of elegance derived from the intricate tearing by her little finger when she had sat on the table beside her woman and made it through her tears. It had been expensive for what it was. To slight its elegance was to slight the cost: the tears, the long silence broken only by the scratch of tearing paper.

'They put them round the legs of the hams at Schipol Airport,' Ottoline added, to give an air of authority to her activities.

The Girl looked up severely. 'Schipol?'

'In Holland. A very nice airport. Very modern, with good restaurants for transit passengers.'

The Girl looked apprehensively about the room. The conversation had taken a turn so unlikely that she sought some outward manifestation of assurance from the little old lady sitting so primly at the head of a table so vast that Sigerson from his end had had to slide the Worcestershire Sauce to her on an organdie mat although she was only, so to speak, amidships along its great length. There was nothing to recall the contemporary splendours of Schipol. The Girl looked hard at Ottoline to ascertain whether she might be being teased. ...

'My mother,' said Sigerson, 'takes holidays visiting European airports. She flies, for several days, around Europe, dining at Orly, sleeping in the airport hotel at Rome, breakfasting in Geneva in the coffee lounge, and eventually returns here, the final stage being accomplished in the trap behind the jennet.'

The Girl's eyes moved on a horizontal axis slowly from mother to son.

'O yes?' she said softly.

'I find the decor of airports refreshing,' Ottoline said, out of an impulse to make conversation.

Ottoline was not good at making conversation but had always tried hard, deeming it an art incumbent upon a hostess, a position into which she had now been forced by Sigerson. To pay him back she spat out a splinter of bone, picked it up delicately and flung it behind her to the whippets. They screamed in ecstasy and fell quivering to the floor. Sigerson winced.

The Girl looked away from him, still seeking some indication of veracity in Ottoline's statement. The cruet, silver and complex beyond the demands of any guinea fowl, glowed softly behind the verdigris of its ornate tray; filigrees of unravelled threads splashed from the lace mat beneath her plate across the dark Spanish table; her immense plate, cradling in its depths the leg of the fowl, a stain of white salt, a tide of pale gravy and two empurpled eyes plucked from a potato, stayed before her as it always had been, a thing of weight and grandeur off which passing innocent or insignificant strangers ate and then vanished out into the night. She thought there might well be something comforting in eating from a cardboard carton, which was even more transitory than one's self.

Ottoline was saying, 'I fly on fine days only, so that I can look down at the land.' She added, 'I like land. I have never, for instance, flown to America.'

The Girl said, 'Do you visit the cities where you change planes?'

As she had expected, Ottoline replied, 'Hell, no.' And then, as if in explanation, 'I was married, you know. Sigerson's father. He was a professional traveller. He wrote a book once – you may have read it –'

'Ottoline!' Sigerson said warningly.

'– called *Food and Phallus in the Lower h'M*.'

'The "h'M"?'

'A tribe he lived amongst for a time – he was an amateur

anthropologist —' his son explained hastily. 'Quite a good one for his time. He was very appreciative of economic parameters, more so than most of his contemporaries who were little better than collectors of after-dinner stories. ...'

'Indeed he provided one himself — they ate him!' said Ottoline, adding, for decorum's sake, 'y'know!' — an expression she had picked up from the phone-in programmes on the wireless.

'Did they really?' The Girl leaned across her own reflection in the deep wood and peered at Ottoline. She did not believe it. No, definitely not.

'Well,' said Ottoline, 'let's say some bits of him were missing. ... Shall we speak of something else during the pudding? I think Aelebel has prepared a spotted dog.'

'A "spotted dog"?' said the Girl, who had met many Dalmatians in Wilberforce Close.

'Are you feeling well? Both you and Sigerson have a weak look about you. Perhaps it's catching —'

'Catching?' echoed the Girl desperately.

'The rabies. Sigerson told me before dinner that he had rabies. And now he definitely looks, well, palsied. ...'

'OTTOLINE! I insist that you terminate this idiotic conversation. It is most ill-mannered of you to unnerve our guest in this way.'

Sigerson almost rose to his feet and then resorted to wiping his mouth with the bit of the mitre on his napkin that hadn't been laundered away. He cursed Ottoline for choosing the Girl to start up this sort of conversation with. Heavens, he thought miserably, it was downright rude. ... Spotted dog and rabies indeed. He wiped again hastily.

'Dorothy,' he said, 'you are being misled by an atmospheric *non sequitur*. It is true that some bits of Daddy may have — er — added to the subsistence of the unfortunate h'M, but you yourself are not being required to consume a Dalmatian — or carriage dog, as my mother calls them —'

'correctly.'

'— as my mother correctly calls them. Nor have I got rabies. We are about to be served something with suet and raisins —'

'Currants.'

'ALL RIGHT, Ottoline. Currants, then. And when I told my mother that I had rabies it was a vain attempt to forestall just the sort of conversation which you are now experiencing. I hope you are a little calmed?'

The Redness came. It came pounding up from her lap, beating through her upper arms and neck, and burst forth in a flood of metrically increasing suffusion through which she could speak but thickly. 'I am not so stupid, Dr Ottraine, as to have been misled by your mother's attempts to put me in what SHE considers to be my place!'

'O, gracious,' said Sigerson furiously. 'For heaven's sake, don't start rowing. Here, Ottoline, you really are the end. Now look what you've done. ... Dorothy, for goodness sake, don't be childish –'

'AH! Look, we are to be rescued from wrath by a pudding!' cried Ottoline, wriggling in her high chair as Aelebel entered, bearing aloft in the manner of a Yuletide ceremonial a large pale hemisphere from which a steamy odour and some blackened dried fruit protruded. 'Set it down in front of me here ....' Standing to cut it, she seized a disproportionate knife, nudged Aelebel, winked at the Girl, plunged the weapon into the heart of the suet and shouted, 'WOOF, WOOF!'

One whippet had to be removed.

Sigerson rose to his feet. He smacked the table in a wild attempt to achieve their awe, or at least their attention. His hair flopped over his eyes, and his long, clever face disintegrated into a palimpsest of all the rages he had ever suffered at the hands of a beautiful woman who had never allowed him to call her his parent, his dam, his Source ...

'Aaah, Ottoline,' he cried, 'what do you want? What do you WANT?'

His voice rose above the howling whippet and the singing winds in the stones and wailed among the lights and the ribs of the stony ceiling, bouncing and smashing amongst the shadows and the dust until drop by drop every demand of hers on men came coursing from the stones in bloody streams, and he screamed at her for murderess and witch and killer. ...

'Damn and blast,' yelled Ottoline, 'the tiles are off again! Here, Aelebel, put the gravy boat under it and fetch a bucket –'

Splat, splat, splat, of his father's blood and the other man's, and now his. Splat in the summer rain storm, laden with bromides and fluorides flailing the stones, the homes, the features of the Atlantic Shore. Splat through the generations, dropping away in the slow erosion of kind. Splat into the gravy boat where the cooked juices of the grey guinea fowl congealed and gelled.

Ottoline ran around the table and pulled his black hair – jerk, snap! on his vertebrae. 'Don't just ignore it – it's a tragedy – a happening – an occasion – an assignation with Poseidon. Get up and deal with it – fetch a pail!'

He hit at her with his hands, flap, flap, like a corpse stirred by the beat of a vampire wing-tip.

'Assignation with Poseidon – it's bloody inefficiency!' Sigerson bellowed at her.

'A pail – a pail' cried the Girl.

'Stuff the potato dish under it, it'll wreck the Aubusson. Quick, quick!'

'Quick, quick, the cat's. ...'

'The coasters, the cabbage dish, the fruit bowl ...!'

'Hasten, hasten, fetch a basin.'

Ottoline leaped about the room setting the shadows into a gigue upon the unwilling walls, creating new and unnecessary winds and eddies where none had been, sparking and shouting and setting her little hands beneath the drops to catch the sweet drips, jerkily as a marionette from the rheumatism and the rarity of dancing to measured rhythm. The Girl ran about behind her, co-operating with self-possession now that the weather had entered indoors and was crying out to be dealt with. ...

'Quick, quick, the sweet dishes, glass bowl –'

Up she goes, up, up into the dark upon the ladder, rung after rung broken and unsteady, leaning herself over the gutter, a mad gnome called out of the hills by the war-whoop of the Skerries' horn and the spears from the ocean, Enemy One the Wind clawing at her head and neck, and Enemy Two the Rain slithering around her heels to bring her down, and Enemy Three the Tarpaulin from the barn beating her about the arms and body to dislodge her from her scaling-ladder while Enemy Four, Sigerson the Treacherous, scrabbled at the bottom and squealed, 'Ottoline, come down, come down! For heaven's sake, you'll be blown away! For heaven's sake –'

'Hold tight – oh for goodness sake hold ON –'

When Enemy Three is fixed and the Aubusson saved, then Enemy Four awaits below.

Inexplicable in the howling rain and the wind stupefying their ears, Ottoline turned about on the ladder. Facing outwards and downwards, looking at them as if there were no barrier between her and them she sang, loudly over the storm:

> 'The lion in the fuchsia went roar, roar, roar,
> As he swiped at his Mammy with his paw, paw, paw,
> The lion in the fuschia went roar, roar, ROAR!
> O, hodie!'

Ottoline reached for the thermos of coffee which she always took to her room. She poured out a cupful into the plastic top. She lit the candles set in silver sticks among the green plants; the brilliant geraniums, polygoniums, African violets, polyanthus, begonias, tiger-lilies, carnations, miniature roses, asparagus ferns and gunmetal plants that stood solemnly and greenly attending her. She removed her smoking-jacket and Italian scarf and flung them through the double doors into her bedroom. Stretching her legs and laying her hands on her thighs, she sat in the wicker rocking-chair and reached for the dials of the old, electric wireless. The green light flickered and ran along the glass.

'You are listening to BBC Radio Two, 693 kHz and 90q kHz. This is You and the Night and the Music ...

Ottoline Atlantica sipped at the coffee and watched the moon traverse the intertidal rocks below the window. The bladderwrack lifted and gleamed, and the beating trembled in the hollow places in the walls. A cigarette burned between her fingers, the ash falling onto her lap. She smiled slightly.

Ottoline Atlantica.

Meanwhile,
Back in the eighth cell...
Dorothy Lambert drew pin-men and admired the view. She had dragged the top blanket off the bed and wrapped it round her feet. It kept the breeze from what someone had once imagined was a fitted casement away from her naked feet. The casement did fit: it fitted the hinges cemented onto the carved jamb. The hinges projected because the manufacturers in Tokyo who made them had not taken the carved vine leaves and grapes which ran up and down the jamb into account. They were stuck out from part of the stem, and the casement hung listlessly from them. As a result, there was a gap of about four centimetres between the vine and the cut-price frame. The vine itself had been cut into the original severe line of the light by a later hand than that which had carved the first, Cistercian window in a wan attempt to embellish the stringent lines. The moonlight, slithering over the high roof of the east range, plucked at the stone leaves and slipped, chill as a caress, over the rotund little grapes and the rubicund memories they evoked.

Beneath the roof Dorothy could see Ottoline's lit window. Through the glass the luxuriant foliage waved and swam in the yellow candles like a rock-pool on a sunny day. The image lay upside down on the sea-salted night, dim, aqueous, mobile in the shifting draughts.

Ottoline had switched the generator off when she retired, and the Girl – Dorothy, as she became when she was alone in her room – had been provided with a Tilly-lamp which filled the silence left after the beating of the generator suddenly ceased, with a muted hissing and buzzing like unlimited mosquitoes. Dorothy was alarmed by the Tilly. She did not know what it was, how to regulate the light for reading or how to extinguish it. It swung from a hook in the ceiling that was an exact replica of one she had seen in Madame Tussaud's impaling a man by the bowels, whose solid blood and gut were reflected on his waxen torso in identical shades of mauve, crimson and blackish greens to those colours which the Tilly cast upon the erstwhile whitewashed walls of the eighth cell.

At the heart of the Tilly was a flimsy scrap of white muslin and below this and around it a clutch of white-hot flame emerging from a highly combustible blue tin belly. The whole was surmounted by a frail little bulb of thin glass with a smoke-blackened rim. Dorothy gave the object some attention and came to the conclusion that the muslin was not burning. She decided that Moses's Burning Bush must have been a very literary description of a similar object which had struck similar awe into the heart of the unsuspecting. She almost expected it to burst into speech and tell her to take her shoes off. That it did no such thing could be attributed to the fact that she had already done so. It had been alight when she came into the room, sodden and on the verge of hysteria after the frenzy with the ladder. She had studiously ignored it until the generator stopped with a dying whoop of triumph and all the lights in the building went out except such as flickered or hissed. Then she had regarded it carefully.

Along with the lamp had been the unexpected sight of her luggage, which had at last arrived. The cell was transformed by the business of her accoutrements. Long skirts, books, files, pencil sharpeners, a camera and a suspender-belt in a cloth cap for safety, a photograph of the World Champion Canary (in colour), a bundle of photostat copies of articles from journals, a roll of graph-paper and a quarter-inch map declared for action and purpose. No good scholar goes to Coimheadach without a purpose.

Dorothy had unwarily turned her cases upside down on the bed with a grunt of possessive relief before ascertaining whether there was anywhere to put the contents. Behind a rod from which drooped a cretonne bedspread attached by sailmaker's thread she found a clothes hook stuck on the wall, the kind that had a sticky back which adheres to the surface to which it is firmly appressed. It was half an inch long and made of yellow plastic. Dorothy hung one of her six skirts on it, tentatively, and it fell onto the floor in the waistband of the skirt. The rest of the wall surface was innocent of projections. Dorothy hung her skirts over the foot rail of the bed. Her other garments she put grimly back into the suitcases from which she had taken them, then stowed the suitcases against the bare wall and sat on them. Her face was as red as the blood of the

Impaled Man. The draught blew a copy of Sigerson's latest article on the development of Rosary Prayers into the ink bottle top, which was sticky. The lid turned over, in slow-motion, as if reluctant to be interfered with by the Atlantic wind, and settled on the photo of the canary. A bronze ring formed as the strain dried in the salty air.

Eventually Dorothy went to bed. She sat huddled against the brass curliwigs in her print pyjamas and tried to read. Eventually Dorothy stopped trying to read and tried to go to sleep. The Tilly spat.

Eventually Dorothy went to sleep and then the Tilly spat twice. Five minutes later the mantel burnt through, and it blew up in a sheet of flame, bursting the glass and scorching the ceiling. Dorothy extinguished the fire with the bedspread and cut her wrist on the glass. Scorch marks made her papers brittle, and the whitewash, now undeniably black, drifted from the arched, asymmetrical rib and whispered onto the bed.

Outside a seal barked and the tide turned. Dorothy, who was exhausted, cried.

Meanwhile
Back in the *necessarium*
Sigerson with his pants about his ankles blasts his mother with words of hate. He does not read in the *necessarium*, nor construct new religions, nor even cry, but sits there like a phoenix, rising and falling gently on his gluteus maxima, his eyes glazed and his jaw agape, hunting up and down the alphabet of both languages for syllables or signs to construct his rage, not satisfied with the soft plop! plop! of his misery falling like tears from him into the frigid new bowl out of which icy nest mews forth still the moan of his mother's morning weeping trickling in the thick, heraldic colours of the fuchsia tree.

And in the Grange
Mary-Rose stands in her drawing-room watching the moth trying in vain to enter, beating and flailing at the invisible. It shakes, vibrates, consumes its tiny energy in explosions of power and force;

crump, crump, crump against the refined silica that it guns against.

An emerald epitome of photosynthesis, perfuming the night, glinting with jewelled dew, Mary-Rose has drawn the moth to the lighted pane, a vision of Paradise in the salt night. To the moth she is the plant of plants; the supreme achievement; green beyond the greens of this world; fresh with diamonds sweeter than the dew of dawns untold, perfumed from paths beyond the stars.

Mary-Rose will not open the window tonight. She has travelled a stony way to find windows of her own which she need not open. 'Fergus,' she whispers to the moth, 'Fergus?'

Whilst in the conservatory over the *slype*
Ottoline Atlantica falls asleep amongst her potted plants.

> '*Perfect was the prison of Gweir in the Faery Fortress*
> *According to the tale of Pwyll and Pryderi.*'

VII

AGAIN IT WAS morning. And the Daughters of Morning were waiting for her when she woke. Again she succumbed to them, hugging her stringy arms across her breasts, the corded muscles churning the sour milk and the youthless forms of the grey, stiff nipples. She lay among them, ridden by them; their statuesque thighs straddled her, working on her shoulders, her shrunken belly, her thighs, even her face. Tears dribbled from the outside of her eyes like a seal's tears, stroking her cheek bones and ears with cold, wet tracery. Under their implacable grasping she moaned and barked and twisted her head so that her sharp little teeth gleamed in the light from first one and then the other of the still windows which Mihilanus had built. And she never asked why.

Later she looked at the windows and saw the grey rain still streaming down them, and saw the sky as thick and mobile as mucus and remembered the night. She thought of how she had climbed up the ladder in the gale to Gilles, gargoyle on the east drainpipe; how she had placed her lips on the carved stone and kissed with her tongue-tip the rotten-sweet rainwater that ran from the open stone mouth. And now her tongue was sticky and foul with the taste of her daughters' anus. She shook her fine silvery hair across her eyes and her lips and her wet forehead, and it stuck to her, a web of unkemptness pinning her down onto the crushed pillow. When eventually she found the battered Woodbines on the floor and lit one with a sweaty hand she sucked and mumbled at it and grew less dizzy. She coughed a bit and spat into the yellow scarf, and then lay back watching herself and the day coming closer to each other, until finally they resolved into the same focus. Sourly she reached out for a whippet and screwed its ear roughly in her fingers. It panted and came back onto the bed whence it had fled earlier on. Its fellow still cowered under the tallboy, its tail pressed right against its hollow belly, its hocks quivering with terror. They were afraid of her. Pinell had been afraid of her. They were all afraid. Aloud she shouted, 'Is there no one left who can make me afraid?' But there was no one there to answer.

She smiled a little, accepting. It was revenge. The Daughters of Morning who came around her, enclosed her — they were revenge. She did not know or greatly care whose revenge, but it was a part of what they were. They dragged her up, drained out of her that which she harboured, as if they remembered the many nights when she had sucked at the seed of the man who had come to her that single summer; drained him; used him as a lance as the old women used the iron knives to lance the fistulae, as Ursula had used the goad to open the flesh of her beast on the hill. She had no interest in where he had come from or where he went when he left or what had become of him. What had become of him was the daughter he had left in her, the daughter she had dragged out of him into her bruised vagina and then had taken to the nuns in the pale asylum on the cold, unspirited mainland. Nor had she ever wondered what became of the child, for what became of that daughter had been Ottoline's return to Coimheadach and to the greater presence of the Daughters of Morning. And the presence of Pinell's son, too young to tell what had happened there that summer. And to the demands of Pinell himself, creeping back one night with a stuffed armadillo and an ostrich's penis to amuse her. And Pinell's demands in the bed in which she now still lay, still bruised, still unable to tell by which man or which daughter. She had taken revenge herself on Pinell, hauling with her arms on the bars of the bed-head, evading his desperation; shoving with her curly little toes against the footboard, eluding him. Then he had gone away again and someone else had eaten him ...

Afterwards Ottoline kept the curtains, although, until recently, she had only used them as a substance to foster moods upon. She would close them about the bed on still, foggy nights when nothing would happen and then run with them, the rings screeching on the runner, and crush them as tight against the walls as her strength could manage. Then she might laugh inanely or cry out with that harsh sound which Sigerson knew, or sing one of her home-made, senseless ditties about lions or stars or badgers which she had never seen. If she thought about Pinell at all at such times it was only in a sort of amusement that he had hidden his face in the bed so that he would never see to whom she turned.

Now, still holding the chilly metal convolvuli with one hand, she reached out with the other and pulled across the curtain nearest to the door to her conservatory. The worn material kept the draught off her and she liked the sudden peace in her shoulders. For a few moments she picked at the curtain where the lining had come away and fell in a loop exposing the reverse side of the embroidery. She poked her finger right through a little hole, making it bigger. It was unmendable. At least, she could not mend it; Aelebel would not; ergo, it was unmendable.

With the immediate change of ideas which was her way of thinking, Ottoline suddenly thought about the tiles on the factory roof, which could and must be mended. Her shoulders and her hands still ached from the cementing of the drain the day before, and she became sour knowing that it could have waited and would have deteriorated little over the weeks, whereas this new catastrophe was urgent and so she must work two days in succession. The rain streamed down the window. The court would turn to liquid mud, the new drain was scarcely firm, the drinking water would darken to the colour of whiskey. But the grass would freshen.

Today, too, she would take her new, young bull, Dan Dare, to run with the cows beyond the Baun on the far side of the Slieve. Anticipation curled her toes and fingers. Dan Dare was an unknown, unproven bull. It would be his first season. Popplethwaite was a fine beast, she thought of him with pride, but he was complacent. It had occurred to her to run them together with the cows until the day when Dan Dare had charged the jennet, ramming his shoulders and brow against the steel railings of his pen with such ferocity that he had dislodged one from its socket. She had told no one about it, gloating in secret over his vigour. Instead she extolled the virtues of Popplethwaite, praising his meaty loins, his mountainous neck, his pendulous balls, his sinuous dewlap.

The jennet, who had been on the other side of the rail from Dan Dare's charge, developed a curious antipathy to the sheds at the far end of the ruined outer court, and Ottoline had told long-winded lies about its hereditary terror of the sound of the sea which reminded it, she claimed, of the days when the lost Armada had been driven before the gales in these very seas and the mules, jennets, donkeys and horses had been eaten below the hatches by the dark Spaniards with long curved Moorish knives by the light of the swaying lanterns. Sigerson, to whom she told these lies, refrained from inquiring why the jennet, which was eleven years old, had not been visited by memories of these mythical events before. Ottoline wondered a little why he did not ask, and then forgot. She had had a good story to answer with, but she forgot that, too, once she recovered from her disappointment at not having to tell it.

Now the prospect of leading the young bull from the court to the far side of the Baun, a good two miles walk, made her shiver with anticipation. This was something which she must do alone. She did not, now, any longer, trust Aelebel. Were the black peasant to see her, with the beast on its long pole clip, being led from the yard, she might, thought Ottoline, either scream, in which case either or both of them would probably die, or attempt to dissuade Ottoline from her enterprise. The true Aelebel would scream – out of ecstasy and awe, a rude, dionysiac ululation. Such a demonstration of appreciation would upset the bull, and Ottoline, unlike the jennet, would not be on the other side of a steel barrier when it happened.

On the other hand, the true Aelebel, in the manner of peasants, was ageing. The true Aelebel was on occasions unpredictably absent, and a strange, weak thing in her would reveal itself. Aelebel must, in the end, give in, as we all give in. Auntie Bridie had been like this, afraid, defeated. Old Mame already has her coffin, ordered from the mainland; it stands upended in the pigsty outside her back door, and she bribes Rory with rum on Fridays to have it lined and brass handles sent for. Auntie Bridie, who had nothing to bribe anyone with, had crocheted her own winding-sheet towards the end. So, too, with Aelebel. She was turning towards Ottoline, as if Ottoline were coffin and shroud and safety against the inevitable granite down into which she was going. And as old Mame rubs linseed oil into the wood of her box, so Aelebel has nurtured and watched over Ottoline, tending Ottoline against the day when she would be needed. It was in the manner of peasants to know that rock is colder and harder than flesh and that tides which ebb will flow.

Ottoline knew this new weak Aelebel almost as well as she knew the old true Aelebel. She recognized as much with her body as with her mind that the grasp of her woman's hands upon her was no longer a bonding but a laying claim. She knew it well because it was to her the same claim that Gilles and Rory and the whippets and the decaying gutters laid upon her and she accepted it as she did theirs. She was all there was. Even this she accepted because of its untruth, for in fact, and to her, she was all there was because she was Coimheadach. Island, abbey, habit. Dead men and dying women and Ottoline Atlantica and the mornings on the granite when the light came first over England and the mainland and then came in the end to them to show that there was indeed not six feet of soil there to be buried in; this was all the morning there was.

Ottoline lay in her scandalous bed, no hollow in it where the eaten man had slept or the babies had been forced out into Mihilanus' brilliant stare, but reeking of bad dreams and sins committed in thought and word. Dog hairs, her brassière, Mary-Rose's rent cheque and ammunition for the rifle littered the place where she had made adulterous love, and a few grey hairs stuck to the rubbed patches on the iron bed-head where she had once hauled herself away from one man and heaved herself down upon another. This was no woman but a beast, tight-bonded and structured into itself, without any capacity for obligation or imagination, a thing like a god needing nothing but appeasement and satiety. Ottoline Atlantica – a cue for laughter, as irresponsible as Heliogabalus flaunting herself upon her own disgraceful altar.

She screamed for Aelebel.

The seal was barking again. He must have hauled up on the rocks below the very abbey itself. Just round the rocks from the jetty there is a platform of flattish rocks ending in a shallow overhang out of reach of high tide but littered with the pebbles of old storms. It is an ideal place for a seal nursery. He had come because the cows would come. She knew that in a month or so the young cows would surely come. She knew it suddenly, not aware of the second which divided the knowing from the not knowing. Her hand released the whippet and rested on the box of ammunition. The guns were downstairs. Beneath the bed the old sealskin rivlins lay where she had kicked them. The warmth was worn out of them by the stone floors.

She screamed again for Aelebel.

To shoot a seal. A grey, spotted bull seal. She would wait until his head was up, scanning the rock platform with his big, myopic eyes. He would strain his hearing, and his nostrils would bulge open. She would shoot him when his head was up. His red blood would spill and wash over the rock where he had hauled himself half out of the running tide, and it would stream and unravel in the swaying swell and kelp about the water edge. Crimson skeins in the water like the crimson of a judge's robe. He would look out of his fish-haunted eyes at her in the uncertain brilliance of daylight, landlight. She, redeemed by the seal's death, would look at the judge's crimson: 'Yes, m'lud, I shot a seal. Bastard's been eatin' my herrings for seven years. Yes, m'lud, no m'lud, stick your arse in the mud, m'lud. A woman who hasn't killed is dangerous. I shot the grey bull, saved the life of my relatives and domestics. ... Thank YOU, m'lud –'

The shot would have to be perfect – and single. The rifle steady in a parting in the seaweeds on the rock she would hide behind, the barrel resting on the steady granite, the quartz, mica, felspars. The point and the little V of the sights would come gently together, polite as they were made to be, mating there in front of the bull seal. Then she would wear him on her back and on her feet, lie within him in blood-warmth. The seal's death rose up in her and she lay against the worn linen pillow-case watching the sky cannily, cunningly, for the wind, the rain, the tide-signs.

Coming in with the tray, lugging the silver up the stone stairway and along the stone floor and through the paltry door into the washed light of Ottoline's room, Aelebel saw her and recognized her.

Ottoline Atlantica, my love, my bitch. ...

O o Dry Scalp, what does a man with Dry Scalp or herpes DO? What does he DO?

How does a man whose truth is in unreality persuade himself that a real woman can love him? If he has any of the imaginative man's common distribution of femininity he can become both the loving woman who sees and understands and still loves the culpable naked thing he is (this is an acquired trick) and at the same time be himself and the recipient of the support given.

Sigerson was such an imaginative man; he had his share of femininity; he liked women and was liked by them, not as some rather droll bachelors are, nor as an object of concern or a provocation for illicit maternity, but for his imagination. He understood them, not passionately or obviously but quietly. He was like them in a lot of ways. He had the same ability to imagine sensuous things; he had sympathy with the sort of fusses they made over minute mundanities, sprung from physical selfishness; he made the same sort of minute fusses himself and recognized them with companionship in others.

In his relationship with Mary-Rose Sigerson had become increasingly capable of achieving a strange dichotomy in his experiences whereby one part of him was in fact being, or experiencing, the feminine part, supplying the emotions he had no other outlet for; indulging the softness and sentimentality he had inside him which neither his work nor his usual life gave expression to. Her intact self-absorption allowed him to indulge himself in all his less acceptable fancies and rest assured that somewhere, inside the covering of herpes or Dry Scalp which embraced him, he would be tolerated and even loved by her, not despite his faults but almost because of them.

As the years passed Sigerson became tolerant of Mary-Rose in that he no longer found the existence within him of a perpetual 'fantasy' — for he was unable to find a better term for his relationship with Mihilanus — a hindrance in his understanding of her, but rather that by exercising and indulging his imagination in this way he had developed, if in a somewhat incomplete way, a whole gamut of experiences and emotions which his fellows, notably Geoffrey, were still struggling their way through. He recognized that this was valuable, and had he not been surrounded by young men using computers he might have, as he termed it, 'got away with it'. He might have succeeded in managing Mihilanus and Mary-Rose and himself.

It was all unclear to him, confused, too personal, too deeply buried beneath his conscious self-protection, but somewhere, this summer, there was going to be a confrontation between Mihilanus, himself and Ottoline.

Ottoline.

Ottoline Atlantica. One who had no need of blessing or of forgiveness. Ottoline, who embraced his periphery on all sides save that where Mihilanus was and who, in the event, might be found there, too. In the night, when he was sleepless, the enormity of this undertaking appalled him; he lay in his bed, as he had lain as a child, shivering in fear of Ottoline, of her hatred; above all, of her ridicule. There was about Ottoline a purity so severe, so luminous, that his own darkling mentality recoiled in horror as a worm from a sheet of shimmering glass.

What does the man with Dry Scalp DO? Does he take his tormented, itinerant scalp to his mother that she may search out the lice and nits, and kill them? KILL THEM between her bloody teeth —

O o Dry Scalp.

Once, on his way to a conference on late mediaeval dialects, Sigerson had stopped for coffee in Durham. Near the Warming-Pan, where he had stuffed on éclairs and cream at the hands of a distressed gentlewoman with light-blue hair, he had found a junk shop and, being unready to start driving again so soon and somewhat eructatious after the cakes, had entered. It had been dark. A clock ticked, aggressive in its unmetrical antiquity. Tick – and it would hiccough, grind, tock-tick and snore. For several minutes, amongst the Pelham bits, Maori spear-throwers, and the echo of the door-bell tinkling in the incurved depths of a cracked bedpan and an Alexandrine coffee service, he had stood, ghost-Sigerson, devouring the unsteady beat of time, meaningless with asymmetry and surfeit, in the dusty rejects of personality, need and entity. When the clock finally stopped and, ah, remained at last quiet, he had said aloud, 'Gracious, how quiet – how quiet.'

Palpable finality settled dust-light about his shoulders, weighed on him, weighed on him –

'How quiet,' he repeated, wondering into the absences crowding him out.

'This,' said a soft voice behind him, 'is quiet. Look. You have no sense of extremes.'

A man had been sitting behind a brass tray whereon bundles of forks were offered, meatless forks tied together in bundles of five for £1.00: three Woolworth's, one Georgian (by mistake) and an L.M.S. crested – rare now, collectors' pieces, nostalgic. The man held up an old violin. The D-string was broken. The man touched the broken gut so that the hiatus gaped. Indicating the space between the snapped ends he said, 'Here is quiet.'

The man had held silence across the palm of his hand.

Staring at the silence, Sigerson had backed out of the shop, and the bell tinkled as he closed the door from the street.

> '*The bells of hell go ting-a-ling-a-ling*
> *For you but not for me –*'

For Sigerson the strange man had stayed forever behind the tinkling door, locked into the gloom, staring at the silence in his hand. He left a man in hell, or in purgatory, or in some unnamed place where things and their absences meet. The stubble on his jaw, which with twelve hours more growth would have been a beard, never grew again. It was in the space between the broken ends of that string that the grey gull, Sigerson-foetus, fluttered in the thickening mist which sighed up from the ebbing tide.

The strange man in Durham had shown Sigerson a space into which he had, resisting, entered. It had been a trap-door. He had sprung the trap himself ('Mihilanus,' he said in his head; 'Mihilanus,' he said with the palms of his hands and found only silence lying across them). Now he cursed the man in Durham who had shown him an extreme in material form. He thought of him as 'D.' – also D for Devil, for Damian, for Dark, for Dialectic. All these things which had been personal, and therefore finite, were now shown by the stranger, D., to be infinite but still comprehensible, although no longer of endurable proportions. D. had shown himself to Sigerson, by speaking out of turn before his beard was fully grown, as a portent or a paraclete, and not as a man, and Sigerson had allowed him to grow in this guise inside him. He had made of D. a vast spectre, a consummation of detachment, entirely terrifying because entirely negative. Emptiness; Silence; Nothing. Sigerson had been prepared to condone the existence of such vacuities within himself, considering them in some way a personal defect, the congenital inefficiencies of an ill-assembled mind for which he was not to blame and with which he had learned to contend. D. had destroyed that assurance by ridiculing the scale of Sigerson's appreciation. Now he was left, trapped in by infinity; by the knowledge that another man could tolerate in infinity those absences of virtue which had been to him as intolerable as personal defects. Like a Greek chorus Sigerson's tortuous morality had sung and sung and bewailed the import of the solitary messenger, running to Durham to deliver him his doom among the valueless coins and the stopperless ketchup pourers.

Wrecked, Sigerson gazed at the spiritual sea; at the yellow evening thick as paint with salt, fluorides and bromides filling the sky, thickening into bulk and density what should be pure and rarified; from the ochreous wall of sky he turned on his side; mica, felspar, quartz blocked out the universe; from the living rock up over the brown horizon, inhospitable, unresponsive to the bulk of Coimheadach Abbey. A stone structure where Ottoline lived.

Which of all these principals must he call *mamma*? The sea, the air, the rock, the woman. The tremendousness of Ottoline and her motherhood was of no less stature than the rock, the air or the sea.

He had come down to the sea, sprawled himself on the platform of the cave mouth where Cyril, saint, had once stammered out inadequate replies to the interrogation of Rehemagnus, grass of my lord the king, a man who had lost touch with his dream. What use was the tortuous pursual of facts which could never be clearly known, never recognized except in part by being so starved of human contact that he must burrow down below the granite chips to come up with a little love and a little recognition of the eroded skull caps and broken crockery of women so long dead that it was not always possible to say if they were women or young men? What illusion of concern could bring a live man only to the feet of the dead? Cold man, cold as stone. Somewhere over his shoulder D. looked out beyond him to the empty black boats beneath the empty sea and said, dogmatically, to nobody, 'Only in total loss is there any solitude at all.'

Down on the cliff, Sigerson knew this was true. He was not alone, however lonely he might be. He was fighting all his fragments to bring them together, and by doing so he was recognizing them and giving them actuality. Thus he was not alone, but had three men down there with him and was behaving like a dealer at a fair, wandering from one to the other, prodding at them and poking intimately to see which had the most rewarding potential. But unlike the dealer he had no experience, and he could not refuse to buy. It had to be one of these three or none at all. Despairing he glared from one to the other, while D. stuffed his hands in his pockets and looked on, grinning and whistling softly to himself, only half-concentrating. Geoffrey saluted him gaily; the sun shone on his side-burns and his marvellous waistcoat of lilac silk, but there was a patronizing tilt to his brow and his top lip was slightly curled, as if in distaste. Fairs were not Geoffrey's métier, and he made it obvious; Sigerson had a moment of panic when he thought that Geoffrey would spot D. and that they would go off together for a drink, iced Beaujolais or Campari, at some shaded table beneath the awnings and would discuss minuets, leaving him here, poking hopelessly at the three hobbled to the line.

Into the dingy plurality Mary-Rose skithered on her bare brown feet, a long dream of freshwater rivers, of hollyhocks, tramlines, vaginas, furrows. Startled by the sound of her soles among the granite flakes, he blushed furiously as the image came to him. The sunburned feet, slender, came to rest beside his face. Extended, relaxed, the spoor would be delicate and fragrant: the slot of the inland deer; the slot of the favoured woman. How the deer comes to the shore for seaweed, at great hazard in times of crisis. The woman, this woman also, looking for salt amongst the litter, amongst the rusted rowlock, the limpet fallen at an angle, the exploded wrack, the torn feathers, Ottoline, the blackened anemones and the spent cartridge and pure spines of redfish.

He looked up to her through the receding blush to find her face. Her head was inclined, Pieta-angled, but as he recognized the pose he found it was merely inquiry.

'What a marvellous place to work,' she said happily, gazing at the sea which for her spun and winked and rippled coolly beneath the ledge.

'Work?' he said, startled, that she should be so perceptive about his thoughts.

Mary-Rose indicated the papers beneath his hip which he was using as a buffer between his bone and a peculiarly agressive quartz vein.

He had intended to sit by the sea and try in all honesty to capture something of the isolation of Coimheadach in an objective, almost literary manner. It had been his intention to use the physical setting behind his work as a barrier between it and his own subjective disinclination to proceed further than the title page. He imagined himself as a student of Brontë or Joyce might haunt Haworth or Sandymount, seeking to cut off artificially by claustrophobia the wriggling worms of individuality in the brain – the pox-box of disinclination and reference, of visceral consciousness and vision which lie between a man and his work, and which, because of the violent relationship between him and this work, had become impenetrable and paralyzing. Instead he used the work as a cushion for his dry bones. He had drowsed on the softness of inertia and wantonness, and had only seen D. and Geoffrey, displaced in the mist.

Seeking out sensible perception he screwed up his eyes to look at Mary-Rose, as if the mimicry of purblindness might enable him to see more clearly. Very suddenly he perceived her, drawing back slightly from her feet as if the clarity revealed something unexpected or strange; as if the extraneous gesture had produced an artifact which he had not sought to make. The odour of her flooded his nostrils, spurious upon her yet innately of her; so far from the odour of flesh that he, who knew a little of such matters, realized that the sacs whence it was distilled could only be of the most vicious of rutting male mammals. Ecstasy at such irony, such equivocation, tugged at his mind; he wanted to laugh, to roll on the thin grass, to throw stones at the blue, silly sea.

Seeing him smile, she tapped the papers with her long finger, and the varnish winkled in the summer sun – Phare Miranda it was called, applied with Chinese dedication, Chinese perfection, right down to the clipped cuticle, no white moon showing, no mordant white between the brown flesh and the shining pink.

'You have brought work to me. I was doing nothing,' he said, still watching her fingers.

'From above you looked so absorbed. I couldn't tell if you were sleeping or so deep in thought that I should be ashamed of myself.'

'O, you must never be that!' he said quickly. 'You must never be ashamed or at least never tell me if you are! It would destroy all my confidence in you –'

'What do you take me for, then – shameless?'

'My dear,' he said flatly, 'my shame needn't affect you in the very least, unless you are prepared to let it.'

'Then why mention it?' she asked snappishly. Her brows contracted and the set lines that he knew belonged only to real, sure women stiffened her face into an actuality beyond mind-picturing.

'Why not? Why conceal, for no reason, something which must be obvious to you? What is the point, until we are sure if you, well, want it or not?'

'And if I don't?'

'Well, then we can indulge in concealment, and unacknowledgement, and all the other negatives you like.'

'We? Don't you mean you?'

'Am I being presumptuous? I am – I can see it. But what else did you expect? I'm not a schoolboy; you may be my mother's – "lady", but that doesn't exempt you from my perception.'

He could not see through the glasses what her eyes might be doing. She was angering him. She was angry herself. The wind unsettled them, irritating their skins, blowing fractious hair into their eyes, mouths. They both wiped at their faces crossly. The grasses showed their white undersides.

Mary-Rose stood up. She said briefly, 'Don't you think this is rather a pity?'

She looked down at him, sprawled at her feet. His lank hair was immature at the sides but contrarily thin about the parting. His neck was thin, his chest flat. But he was big, real.

'I don't want this!' she said involuntarily. 'I don't!'

Sigerson heard the protest, and heard behind it. 'Don't you?'

'What?' she shouted over the wind.

He thought she was going to kick him. The dark-blue gym shoes were close to his eyes, and he could smell the rubber from their soles, wet from the walk down the cliff.

'My dear, I should not be behaving with nearly so much reticence if I did.'

'What does that mean?'

'No, no, please don't move. You ornament my shelf. Isn't it a forbidding spot? To think that the old man – Cyril, you know – lived here for numbers of years. No wonder his arthritis gave him trouble –'

He rolled onto his back and looked up at Mary-Rose. Her fine hair drifted like lace in a summer window. Through the tinted lenses of the big glasses he could see the fringes of lash, the moist ivory of the eyeball; peeping Tom into the interior of a summer room, darkened and cool. Like Tom he prowled round peering; he gave no sign that he wanted to break in, to enter, to participate even as a vandal in the shaded interior. It was sufficient to stroll, cautious, tiptoe, peeping about the walls, glimpsing, fabricating tableaux, a thief who would take nothing that the owner would miss, vicariously stealing, hands deep in the vine upon the sun-warm wall.

'Tell me about him,' she offered, squatters' rights in an uninhabited structure.

Sigerson looked surprised. 'There's a *Life* –' he began doubtfully, unsure that her powers of attention would carry her through anything heavier.

'Oh, Lady Thingy's? I read that. All about the birds and the bees!' She laughed. 'Isn't there anything else? Isn't there some weird story that turned up lately?'

Sigerson digested the question carefully. '*Rehemagnus Report*, you mean? It's in the museum. It doesn't tell us anything, only that Cyril was a bit old-fashioned in his outlook, and had a cataract, and that he was not politically inclined. It's only important because it proves that Cyril existed, which was open to doubt, and that the king had spies going about sniffing for disaffection. This one, Rehemagnus, only got here by mistake. He wasn't looking for Cyril – he didn't know Cyril existed, probably. He was shipwrecked, or that's how it most probably was, and came over from the headland to take seal. This was a breeding ground or something in those days. They still come from time to time, but not often. ...'

He stared down at the jetty at the foot of the steps. The sea was dark under the overhang of the cliff. It swayed, frothed a little and stirred the wrack feeling over the surface. In its deeps the rock was purple, indigo and black. No light twinkled; all that was further out, out of the shadow of the granite and the mountain. On the far side of the jetty gulls wheeled above the spot where Rory had gutted the mackerel for Aelebel. It looked cold down there, at the bottom of the three hundred and five steps that Gilles had had cut in the cliff face that the monks might bring the chilly flesh up out of the boats. They still came, the lobster, the big crab, the seal.

'Spies?' she whispered, softly.

'No,' he said. His voice was very deep and quiet. He spoke without expression. The sun danced across the shelf of grass outside the cave. Feathery clouds teased it, swung it among the short grass, the sea plantain, the few impossible harebells. 'Not spies, tempters.'

He shut his eyes against the sun, cowardly in case she should look at him or he at her. He did not want her to see him, to see that the acknowledgement was without meaning. He did not have enough courage to roll back onto his face; so large a gesture would be given meaning, the lesser one might escape uninterpreted. But Mary-Rose did not see the gesture, for she, too, looked away. Behind the smoked glass her dark slanted eyes widened between the mascaraed lashes, widened and closed. A little pulse beat at the outside of a lid. Fear made her shiver in the sea wind.

'NO,' she said loudly. Then she laughed again, a brittle, high sound, slightly neighing through the very English long nose. 'There's nothing much in the way of temptation here –'

'Yes there is,' Sigerson said. He kept very still. There was still no expression. 'You tempt me.'

Mary-Rose moved, deliberately lethargic, as if she did not understand, would not be trapped into understanding. She pushed herself up on her hands to demonstrate her freedom from their words, from any contact they might have.

Afraid that she was going to bolt, Sigerson opened his eyes rapidly and glowered at her. He got up quickly and stood too close to her. But he stayed that hand's-breadth away, still scowling, flattening his hair with both hands.

They stared at each other. They did not want each other, they did not even terribly like each other, as close to as that. But the thing had been born, had generated in the wind. The cliff cut them off from Slieve Coimheadach; they were isolated on the shelf where the old man had spoken with the spy. They were alone, as the old man had been, and society was forming between them, as if had imposed on the old man and the king's tale-bearer. Question, contact, answer.

Still staring Sigerson said, 'I don't want it either, but it's happened.'

Mary-Rose shrugged sulkily. She knew it had happened. She could not walk away, not now that the thing was there on the shelf with them, not now when the contact had been made, the realities expressed.

'You talk too much,' she said accusingly.

'O, talk!' Sigerson cried shrilly. 'Talk! O, yes, I talk a lot – what else have I got to do?' The despair belched up inside him, burning; he thought he might cry, or giggle – the wind tickled his ear.

'Damn this awful wind!' he said.

Mary-Rose was astonished, and she looked at him closely again. His eyes, which had been so blank, so physical, were full of expression. The whites had little veins, the lids were heavy, the pupils large for the high, bright light on the shelf. He looked desperate, as if some exquisite pain was flooding him; as if he had memories, or a terror, or some enormous emotion of which she had been unaware.

'You're not in love, not with me?' she said incredulously, speaking the thought as it came to her.

'O, gracious,' he said.

The desire to recognize himself as beloved fed into his hands as an appetite. He twitched them and covered his mouth. He desired to touch her mouth; the tiny wrinkles in the wind-dried flesh tweaked his arm muscles and he turned away, vulnerable.

Mary-Rose's lips tightened, and the lids of her eyes rose to cut off the lower crescent of the dark pupil. Little seams and creases ran from the lids across the tanned skin. The salt on the wind etched them a little, memories ran along them like slow rain-drops on a wire. With his back to her she was suddenly alone, the society they had held hardened by the loss of his face. Alone on the shelf where the old man had been alone for God knew how many years. The ocean stretched out to a Baltimore and a Newfoundland eradicated by Ottoline, so that the ocean stretched out for ever. She stared at it, but it made no sound, no syllable of instruction, even of existence. The seaweeds she painted and ran her delicate fingers up and down lay upon it, drifting, careless, directionless, subject entirely to the ocean, utterly subject to its own futility. O, what shall we do for our ancient sister, the seaweed, for she hath no roots? The trees, drowned in the warm soft growth of the peat, mourned, and the moss closed about the roots, and the gentle suffocation caressed like death in the lignin, in the bark, in the shiver of the ultimate leaf.

'O God,' said Mary-Rose.

He turned, but the clarity with which he had seen her before was gone and only the faint perfume came to him, for she stood upwind of him. The wind brought tears into his own eyes, and he made a silly little gesture, indicating them.

'I'm sorry,' he said, 'but I have no excuse —'

'Well,' she said, 'is there ever one?' Smiling a little ruefully she held out her hand and he took it, and together they walked sadly up the cliff path.

Ottoline stood by the shed in the outer court. She had seen the seal from the top of the ladder when she was replacing the slates on the roof. The damage had not been as great as she had been expecting, merely two large slates which had slithered apart and downwards so that a runnel of rain trickled into the roof cavity directly above one of the worst cracks in the ceiling of the *factory*. The insistent fall of water had suggested a great gap, and even when she had climbed up and tied the tarpaulin over it in the night she had not been able to see, nor had she tried to, whether the damage was extensive. She had replaced the same slates, tapping up the little lead brackets to hold them firm, cast a sly look at the top of Gilles' head and tried to stick a cigarette behind his stone ear. But the carving was too weathered, and the cigarette fell out and dropped into a puddle below, where it turned brown and the tobacco began to drift out of the split seam. Then she had watched the bull seal. He had been sleeping, breaking surface for a few breaths every five minutes or so in a circle of disturbance. She was too far from him to see any details, just the widening rings of his emergence and the dark jut of his head. And then he would drop quietly out of sight into the heavy grey swell and go down where he had come from. Where she could not follow.

She had come down the ladder slowly, thinking about not being able to follow him, and had gone to the long stone passage to fetch her gun. The smell of the gentle oil and the smoothness of the long, cold barrel brought out little pricks of sweat under her breasts, and the hair between her legs tingled. She stood blankly, the age-blackened stock against her cheek, the barrel straight down her body to her knees. She did not resist. Tension blurred behind her eyes and she shivered. Then she had hurried to her bedroom to fetch the ammunition, mumbling to herself, her cigarette twitching between her lips.

In the room which kept Sigerson away from her she had found an enormous pair of driving gauntlets. They were stiff, and there was blue damp across the palms and along the seams in the leather. They were too big for her, but she pulled them on. Then she fetched her father's funeral bowler from the top of the chest, took a swipe at the dust with the back of her sleeve and smacked the hat down over her ears. She had put some extra bullets in an oilskin pouch which she slung on her shoulder, taken the gun and gone down to the sheds for the bull.

Propping the gun against the stone lintel, Ottoline peered carefully around for Aelebel. No sound or sight of the great woman helped her. The jennet, hobbled in the courtyard, coughed and lipped in a desultory way at the mud. There was little for it to eat. Ottoline whacked its behind with the gauntlet, and it hopped unevenly towards the inner court. She shooed it through and propped a sheet of asbestos roofing across the gateway to keep it in. Then she wondered which roof the asbestos had fallen off and sighed.

In the gloom inside the shed it was dry and the light was silvery, coming as it did through the cobwebs and reflected off the sea and the stone. The bull was standing near the door, his head down, hock deep in manure and dried turf bedding. A swallow, disturbed, peeped out of its grey nest in the beams and watched carefully. Ottoline did not speak to the bull directly but spoke to herself about him. About his strength, about his meat, about his near sanctity. He stood ritually, his head low, the ring in his wide muzzle gleaming and the red rings in his eyeballs gleaming. His shoulders shone like used ebony and his pale, outspread horns were tipped with black as deep as jet. In the dim light the blond stripe down his spine outlined the length of his straight back, and his bulging forehead was dense with coarse curls. The muscles of his forelegs bulged out beneath his massive shoulders, and his knees were vast and flat, paling into golden cream beneath the caked, dried muck.

She spoke to him of all this: of his sinewy, light hind quarters; of his speed; of his flexible, mobile carriage, structured for savagery, not for slaughter. She spoke of what he was to her – her wealth. She clipped the spring-hook on the end of the long pole through the ring in his muzzle and stood away from him. There was no love, no communication, between them. She loaded him with fantasies, but he ignored her. She led him out of the shed, picking up the loaded gun and carrying it in the crook of her left elbow, both hands at the end of the pole, the gauntlets' grip firm, sure, immobile. At the other end of the pole the bull came with her. He was not following her, he was coming. His detachment hardened Ottoline. It rose in her throat, a lump of strength matched with the bull's, a hard core of possession and will and purpose and security. Her bull made her.

For a while Ottoline did not think or dream at all, just walked along the track above the sea. Terns and fulmars swung on the wind, and in the grey spray a shag brooded over the wrack, as primitive and ancient as the shape of the rock it hunched on. With her head and hands protected Ottoline strode among the granite boulders, the quartz pebbles, the sea mist, the back-bred primitive bull which she had called into being, the primitive shag which had never known change. Out in the sea the seal surfaced, moaned and dropped idly down.

As if to balance the event, Ottoline's mind sank with it, down among the dreams and the things which she was. Back down into the vision she had.

Walking, before the walking trees, walking, wading inshore through the moonset on the rising tide to take possession. In a mauve invisible sky terns and petrels proselytise the Coming; light shafts in the thick air mumming Crow. *Watirs wap and wawys wanne*, and the long black boat emerges — or submerges, what matter. When? Where?

When was it that the sky was so thick with the salts of the seas that, ochreous, it lit down on the intertidal regions; thick, invisible sky, no sky, no meeting place with the sea, acushla-acushla on the green backs of the limpets, the indigo shimmer on the mussel?

Where was it that they made landfall, carrying a hunter's moon between their horns, moons laid flat and placed in time by their coming; brine to the fetlocks, dense, rimed, terribly from the sea. From where?

Forearmed against imagination they bear on their forehead the awful bone; the bone that labours against the weight of the horns that sweep from headland to headland of the bay and pierce the side of each headland from which no water flows.

Where? When

And when they walked, and where they walked, no man met them.

No man saw the dim silhouette gather colour and sound and stench, swishing between the ultimate ripples, dewlaps, balls and udders streaming, the first cloven hoof on all the sands of the coast.

In myriads they form along the shore; the tide leaves them; the sand dries, lightens around them. A line, wither to wither, terribly black from the sea, they stare at all the unmarked sands of all the shores of all the coast. The tide has pulled out from under the sky; the sky, the mist, rests flat behind them. Through the thick sky they begin to walk. Inshore.

It is no more than a vision. A haunting picture structured into the mind. It is a vision composed of many elements; the end of manlessness, the end of time unacknowledged, times so huge that they are not times but movements conducted towards a Here, a Now, ha! which is already gone – taken a powder in the Long Night which is itself only a speck, a locality upon an elipse which itself moves. But not Towards. And another element, trees; static, biggest of living things but still, rooted down into horizons measurable in terms of time, which are, in fact, place. Ambiguous trees, sucking nutrients from the pterodactyls or the god's metals, what matter, but INCAPABLE OF MOVING. But, and this is the irony, every leaf drawn from every twig, from every branch from the specific direction of the trunk, still as iron in a pool, is movement. Is the infinitesimally minute movement of growth answering the slant of the sun, an arbitrary gust of wind, an accident of shadow cast by the growth of another tree, of a depression moving east, of an evening overcast in June. By warmth, by the flash flood and nothing so dramatic, the half-hour more or less of rain one day, one day in time acknowledged, the cloud, the weight of a rook's nest one spring and not the next, are the shape of the trunk, the branch, the twig, the leaf, season by season, day by day, minute by minute. So, the still trees are moving. And seed by seed, breeze after breeze, directed by the growth of the trees into places sheltered by the trees, or unshadowed by the trees, the seeds move and fall and grow or die, across time and across place. Because the cattle walked before the trees, and turned back, lazing colossally in the unshaded sun to chew the cud of last year's weather, last generation's itch scar on the bark where the little, starchy suckers are.

And another element: among the trees the Man walked. Adam? called God in the evening. Adam? Knowing he HAD to be there among the trees. Man acknowledged, in time acknowledged. In Eden, or Enniskerry or Ben Eighe. Adam could not until the garden was; then, localized and temporized in fact or in story, Adam came, and with Adam the break of time acknowledged. And Adam took the fruit and ate it, and the story doesn't say what he did with the pips. With the five implicit trees that grow out of his crotch in the genealogical tables, stretching out tendrils and tributaries to fill up the whole page as his monstrous piddle burns up the garden and all the gardens growing from it, beyond where the angels stood with flaming swords which he could not put out.

And another element: the awesome cattle, the herds of aurochs, moving, walking around the trees, around the skirts of the forests, and man, the herds of Adam, the progeny born in the waters of his piddle, spawned in the water he made, glutting on the pips, crushing the pips in pits, long-houses, earth-houses, masticating slowly in a painted shawl, devoid of humour in the evenings after Eden, with malaria-yellowed eyes and pompous, protein breasts; old men eating the forest, old hyena-women devouring their own placenta. Peering into the still pools of Roundstone and Redbog, the shallowing water reflects the crump of the Tree of Life as the forests fall. When, at last, in the silence, the stricken eyes are raised, what is there to see but the blasted heath? The stricken oak we know; the gnarled and stunted birch; even, astonishingly hanging over the Oare, the blasted beech. But whoever read of a blasted tulip tree? Tulip, arbutus, jacaranda, eucalyptus, the early olive groves that fruited oil and reason, it was Granny Smith that did for them. Granny Smith, with her silky green skin, tart as peroxide or the formic acid in which the curiosities of malformation are preserved, how edifying.

It was only that sort of vision she had about the cattle, walking, before the trees walking, wading inshore through the moonset on the rising tide.

It was no more than a vision, a signal sent by her mind on a utilitarian journey through the nerve ends, and she drooled and whispered over every picture, every idea, every notion that poured into her mind. Quotations, illusions, lost Latin tags learned from a religiously defined annual structure aligned on the secular agricultural year; strained parallels drawn from hen-strutting in Pinell's anthropology books and dubious tales taken as authentic incidents (nothing ever surprised Ottoline): Scraps of Kate Greenaway poetry and Keats, tales from the baun and the bothy heard and accepted in the byre and discussed earnestly over the brandy after dinner; the Pentateuch and Petronius, Pitt-Rivers and Parnell; the lies of Pinto, the lies of Pirandello, the half-truths of the blue Spaniard.

All this was in some way based upon the Vision. The grand vision of the great herds of cattle which had, once, come to the island.

The Vision had originally been provoked by a book of Sigerson's which he had left lying in the chimney of the chapter. Ottoline had been setting the whippets' predecessors on the rats in the scullery, and the rats had won. She had been stirred and enraged at the damage to the dogs, the gobbets and shreds and rednesses of battle, never mind the premonitions of septicaemia, all over the fawn velvety coats and the hurt, besieged eyes the ineffective animals had rolled at her sport. She stood upon a chair and shouted *Olé*! to no effect, frightening the whippets and perplexing the rats. The battle had taken place in miniature: the whippets were low on the ground, the rats jabbered and shrieked in the shadows. Draughts brushed cobs and husks about the floor; the electric light dimmed and waned as the offshore breeze gusted in the wires. The more she had shouted and screamed and stamped her boots on the wooden chair, the tinnier had been the little ringing of her spurs and the higher the squeals of the moidered rats. All outside her and the pit of the pitch was unlit, untouched by excitement; all unaware of the stimulus she was creating. The abbey ignored the noise, did not even echo along the blank passages. Somewhere a shutter banged, alone with the wind, outside the circuit of performance she was making down below the chair legs.

!*Olé*! screamed Ottoline Atlantica, two a.m. in the scullery; !*Olé*, the big rats in a circle churning the motes and dusts in the flags; !*Olé*! the berserk dogs running round and round each other, *e stampada, e stampada* on the seat of the chair of the stand where she stood, ting-a-ling spurs a ring in the *stampada*, making mock circus, bright red bloods, froths and dribbles dark on the grey tiles. Mock. The rats grew accustomed to the din, the clapping and the wild howls, bit one of the dogs and exited a-flourish, bored by the insubstantiality, down the open drain. The dog cried. Ottoline cried. The offshore wind skittered in the wire from the generator. The dog's ear went lustrous under the iodine she put on it, and its screams rang in the stones.

Drawn by lust for blood she went to the chimney to find brandy in the squat decanter. Lying where Sigerson had ruckled up the rug in front of the fire was the book. Already the turf dust had whitened the gloss on the picture. Rolling the brandy glass against her breasts she had looked at it upside down. Deep sorrows settled on her with the floating ashes. The shutter banged again. The sorrows entered through her eyes, her nose, her ears, her fundament; flowed in a great endless flood of silence and ash and the odour of antique winds blowing. To drive it out of her she gulped noisily at the brandy, wiping her lips on a sleeve that stank of rat. Blood drink, it made her belch, gurk out the smouldering sorrows like Mary after the funeral meats – *mater dolorosa*. She had circled the chimney, gulping and gurking, and itching until she could see the picture the right way up. It was a photograph of a painting of an aurochs which had been found in an antique shop in Augsburg in 1827. In Sigerson's book it was representing the economic progress made by selective breeding from the original wild cattle of Europe towards the valuable beef and dairy herds of modern times. It illustrated the principle well. Beside was another photograph of a Smithfield Champion of 1958, a monument of man's self-regard wrought in beef.

But, for Ottoline, the aurochs walked across the page, from east to west, towards Coimheadach. She had knelt by the book, dusting the turf ash off the glossy paper until it shone and gleamed. The overweighted fore-quarters; the lithe, angular hocks; the enormous, killer's horns – here was Ottoline's vision. It came to her, cuddling the brandy glass, that this was the only beast capable of Coimheadach; that to bring this beast to her land, to use her land for the rearing of this and only this beast was not an ambition but an inevitable consummation of something, and she could not fight her wild mind down to say quite what it was. She did not think nor had ever thought of Coimheadach as distinguishable in any way from the rest of Western Europe. To her, as to all of us, Coimheadach is where all other places are distinguished from. Ottoline was too imaginatively poor to contrast bougainvillia and oleander, Oxford Street and the Graben, the Top Hat Ballroom and les Halles with her cavernous sheds and fescue cliff tops, but she saw the strange bull in the picture-book as being as complete a statement of Coimheadach as Sacher's is of a certain sort of Vienna, or Maynooth of a certain sort of Ireland.

It had taken her nearly twenty years and all her money to breed Dan Dare. She had been disorganized and ignorant, but she had tried hard – writing to the zoos in Berlin and Munich, where such animals had been recreated already; importing frozen semen from Easter Ross and Madrid – until finally the Vision had become real and she was leading Dan Dare by the nose above the shags and the cruising seal to her chosen cows and heifers on the far side of the Baun. This generation she did not love. She gave them ridiculous names to weigh down their significance; she protected her head and her hands against them; she had no more sympathy with them than she had with Coimheadach – but the hard passion was the same. It was as hard and as far from love as quartz.

Her arrival at the pasture was without event. She released the bull before opening the gap in the wall, blocked up with a rusty Volkswagen door and the shafts from an old hayrake held together with barbed wire. The herd was over the shoulder of the slope and up-wind from the bull. He snorted a little, but only at the grass and the wind and the clouds and Ottoline's bowler hat, and she had to stand behind him and beat him on the loins before he would go through the narrow gap in the wall. She hit him with the pole, and he lowered his head and grunted at the narrow entry. She hit him several times until he began tossing his head about and a little trickle of urine dribbled from his belly. Then she got the gun and poked at the silken skin above his blond testicles; the barrel made a round, oily stain between his thighs. She shouted at him, butting him higher up under his tail, and suddenly, away from her, jumping clumsily over the dismantled shafts, he went into the pasture, turning to give himself room to go for her. She grinned at him, shoving the hat rakishly on the back of her silvery hair and pointing the loaded gun. There was a little click as she let the safety catch off.

Over the hill a cow lowed. Dan Dare left Ottoline and went about his proper occasions.

Ottoline reassembled the barrier and then sat on the edge of the car door. She was very still. Something within her head went quiet and loose. After a little she cried; not harshly but more like a tired child, a gentle very tearful sobbing; a relaxation of the lungs and eyes. She did not really notice it, herself. There were larks in the gusty sky, and over the top of the mountain a raven drifted, a merciless telling of mortality.

VIII

FOR SOME days Sigerson found himself unable to be at home in himself. This had seldom happened to him before, and never so catastrophically. He was unable to think about himself without thinking of the shock of the betrayal, for so he considered it. He felt like a man in exile, unable to feel beneath his feet the soil type to which he was accustomed, unable to direct himself to shelter or rest amongst alien trees and shrubs whose properties were still unknown. He worked obsessively at his book; at bad times he retyped, checked his grammar and spelling, organized footnotes and started to think about the index to save himself time and tedium in the future. It was mechanical, exact work and tiring. He considered himself fortunate that it was available to him when he needed it. At better times, in the early mornings or after a post-prandial pause, he even made some progress with the text, but he had to leave Mihilanus alone. Once he became entangled with Mihilañus he found himself weaving Sigerson Ottraine – or, worse still, Sigerson O'Treann – into the enigmatic monk, and the monk in turn crept up inside his dressing-gown and settled into the woolly Jaeger as if he were determined to use it for a new cowl.

Sigerson's obsession with Mihilanus turned easily to fear, and he refused to write about him. The man was a trap, a gin baited for him with sympathy and gripping him with dark introspection from which release was at the whim of outside intervention. Only interruptions from outside – the clangour of Aelebel in the yard; the mess-call of the cracked gong in the chapter, swinging on frayed leather between silver-tipped bison horns and beaten with indigenous ferocity; a sight of the Girl wandering about the graveyard pranging the sleeping saints with the iron goad – could interrupt and spring the trap, but he could not organize their occurrence.

Perhaps it was because of the Girl's continued presence that he became lonely, too, in a new and unhappy way. Continually he found his thoughts turning to Geoffrey, and he ached for a sight of the flamboyant spotted tie and the silky side-boards, for the sound of the clear, precise voice with its undertow of Northumberland accent, and its finicky latinate grammar. The nearest he could get to Geoffrey was the Girl, for even if he wrote it was unlikely that Geoffrey would reply with anything more elaborate than a telegram – his usual form of correspondence and one which struck Sigerson as irritatingly extravagant and insufficient.

To the Girl, therefore, he eventually turned, having previously fled from her. She appeared unchanged, her responses and reactions predictably taut and personal. With the Girl he was on the familiar ground that lay astride the Cam, and he walked upon it easily, knowing its pitfalls and secure places. The weather remained overcast and cold after the storm that had brought the tiles off the frater roof, and the fire in the chimney smouldered and sulked, bellying warm gouts of smoke around the chapter, impenetrable with floating particles and white motes. The Girl had made one or two abortive attempts to work in the chimney but had been driven out by the spasmodic appearances of Ottoline, snorting or questioning, by Aelebel, towards whom she was developing an unbalanced antipathy, and by the lack of light, ventilation, heat and table space. Sigerson, therefore, found her in the eighth cell with a blanket wrapped round her knees and a drop emerging from her nose.

She looked up and sniffed as he entered, and he could have sworn that she bridled a little upon perceiving who it was. The Redness made a subdued sortie and then retreated, and her eyes flickered shiftily. There was something about her posture, an apparent control visibly exercised with no betrayal of what was being controlled; a studied uninterest projecting from the heavy brows; a readiness for defence obtruding from between the tightly clenched thighs. Sigerson smiled his most charming and slithered round the door, immediately anxious because there was nowhere to sit down informally except the bed. That was informal; it contained tomes and a bag of apples. He sat between them and his weight unbalanced them. He put his hand out to support them and found that both piles would topple if he removed it, so he was constrained to sit still. Since he did not know why he had come, he did not have a background from which to hustle about and rearrange the Girl's apples.

'Well, how is it all going?' he asked harmlessly.

'Not well,' she said with perfect clarity of diction. She did not look at him.

'What's gone wrong? You were doing some very effective work when I last looked. Can I be of any help, or is it a matter for Geoffrey Cudleigh? He did ask me to help if I could, you know –' He paused, hoping that he would not have to be too urbane before he ran out of words.

'It's not help I'm short of,' she said so softly that he had an urge to put his hand behind his ear.

'Texts?' he suggested, looking at the heaps of scattered open offprints; the open journals, maps, tables, genealogies, scribbled translations, figures and, on one sheet, even a diagram with heavy arrows all pointing convincingly in the same direction. He screwed his neck about to catch a glimpse of what they were pointing at but failed. 'Not texts?' he repeated, less harmlessly.

'No!' she breathed.

'What then? I'm in the middle of a letter to Geoffrey, so if you want to put something in we could save a stamp –' He wanted to talk about Geoffrey.

'I have plenty of stamps.'

It was curious how she had not moved any muscles since he entered, except those required for indistinct speech. Even the sea said a-CUSH-la outside, and Aelebel screamed twice.

'Well?' he prompted with pedagogic insistence.

'I find it very difficult to work –' she muttered.

'I'm sorry?'

'I find it VERY DIFFICULT TO WORK IN THIS HOSTILE ENVIRONMENT!'

'Good heavens!' he cried, taken aback by the volume of noise. 'Gracious!'

'Well, you can't deny it!' she flashed.

'But this is so sudden –' he said weakly, feeling the words were familiar and inappropriate somehow.

'Like everyone is pretending to do one thing and all living out secret situations based on some sort of inner reality that excludes me – deliberately. Like you all go off at night and turn into something else – bishops or sealions or something. Not real people, anyway!'

'What on EARTH could you mean?' he said crossly. He still wanted to talk about Geoffrey.

The Girl, or Dorothy as she was fast becoming in the spate of incomprehensible words, stroked the rug hastily on her knees; it was the same gesture he had noticed in the rose garden. Her face became mulish and dark, the underlip sticking out like a boot.

'Ummn,' he said, contemplating a rupture.

'Look, this is one scene, right? You and me, historians, doing a job with some end in view. And I'm messing up my thesis, aren't I? And why? Because there is another scene with this Gothic send-up everyone is playing at – you, too – all wandering around corridors in hunting boots and oil paint and looking vague as if you were on T.V. all the time. I know it's a send-up. That doesn't bother me. What gets me is why? Because you all go on in this fantasy situation and what do you really do? Like you all go away after supper and even the bloody electricity gets turned off, and then what? I get pushed over here as if I was too young to join in the grown-ups' games, and then you all turn round in the morning and put up little bits for grabs – an artist bit, or an absent-minded bit, or an eccentric, to anyone outside the group. Like you don't want me to look too close at any of you. Like you want me out. But I'm here and, bar mucking up my work, I'm staying till I've done what I came for, right?'

'Uh?'

'RIGHT?'

Sigerson stared at her most rudely. He was totally astonished. Up till now the girl, who to him had been the Girl despite knowledge of her name, had shown not the slightest hint of any such violent turbulence.

After a while he said, 'Yes,' exactly as Nanny/Governess/Tutor had said Yes when his lies exceeded their entertainment value.

'So,' spat Dorothy, 'I'm here. Consider me a fixture till I say so. Right? And I'm not going to be evicted by the mad peasant or the impaled man or your mother!'

'What impaled man?' Sigerson inquired, terrified of being answered – the company his mother kept! – but totally at a loss.

Dorothy gestured wildly at the ceiling, and Sigerson immediately thought of Ghost –

'Anyway, your mother – what's her scene? She's a lady – she's a beauty, and she acts out this freak-out cover-story like she's ignorant and a man. What's that for?'

'A man? What do you mean?'

'She thinks she's a man, doesn't she?'

'Well, she is, you see,' Sigerson said hopelessly.

He had forgotten Geoffrey. Even forgotten Mihilanus and Mary-Rose. He was horrified by the penetration Dorothy was showing. He attempted to pull himself together and start lying, but she was on to him like a flash, spitting and stroking and sniffing the drip back into her adenoids.

'Dr Ottraine, you can string me along so far and I'll dance quite happily, because I'm too busy to bother about it, but not that far!'

'I'm sorry, Dorothy,' he said miserably, 'but I'm getting terribly lost. I think perhaps we are discussing things of greater depth than our conversational tactics will stand up to –'

But she wasn't interested in his apologies, only in achieving some sort of weird reality which forced her into physical action. So she smoothed and stroked and grew denser in her flesh. Her shaggy hair enveloped her head, coursing over it and capping her square face. She had bright eyes, and in the gloom of the day they peered and pryed, and anger whittled away the personality in them. They might as well have been gemstones or fish cuticle so palely acute did they become.

Sigerson was made aware of the density by the way the rug quivered about on her knees; a pastiche of Old Woman, quivering in the pseudo-plaid, a barbarian off a page smelling of printer's ink and the schoolroom; no barbarian, and yet emulating the physical density of one. Physical, physical, real. A double brawl, a *bransle* across his consciousness where he danced the two steps rightways, one step left between his mind and Mary-Rose and his dam *manqué*. He could smell her flesh, the smell of Girl and garment, hereditary smell subsequent from years of eating sponge pudding and treacle and Chicken Maryland in clubs; mawkish beside the sharp stench of milk and stout and salt that to him was no smell but which nonetheless made London natives wrinkle their noses on the main line platform when the mail trains to the west were filling up at night and disgorging in the mutinous dawns of immigration.

So her smells and her clothes, clean and dull with fashion, reeked and smothered him, pressing down the nostrils of his mind so that other scent and trails became lost and muddied and overrun by her neat feet in the bulbous shoes and shiny toenails. Did she scrub them? Polish them with a minute brush laden with stringent lacquer to spread and gel over the horny substance? A shell from the oil hard and artificial, as frightening as bent barbed wire and as transparent. Two steps right and one step left. And again he made the pimp's gesture — *I'm tired and I wanna go home, I'm tired and I wanna go to bed* — selling himself short to himself because of the Chicken Maryland in Wilberforce Close.

'Dr Ottraine,' she said, 'I am in some way unable to understand the situation here. Perhaps I should apologize for having lost my temper. But I'm all uptight and miserable, and I can't get any sense of reality out of my work or — what are you laughing at? You're LAUGHING.'

'Dorothy, forgive me. I, too, am "uptight", as you say, and I can't see that this sort of talk is going to benefit either of us. Suppose you tell me exactly what has gone wrong, and I will do a sort of mental obstacle race and try and explain to you why we live at Coimheadach in this appalling fashion. Would that help?'

In his fervency to correct his horrible laughter and make it sound flippant or dismissive he giggled skittishly at her, and the echoes of his sound tingled in his ears.

The fury of the Girl came at him across his introspection. Jumping up she waved a pale handkerchief in the air, much as it had been the goad, much as he had flapped at his mother the vampire, substituting activity for direct blows. The foreign smell of eucalyptus ranged from the handkerchief in the eighth cell, symbolic of Prisoner. Prisoner. Cleaner a smell than old incense and the diphtheria of Father Silas, captive between the musty walls and the peat outside. Scarlet, she would have bloodied him, too, shouting.

'You've no right to laugh at me! I know what I'm doing, and none of you do! Fooling about like kids with this fantastic place – and you, tossing off snide jabs at petrified hands and ruins – if this place was looked after you'd have a respectable scholar to find out about the hand and you'd see that the place was kept up, not covered with a bit of tarwhatever canvas by a madwoman careering up a ladder in the middle of the night. I'm serious about this place and I'm serious about my work, and if no one else will try and take care of it all, I will.

She strode about between the bed and the door, the plaid rug of her discarded corporeality flung in a lump of obsolescence on the floor. Her footsteps were heavy, strangely coarse beside the light feet of the brawlers in red petticoat.

Earnestly he begged her, 'If I write to Dr Cudleigh –'

'O, stuff Dr Cudleigh –'

Well, perhaps, perhaps. The tentative approach, we would be mutually excellent at it, but no, no, not that sort of help in the folds of the silky polka-dotted cravat.

'But seriously, Dorothy, I AM very tired, and I didn't realize that you were so upset. I only laughed to try and cheer you up – Please don't go on like this, please don't –'

He put out his hand to arrest her stamping, and she saw it, a fraction of a second before it would catch her about the waist. With a hop! she avoided it, and her brows, pencilled heavily by a child with too large a crayon, clamped down over her eyes. Thus visored she surveyed him out of her infancy, her rage, her innocence.

Sigerson sighed dismally. The affair was not to his liking; the event made him sour. She was not being predictable, feminine, known. She was a child.

'Listen,' he said angrily, 'everyone gets like this at times. You ought to take a day or two off from your thesis. Forget Ursula and the blasted bones and go for a good walk –' Buy a new tie and ignore the situation, the Dry Scalp Situation, like me – 'and go to bed a bit earlier. There's always a point where you feel you are just going on and on, not getting anywhere. Gracious, as if I didn't know the feeling!'

'I feel, Dr Ottraine, that if I wasn't surrounded with a group all fixated on fantasy I might get on somewhere very fast. It's not me that's holding up my work, it's the ethos of this place – like everyone has a fix on their genes. ...'

'Uh?'

'Look, your mother. She's a man. Well? And she breeds hideous great things on the top of an earthwork. Why? Like she has a fix on primitivism or something. Like your father was EATEN. Now do I believe that? DO I?'

'Well, you see, not exactly eaten. ...'

'No, I bet not. Just nibbled at for kicks!'

'No, no, you've got it all wrong, he was an anthropologist –'

'*Food and Phallus in the Lower h'M* indeed! So you have an eaten father and a mother who's a man. Don't make me laugh. If you want to run a pantomime, I'm not dressing up in the clown mask, you know.'

'No, no, you look very nice as you are – I mean – DOROTHY, stop being so subjective!'

'You expect me to be OBJECTIVE about this?'

'Listen, you think you're having your leg pulled, do you? What do you think it feels like to get that reaction from anyone who hears that your father was murdered in a bloody jungle and his genitals cooked with a hotch potch of yams and bananas? Would you like to live with that? What do you think I told the boys at school? What do you think I feel like every time my blasted mother gets going on the story? THINK, will you, you – you CHILD!'

Sigerson jumped up and began to thump the table. The apples rolled to the floor, bouncing and bobbing – boiling balls, global origin of existence, his, in a melting pot along with the monkey's fruit and the ridicule flailing at the bars from Them On the Outside – he kicked one, slyly, Oedipus playing ball-alley with a temptation.

'You mean, it's REAL?'

Sigerson darted at her, bunching his hand into a fist and thumping his other palm.

'Yes, of course it's real. It's true. Use your imagination.'

'My imagination has broken – I don't know – but your mother – she said it was a story – an after-dinner story –'

'Dorothy, given that the revolting fact is truth, how do you think I live with it? Listen, she hated him, hated him, and he went off – he always went off on these long journeys – and one time he didn't come back. Because of her. Because she is a bitch ... we all know that, you don't yet. Underneath the poet and the male principal, all the purity and savagery that strangers see as attractive in Ottoline, there is a hard thing – I'm sure some of your psychologist friends would give you lots of impressive names for it, but I myself call it irresponsibility. She is a woman almost without love – she has only ever loved once that we know of. And only one person has loved her. It's this solitariness that I referred to when I said she was a man. ....'

Sigerson stopped and looked at Dorothy. She was leaning against the grilles and gates of the bedfoot, looking at him sombrely, out of her infant face. A string of red wooden beads trailed across her chest; three strings of them, the beads interspersed with dyed cacao beans. When she moved her head they sounded like a tiny washboard at a great distance. They were a sound from the Cam, from the glad decorative world of the computers and positivists. They were a remembering, a nostalgia for other sounds where people did not smack their lips. How dark and monstrous it must all sound to her, he thought. Inexplicable, if she believes it at all, to be in communication with the other side of man.

'Well,' he said, gently, 'you asked for reality, for truth. Do you believe me?'

She shook her head. 'No,' she said flatly.

'Why not?'

'Because it is exactly the sort of story that if I was right, like I said, about your having an obsession with your heredity, about your peculiarity and all that, then it is just the sort of story to fit in. No, I don't believe you. O, I know there are still a few mildly cannibalistic tribes back of the Amazon, but male principals and yam stew, no. I'm sorry, but you go too far with it.'

She leaned backwards, dangling the beads across her hand so that the washboards never stopped drumming, faintly, but near enough to keep them both aware of the distance, as well as the continuation of the sound. Against the sound the drums of savages were impotent. Sigerson realized it and smiled at his story-telling. He had no gift for imaginative descriptions, for atmosphere, for credibility. Beneath the blocked-in brows the eyes were dark again, gloomy with distrust. The very way she stood showed that he had lost all meaning for her: she no longer bridled; she curved, careless, her wide shoulders back, the thighs braced out to take her weight. She was not considering him any more. In her face, in the twist of the eyebrow, patronizing detachment reared in front of him.

'O, well,' he said, 'you'll learn. One day.'

'I know, I know. I'll learn that someone is trying to live it up, in more senses than one!'

The child shrugged carelessly and turned to stare out of the window. All traces of anger had been dissipated. She was let down, rejected by his refusal to help her. She made it apparent, hunching her shoulders defensively, biting at her square thumb nails, dangling the coloured beans between her fingers and staring out of the window at the grass sodden and grey, cluttering up the tombstones. It was not ordinary grass; not green and soft, but bluey-white about the rims of the leaves, blond where the seeds had begun to ripen, and sharp as flint. In the rain it looked as if it might have been made of metal. Evidence suggested that the dwarfs and gnomes, the monsters, fairies, elves and elders who had lived here, for they were not men, could not be men here, had eaten human flesh. So, they ate human flesh, what else was there to eat. They were not men; they were characters in documentary evidence, without appetite or gender, without name or love, and that was all right, too. They could not be men, could not become men by virtue of her literacy; she would send no paraclete of liveliness across the dark water where their long boats drifted, no ghost to breathe them quick.

Smiling brightly she said, 'I'm sure you're right, Dr Ottraine. I'll go out and have a walk. May I borrow a pair of Wellingtons?'

Tired, is it, and wanting to go home? Had enough of disgraceful reality, is it, and the cold rain, stinking of empty limpet shells and slimy wrack? Tired of the little pointed barnacles between the toes, every which way walked, so painful, like a gravel of the soul as Rory's auntie had about the stomach, hunched over the fire and rocking her fever in the débris of a vegetable world gone to dust between her fingers. Sending up messages and smoke signals of singular distress into the sky, and Rory away up the sharp pointed mountain looking for the red cow with the spots on her flanks to bring her to the bull, unable to answer the distress calls away out there on the sharp, pointed mountain. Tired of the repetition, the reiteration, the rhyming slang, the One who was Eaten/the One we have Beaten. What happened to the gate-post, Sigerson? It should be there now, wrought and impressive, rearing its way across this way, shouting Within Here is Home, but half of it's gone. That was a great mystery, how no one ever found it. Where could it have gone? Why, there is no home behind it, the space where it should be ... there is only Coimheadach. What need for it then, for there is no home for it to signify. Perhaps that is why it went away. It had nothing to do. Not a great mystery, after all.

Walking with Mihilanus down the dark passage. Taking his hand and hearing him call, My soul's brother; slumming it in history with Mihilanus, down the twisted, introspective corridors. Catching him close, and pressing him to the heart, 'Get out, you prescient bugger, get out!' Perhaps, perhaps. Hold his hand tightly, get familiar with the ligaments, the thin flags of skin between the fingers which might yet grow webbed, or lose more avoirdupois eating linseed seeds and hazel nuts and coming close as an hallucinogen to the blackbright eyes and the lines etched about them. My soul's brother. My lover. Mihilanus pulling Enemy Four,

Sigerson the Treacherous, away to the pig-stys and the outhouses, and the shotten hovels of the byre; pigging it in History, way out there among the earth-houses of the mind. Stinking of tangled people and closed minds; dark, tortuous, introspective. Peering into skeins and webs woven in the dark — in daytime dark. Asking endless questions to which no reply would ever come, just the sly giggle from the dark, the involved affront of ignorance.

'We wouldn't know we wouldn't know we wouldn't know.' Sucked down into the lanes and wynds in the daytime dark, tenements of history against a castle wall. No way out. My soul's brother, my lover Mihilanus, alley-fugitive in the mind.

'Mihilanus?'

'Mihilanus?'

Ottoline came back along the track where she had led the bull by the nose. Here and there along the rabbit runs and on the thorns of the gorse his stench lingered as if it had been caught in little pockets in the vegetation; as if it must hang about where he had been, for no especial reason, until it sank down into the woody stems and roots and into the thin soil and onto the surface of the granite — for no good reason except that he had been led that way and his passage was to be reserved in this hyperphysical state as a part of the land itself. Where his hoofs had pressed their double crescents down tiny liverworts and mosses, spores and sacs were deformed and re-aligned. Beetles, earwigs and ants had died where he had walked. Yet the great air, cleft by his horns, swung as if the might and weight of his insignia had never touched breathable reality.

The releasing of the bull among the heifers had been an almost clandestine event. Ottoline had had, and had desired, no witnesses. It was for her an act of enormous significance. She had worked towards the breeding of this bull for so long that this act which she had now committed, and towards which she had looked, created in her the sensation not of achievement or even excitement but of a breathtaking release from her anticipation. It was as if she had leaped out from between dank walls into an enormous, gaudy sunlight; as Mihilanus's dead monks had been carried through the dark slype of the abbey into the brilliant extramural blaze of the graves in the cemetery out of sight of the sea. Only a dream, her notion of giving to the island the Great Original of all the stock which had ever grazed, slept, dropped calves, been eaten on the island; this passionate fantastic demonstration of her coupling not with Coimheadach now only but with Coimheadach always, had had the implacable rigour of a dream – of a nightmare; of, perhaps, a labour from which she was now released. A labour, she felt in her daft head, which had given a Golden Calf to Coimheadach, the Golden Calf which was also Bull-God. Striding down the mountain, she came, not to melt down the idol and smash jubilation but to lead the dance. A perverted Moses who had taken the bull-god up to the heights and come down alone. Surpassing Ursula, saint, Ottoline became a patriarch.

'The lion in the fuchsia went roar, roar, ROAR.
As he swiped at his Mammy with his paw, paw, paw,'

she sang. The gun jolted against her right hip bone and occasionally her knee cap rapped the underside of the barrel. Her eyes were full, darting around the inside of the lids, pale, the pupils minute in the swooping, cloud-torn sunshine. Her shadow leaped and fluttered and grew; and vanished when the high clouds streamed across the light; danced out of the shade again – disappeared. Moving unevenly, her fine hair fluttering under the rigid hat, she came and went on the headland only the gun remaining at all times straight and unaffected by the comings and goings in the sky. Sea- and land-birds mingled over her, a wheeling circuit of screaming terns spinning between a lark and her nest; a gannet exploding in a violence of light and spray beneath the languorous return of a harrier's circuit; hooded crows and herring gulls paraded on the same curve of a warren. By her side fescues, brackens and heathers mingled with sea pinks, sea hollies, sea thistles, between the flaring gorse. Her path lay straight down the line of ambivalence where the elements merged.

The fulness of her eyes caught the light so that her eyeballs gleamed and shone in the restless land- and seascapes. The fulness was in her mind, crammed high and impelling in her head and tight in her stomach. It loosened muscles in her wrists and neck and groin which age and the febrile betel-bed had stiffened. The act she had celebrated had been the spending and ridding of an old desire, yet in its wake it brought neither tenderness nor torpor but a hard, bright violence.

To her right, a hundred feet below, the end of the Atlantic pounded the dregs of rock: thrust in to the walls of mica, felspar, quartz. The rock glittered. The sea glittered. They beat together, the tide was coming in. She turned aside from the faint track between two gorse bushes, the urge to squat distracting her. Before she lowered her breeches she laid the gun on the curt grass before her but a minute later picked it up again, leaning her weight forward on her toes, gripping the gun low down about the dark butt. The warm, moist nourishment passed from her body to the thin grass-mat over the thin soil. Out over the sea a cormorant broke the water, a fish shining briefly in its curved, archaic beak. Ottoline leaned forward, her hands running up and down the barrel of the rifle. Obliquely aligned, it rose up in front of her. She caressed the smooth underside of the long gun, and the thick warm curves of the wooden butt. After a while she stood up and moved on down the track, the gun's weight resting in her right hand.

The releasing of the great bull had in some way which she was not interested in analyzing set her free to kill the seal. The bull had not, in fact, taken up much of her time, daily. But he had absorbed her emotion. He had siphoned off all the bright potential for concentration of which she was capable; he had used up all her ability for physical expression so that much of her work around the place had become shoddy or temporary or reluctantly done, as if she were merely marking time, filling in with careless labour the months which had to pass before she set him loose among the élite of her stock. She had not even mended the roofing above the stall where he stood but had merely slung tarpaulin over the gaps in the slates and anchored the whole with ropes attached to great boulders which had bumped dismally against the shed walls in the squalls of spring, knowing only that there was some tremendous carnal expenditure which must be completed before she could channel her strength towards any other end.

Recently, in the pale, high-mooned nights of late summer, she had taken up both gun and the ostrich's phallus more frequently than ever before. She had sat, or stood, for nearly an hour on some occasions with one or the other, running her small fingers up their length, mumuring abuse and begging for patronage at the grave, fading face of Abbot Gilles, gargoyle on the east drainpipe.

Aelebel, moving grossly through the rooms or the courts at night, would come upon Ottoline suddenly and, seeing the sly face or the daft, unseeing eyes, would take away the gun or the stuffed penis and thrust her towards the tortuous bed where she would lie until Aelebel had sunk back to the kitchens, breathing in the sweetish stink of last night's sweat from her sheets, waiting for the night in the bed to pass. But with the gun in her hand or the penis in her lap Ottoline sensed that she was waiting, not for time to pass, but for a crisis to arrive; a crisis which she would meet more as an idea than as an individual.

For Ottoline, ideas were not abstract things, but bright, flashing pictures which she could not disbelieve or ignore. It seemed to her a very simple thing that in picking up the gun with its live ammunition, or the dead ostrich's phallus with its bullock-hair stuffing, that she could fulfill the picture she had of herself. It was a picture without gender, without singularity, without a periphery of birth or death. It was a vision she had of a thing of tatty magnificence, richly robed and ripped by the sea wind; a thing penetrating and devouring simultaneously; a thing whelping on the earth and dripping rich blood into the earth; a thing as hard as the granite chips it was made of and which wore her face; a thing which at one moment she called Coimheadach and at another, Ottoline Atlantica, and to which she never paid much attention.

But there it was now, as she came to the top of the steps which Gilles had cut into the rock face, and with the gun pointing down her thighs it was little different from herself. Together, in the shadow of the granite cliff they slipped down to the rocks where the seal was hauled up and where they shot him when he brought his head round to look at them.

IX

'Aelebel, touch me.'

'Touch you? What for, so?'

'I don't know, I don't know. Generation, perhaps. Make mischief, touch me, bring me back.'

'So you think we want you?'

'Don't you?'

Aelebel reached out the flat hands and took the skull of Ottoline between them. 'Cold,' she commented. 'You're getting over old to be chilled. Where is it you've been?'

'Up at Ursula's Baun, and then by the sea. The gulls are still at the blood.'

'I've got you a lobster for your supper. Come to the fire, so, and we'll warm you. Here, You, put out your hands, rub them, put them between mine then, lovely, put them here in my breast, so, and I'll warm you. Wait now while I put a turf on.'

'Saint's Way. There is a road in town called Saint's Way. Why, Aelebel?'

'St Cyril came that way.'

'He did?' Ottoline asked naïvely, as the truth should be no less known than this. As if the peasant's answer was all the answer needed. Aelebel looked at Ottoline without reserve. 'He did,' she said.

'Perhaps,' said Ottoline staring at the new turf, black against the whitening glow of the old, 'perhaps Ursula trod upon this one.'

'And if she did it'll not burn.'

Together they watched the embers redden and glint. Heavy smoke made auguries about the chimney breast, as if the future were contained in it, as if the past were verifiable in a future created out of repetition and conscious recreation. The flame which would come or not come had an authenticity of which they were neither afraid nor curious. The statement which it would make bore no relation to them, having touched them before and passed on a thousand years ago.

'Touch me and bring me back,' she said again.

A small flicker licked at the side of the turf. Here, on this heather, on these red cotton stalks, no saint had trod. It was a fact of no importance; its truth of no significance. Only the present warmth and the present sweet smell, trodden in by the antique lay, were of significance. Saintless, she was nonetheless warmed. She made an effigy of her own past and her own future by posing with her hands in the peasant's breast. Mary-Rose, coming up to the abbey for the evening's milk, found them that way, postured by the chapter fireplace.

Mary-Rose drew a deep breath and paused consciously at the door. She stopped to gather the picture in her mind and pin it firmly onto her interior drawing-board. The pins she used were sharp; one of adoration, one of jealousy, one a little tainted with lust and the last with vanity. Inclining her smooth head against the warped jamb she regarded the exterior and the interior pictures sombrely. 'God, you are lovely,' she said to them both.

Ottoline took against this remark, not seeing anything very lovely in Aelebel. 'Don't be silly,' she said snappishly. 'I'm cold.'

Aelebel turned her about and placed her lips in a great O against Ottoline's shoulder blades and puffed. The hot steam from her insides rushed through the black barathea of Ottoline's grandfather's hunting-jacket and through the silk of the shirt that her mother had been At Home in, once, on a cold day to nobody, and through the purple cotton vest onto her skin. It went through that, too, and into the very bone.

'Ah,' she sighed, 'a hot potato!'

'A hot potato?' Mary-Rose advanced crossly from the door to see. She was angry with Ottoline: once again she had disrupted an image of very poignant beauty. It would be an effort now to remember against the day when she would commit it to canvas. Against the day when she would be an artist.

'Give her a hot potato, Aelebel,' Ottoline commanded.

Mary-Rose felt an instinct to turn away, but she took another step forward and gritted her teeth. She felt martyred and silly. She curved her spine and felt the coarse hands grip her forearms. The fat on them was chilly. Mary-Rose's gaze slithered from the desperate eyes of the pink tapestried Leda on the stone wall and came to rest on the fingers about her own arm. The nails were deep in the cotton of her shirt. There were black crescents beneath the nails. Mary-Rose turned slowly and her eyes met the black peasant's. Slowly, Aelebel took her hands away.

'Can't,' she said quietly.

'O, for heaven's sakes!' Ottoline said pettishly. 'Stop emanating, the pair of you.'

'I'm not. I'm on my way to visit Sigerson.'

'O, hell and damnation – he's been emanating all day. Do something about him, will you, and quickly. I don't know what's the matter with him. He looks as if he needs a draught. Can't you DO something? He depresses me. I don't like being depressed. It's so sticky.'

'Sticky?'

'Great wafts of glycerine misery cluttering up the conversation. Not that he can converse, but he used to make an effort. What do you want to see him for, anyway?'

Mary-Rose made an eloquent little moue. 'I wanted some un-cross company,' she said winningly.

'Well, you won't get it from him. He's been badgering the Girl with the Birdcage all afternoon. I heard him yelling at her. He called her Dorothy and all.'

'Any reason why he shouldn't? It's her name.'

'Tarty!' Ottoline wiggled her bum and put one finger to the side of her nose.

Mary-Rose turned her back in disgust.

'Here, You,' Aelebel said to Ottoline, 'don't annoy the lady.'

'Why not? I'm a lady, too, aren't I? Well, AREN'T I?'

Silence,

'We – ll. ...' said Mary-Rose at last.

Ottoline jumped at her furiously. 'What the hell do you mean, "we – ll" ' she mimicked. 'I tell you, I'm a lady. I'm a damn good lady! I make a better lady than either of you, so there!'

Mary-Rose backed hastily away and came up against the little table in the corner. It wobbled and the black leather column thereon quivered.

'Watch out!' Ottoline shouted, nervously. 'That's precious.'

Mary-Rose still felt compelled to answer Ottoline, who shot sparks about the room and whose hair bristled with static electricity against all likelihood in the damp air. She had not meant to quarrel with Ottoline. Ottoline was valuable. Mary-Rose grew angry and bitter against Ottoline.

'You make a lousy lady,' she cried, gripping her hands together and wringing them. 'You are beautiful and you won't BE beautiful. What's the use of you, if you won't BE what you are? I've lived beside you for four years and what have you ever done but destroy, destroy, destroy –'

'ME?' Ottoline said, poking her head forward attentively. 'ME? DesTROY? What have I ever destroyed? I'm creative, I make things ... more things than you do, with your sea-cabbages in the sunset. If you want to know, I think your sunsets are a bloody sham! Why don't you stop making assignations with my silly son at one a.m. in the morning and do some WORK. Why don't you paint something. A picture OF something? Sunsets, indeed. ...!'

'I've never had an assignation with your son at one a.m. What are you talking about?'

'I'm referring to your assignations with Sigerson in the slype after midnight! That's not ladylike, either, if you want to know. Running round other people's grounds in the night and whispering in their slypes –'

'My dear, it sounds spine-chilling. I'm only sorry it wasn't me!'

'Then who was it? Who was he muttering to – a tape recorder?

That's what he says, but I know he hasn't got one!'

'Perhaps Dorothy. ....'

. 'No. It was before that Unlikelihood descended on us.'

'Well, I can't help you, Ottoline. It wasn't me. Why don't you ask Sigerson?'

'O, WOOF,' said Ottoline, suddenly dispirited with it all. There seemed to her to be no future in arguing with Mary-Rose; it was too serious. Ottoline was not capable of argument. She liked to fight, or to be at amity with her companions. Argument seemed a poor wee thing by comparison with either. She walked carefully round Mary-Rose's elegantly faded denim legs and bestowed her exhaustion in the chair beside the table. Absently her hand stretched out and began rhythmically to stroke the leather object. As she caressed it the smooth cool surface lulled her fingers, and the tight muscles began to ease. She sighed deeply.

'You make me old,' she complained. 'You don't LOOK at things, Mary-Rose, that's your trouble. Here we have a really stimulating small situation, and will you look at it? Will you, hell! I give you Sigerson whispering in the slype at one a.m. and all you do is say it wasn't you. Well, it should have been you, and if it wasn't, why wasn't it, and who WAS it?'

This was one question too many for Mary-Rose, who was only wondering about the last one. She put her hands behind her neck and ran her fingers through her hair, pulling it down about her, a beautiful veil, a Mary-Roseness to hide beautifully in.

Ottoline stretched her legs out and kicked moodily with her toe against her other heel. Away from them Aelebel continued to emanate, and Mary-Rose glanced obliquely down at Ottoline. She was so exquisite, said the pin in Mary-Rose's drawing board which wanted Ottoline to be exquisite; so frail and delicate and mauve-coloured and so totally HORRIBLE in her boots and frightful jacket, scowling away at the smouldering fire and wiping her nose on the back of her hand. There were lines on her face, and dust had got into them and etched them black and savage. She looked as if she was wearing a pinny and black stockings, as if her hair was in pigtails, but that was an illusion. She wasn't sepia-tinted and blurred about the outside, and at any moment she might leap or march tremendously. ... The pin of adoration stuck hurtfully into Mary-Rose.

Ottoline said, 'It's distressing for a lady in my position to be surrounded by dead ends.' She looked up at Mary-Rose as if accusing her of this singular shape.

Mary-Rose bridled. 'Well,' she said, 'and what is your position that dead ends are so destructive to it?'

'Ongoing,' pronounced Ottoline and looked smug.

Mary-Rose snorted disbelievingly. Aelebel took a step from the door where she had been hanging about looking menacing. Ottoline tossed her silver head and smoothed the skirts of the frock-coat as if someone had complimented her. Ottoline looked portentious. 'I am about to *floruit*,' she announced.

'O, God. What next?' said Mary-Rose in disgust. It was the pin of jealousy that happened to be doing a Judith in her, now. She shrugged as if to shift it.

'You keep quiet, You. D'You hear me? Quiet. ...' said Aelebel.

Ottoline turned towards her. The mauve eyes widened and began to fill. 'O, Aelebel,' she whispered, 'can't you stop it? Can't you stop it all goin' off sideways and tell it that I'm here, waiting for it to catch up? Can't you, Aelebel, I'm ready now ... and one day quite soon, I'll be ... I'll be too mad.'

'Now, you lay off of her. Go on, go on, out of here, and find MR Sigerson, and leave her to me. ...' Aelebel lunged across the room at Mary-Rose.

The pretty scene smashed into fragments on the hard floor. Ottoline stared away at something only visible to Ottoline, and tears began to swell from the blossoms in her eyes. Mary-Rose hurried out, her long legs swinging.

Much later, the Girl found Ottoline in the warming-room. She strode rapidly up and down in front of her. Every time she reached the wall she turned so fast that her long skirt whipped out and spun about her ankles.

'Madame Ottraine, believe me, no harm could come to your papers. If you would just allow Dr Ottraine to have them for a day so that I could look at them in his company – surely you would be satisfied with that? I won't even touch them – he can handle them and I will just look. Please, what possible harm could come of it?'

Ottoline folded her arms like Napoleon and watched the Girl, scowling. She was slouched on an Italian Savanorola, and her legs stretched out across the floor, her back rested against the tattered *Robin et Marion* in *gros point*, and a stain over the cyclamens on the grass showed how often she had sat, thus, resting her head in the same place, in the same field of flowers. Above her she could sense Robin, as he had played with her as a child when the draughts brought the dance home to him down the centuries lost in the tapestry. She and he had danced here, to the westerlies and the cold nor' easter, in the glow of the turf fire, in the inspiration of fleeting spring suns on spring tides flashing and becking through the three tall lights of the stone window. In the dust, as children. And here he was, still, brown arm outstretched above her head, a caress, a signal, a personal thing in the room isolating her as her and Robin and their past, different in quality from that of the others in the room. '*Venes après moi, venes après moi,*' she sang with him, in her head, as she stretched out in her place on the stool. Because she had Robin, she had security. No one else in the room had an ally the way Robin was her ally. She turned her head, a caress of her grey hair on the frayed wool. Robin.

Dorothy noted the way the old woman scrubbed her head against the Arras work and shivered – things like that should be in museums, not clogged with ash, hair grease, balding in patches where irrational fingers had picked. ...

'Please,' she ended up, weakly, unable to think of anything at all that would soften the obstinacy of old Boney, scowling on her campaign stool.

Ottoline sighed and smacked at her stockings with a fly swat. 'I wish,' she remarked petulantly, 'that you were less importunate. Now that is a long word, the sort of word my son uses, so you ought to understand it. The position is quite clear. I do not wish the Coimheadach papers to be published, even in part, until I myself have been through them with my son.'

'But I don't intend to publish – I'm only looking for a few facts –'

' "Fact Finding Expedition" into the lives of my ancestors, as if there was any point in going on an expedition if it wasn't to find facts — what else does one expedition for? Blind-man's-buff in a jeep? When I was a girl I had a governess called Miss Holt-Poulter and I used to play Blind-man's-buff with her and when her eyes were bound, do you know what I did?'

'Madame Ottraine, I wouldn't begin to guess —'

'I used to lie on the tallboy and tweak at her fitchew with my fishing line —'

'Madame Ottraine —'

'O'Treann.'

'Madame Ottraine —'

'Your vowel sounds are VERY ugly, dear girl, but let it pass. It was a mackerel line, actually. I wasn't allowed to keep trout lines in the bedroom, because in those days the seal weren't here and the mackerel and salmon were very prolific. Now the poor buggers get gobbled up as soon as they come within trawling distance. But I shot the old bastard. Right in the throat. It was a good shot —' she said gently, rubbing her hair against the flowers of the forest and feeling Robin signalling to her out of the dust, 'straight as an arrow. I had my glasses on, you see —' she explained, lest the Girl did not realize the care that had gone into the dying.

'Yes, quite.' The Girl made a premature turn, not having reached the full length of the room. Her eyes were showing their whites again and rolling a little as if the muscles were weak. The anger burned around in her head, dull and hot like a bruise. She had made up her mind that tomorrow she would leave. There was no point in any of this. It was futile, silly, a waste of time.

'WHO did you shoot? she asked sarcastically, not believing a word of it but believing in her stomach, knowing that some death had been occasioned, demonstrating by her tone how impervious she was to the old grey bitch, denying the gut-knowledge of the old bitch which told her that it was no lie, just as nothing else had been a lie – Christ, that poor wretch, Holt-Poulter, what she must have gone through! Suddenly she thought, I wonder how many men she has killed? And Wilberforce Close trapped her in and she thought how indoctrinated by this sodden nullity she had become even to wonder. Killing men! Crossly, having caught herself out, she said, 'Well, who DID you shoot?' like a child, pert.

'The big bull –' Ottoline said dreamily, caressing the thought of it, caressing the cyclamen on the forest floor, caressing the murders and the blood and Robin and the brown little pointed children who had jumped about in the white motes of the turf, children so like and so unlike the daughters of morning, of Auschwitz, Liverpool, Los Millãres, Coimheadach.

'O –' said the Girl, infuriated by her relief.

She loathed the big cattle on the hill. She loathed their barbarous shape, their fleshiness, their mean red eyes, their black-tipped horns, so spread, so vulgar, concomitant with their size, a nightmare out of Grimm's tales. She was embarrassed by their continual mounting and farting and the projectile evacuations of the bulls when they galloped. They smelt, not milky or branny or meadowy like the cows she had hitherto come across, but sour and virile, and her hatred of Coimheadach became centred on the monstrous anachronistic brutes up in the Baun. She hated the way the old bitch's circumscribed mind went round and round the cattle, circling them in pictures, fantasies, evocations, allusions; never still, always circling round and round the cattle. ... She was glad to hear that one had been shot. She did not want to know why. She did not want it stewed for dinner.

'He was eating my fish,' Ottoline was explaining.

'Your tins of herring?'

Dorothy had heard of the picnics in the Baun – she did not believe in them either, and yet she did believe, detecting a fishy stench off the oxtail broth. The oxtail broth had come out of a tin with impeccable ancestry; it had been the tureen into which it had been poured which had imparted the fishiness, but the Girl did not know this and had attributed the mixture to the predilection of Popplethwaite for soused herrings, of which Ottoline had gaily informed her whilst splitting a Claddagh sheep's femur with a poultry shears to extract the marrow. This innocent little scene had taken place beneath the bucolic leers of the ancestors the evening after the rescue of the Aubusson carpet and Ottoline had stood against the carving table, a monstrous slab of Irish Chippendale much embellished with curly-headed bulls with ram's horns and claw-like feet clutching spheres like the roc its eggs. Ottoline's mouth had been wide with concentration and her jerky movements reflected in the mahogany, so that the Girl had seen the action simultaneously from right way up and upside down – and neither sight was comforting. The marrow, when she was offered some, tasted of soaked Hovis and cabbage-water to her inexperienced palate, and she had some difficulty forcing it down, while watching Ottoline drag hers out in grey gobbets with a chutney fork, slouched over the Chippendale, salivating and sucking, and wiping her mouth on the sleeve of her spotted shirt.

'Fee, Fy, Fo, Fummm!' muttered Ottoline Bonaparte now, tickling her instep with the fly-swat. 'Don't be a fool – why should a seal want to eat herrings out of a Fortnum & Mason's tin when he can get 'em fresh out of the ocean?'

'A SEAL!'

'Yes, you silly girl. A grey bull seal. He was eating my fish – I told you.'

She explained, as to one ignorant, her fear that the seal which were increasing in local waters, might be selecting new breeding grounds. From time to time, down the generations, it happened. Inexplicably, colonies would appear from the depths, cruise, haul up, breed, mate and vanish after a lapse of years. Something to do with sunspots, she thought, or long-term shifts in the patterns of the currents as the coastline altered, century by century; of movements of windbelts, of the earth's axis; pressure, perhaps, of the shoals unknown; unguessable pressures in the alien element; pressure of population or the atrocities of Sedna – she did not know the reason, but it happened, now and again. She feared for her fishing grounds, for her kelping for manure, for the Claddagh sheep who lived on the rocks and seaweed and which she ate with relish for the iodined flesh and the delicate little bones. She feared the parasites the seal brought to the fish, the dirt, the noise, the vast mounting tension on the rising tides when the cows came in to give birth. She did not want the rotting placentae swinging in the beaks of gulls, the scarred corpses of the moidered calves, the encroachment upon her territory of a society so formal, so bleak, so stringent, so unutterably strange. She feared the colonies, she said – Ottoline, who feared nothing. So like women, she said, the predatory front grip and the vicious claws scraping on the rocks; the lonely infancy of the stranded pup as the cows turned again to the ugly, cruising bulls. Up and down, up and down, prefacing their eternal pregnancy; the mystery of that pregnancy, perpetual, unyielding, ceaseless. She feared the wailing voices, the harsh antagonisms, the strife, the formal loneliness of the seals. Too like women, she said; the enormous eyes, for finding the fish silhouetted in the luminous waters above them; a woman's enormous eyes hunting up and down the soul to devour the Christ-Sign, the ichthos in man, which distinguished him from her; Ursuline eyes, she said, thinking of Cyril, saint. She feared the arrested pregnancy – the appalling dormant days when the foetus lay latent – alive? How alive? The hundred days' horror, the fear of still-birth – the superstitions and awes of generations of women, sluttish, lonely, ignorant. O yes, she feared the seals. And the ugly grey bull had been cruising now, on and off for years, seeking territory, never taking it, but this year she had been more afraid than before. This year she had to kill him. She told how beautifully she had killed, how swiftly, how accurately. Leaning her head at Robin's feet, how the act of the death had been a signal of her care, her love for the threat of the big bull seal.

'Seals,' she said, 'are women's work. He was a danger to me; he added to my life; he GAVE. I suppose I loved him, in a way. Loved the rising attention I had to give to him, waiting every summer for him to come, to regard my territory, to postulate claim. I loved the danger of it, the threat. This year, for the first time, he hauled up regularly. Then I came. ...' Her eyes were dreamy, enormous, indigo eyes, as a woman's eyes are when she dreams of mating. 'There are,' she snapped abruptly, 'enough women here.'

Dorothy Lambert drew in an enormous breath that drew the damp, clogged air into the outmost filament of the outmost tubes of her lungs. So thick with salt and turf was the breath that she coughed asthmatically and wheezed. Ottoline watched her patiently while she suffered. Ottoline tormented her bunion a little with the fly swat and waited for the Girl to go away and cough somewhere else. But the Girl wanted to know if Ottoline always shot her enemies and whether her last remark should be taken in the light of initiating hostilities. She also felt positive that there was no safe way of acquiring this pertinent information. She remembered having decided at various times that Madame Ottraine was mad; a man; a great actress in the tradition of Bernhardt; a silly old fool. She now remembered the eaten Pinell. She remembered the apparent carelessness of Ottoline's athletic grip on the long, razor-edged goad; she remembered the spitting and the gluttony attending the awful, eucharistic dinners in the whispering refectory. ... She whooped and said, 'You give me the shivers.'

Ottoline was a little disappointed. She confessed as much to herself. She had aimed at distracting the Girl from her avowed intention of peering at the Coimheadach papers and at the same time instilling into her some sense of her own mounting irritation. Instead the silly girl had got the shivers. She was obviously too unused to the intricacies of civilized diplomacy to appreciate Ottoline's conversational subtleties. She probably came, Ottoline decided, from a rather common home, making a mental note to inquire from Sigerson about the matter. For unless you were a Lady of Leisure, she reasoned, you would not have sufficient time to develop the art of conversation, which was, after all, a skilled occupation. Of course, if you weren't a lady at all — but there were a few matters in which even Ottoline confessed herself to be imaginatively limited.

'Can we,' said Dorothy, straightening up right in the middle of the room and glaring like an enraged macaw, 'be a little more DIRECT, Madame Ottraine?'

Her worst fears confirmed, Ottoline in her turn sighed deeply, but her tubes were so coated with nicotine that the dust and damp hadn't a hope. 'I suppose so,' she agreed reluctantly. 'But won't it be a bit dull?'

'O, for God's sake!' Dorothy cried, flinging her arms about and generally coming apart at the waistband and in the nerves. 'It may be dull to you, but it is my work! I came here to work, you know —'

'You came here to put something in that empty birdcage,'

Ottoline contradicted her. 'You came here to my house with an empty birdcage, and you have been here ever since because you can't find a bird to put in it. Well, Girl, this isn't an aviary – I have nothing for sale in any of my cages. You can't put your hand in and grasp a bird and pay; put it in your stainless steel cage and march, trumpeting, out. That's the way small boys buy bull's-eyes. The things in my cages can't be bought – can't be paid for. Do you understand, Girl?'

The Girl did not answer. She stood in the middle of the room, on the flags, one foot in its sandal across the worn edges where two flags met; one red, one brown. Her fingers tangled in the many rows of beads about her neck; cacao seeds, pomegranate seeds, coffee seeds, melon seeds, on a thin strand of gut. Ottoline looked at her levelly. There was no expression on her face. Cacao seeds, melon seeds, strung on gut – poor Pinell, so long ago. So long ago that it didn't matter any more.

The Girl did not answer; she did not understand. She thought of Ottoline as a shop-keeper with a tinkling bell and a counter piled to heaven with junk, bull's-eyes and canary seeds and rat poison and rope, and a bell that tinkled as the door shut.

> *'The bells of hell go ting-a-ling-a-ling*
> *For you but not for me.'*

She did not understand; she had only come for bull's-eyes. Why were they not for sale?

Slowly, as the silence drew along the cold warming-room, she became afraid of the old grey bitch. Ottoline stared at her, as if she could force understanding in through her eyes; force learning, force feeding of the wit. In her effort to avoid the pressure, the Girl shook her head from side to side and turned away, her wide chest stubborn and solid. The old grey bitch was hunting her now, sniffing at her, rhythms of tension running like tremors across her skin. The Girl wanted to run. She looked around the room; there was nothing much in it; a dead fire, a comfortless mantel of carved stone and faded green paint, a tapestry drifting in the draught, a wild brown man and the old grey bitch, straddling the campaign stool, head up, sniffing. There was nowhere to run, no cover, no exit, except the door that led deeper into the viscera of Coimheadach. There was not even a direct threat, just the pressure of the Bitch's presence. The Girl lifted her hands as if to ease the weight, and the thin lips curled up about the Bitch's teeth, there, between her and the door.

The wind snarled among the fire-dogs.

Then suddenly the sunlight lashed against the three lights of the window – a lamé shield of dazzling imminence, a screen of sunlight dropped behind the grey mullions which tore the darkness out of Ottoline's face; which struck satin sheens on the black firedogs; which flung Robin, his hand to his eyes, reeling backwards into the shade, and which plummeted upon the Girl, alone, no longer alone, encased in light in the middle of the floor. It hit right through her, and as its warmth flared through her body, through her stomach, through her throat she dropped her hands and cried, 'There! There isn't anything to get shivery about! You tried to worry me, didn't you, with all this fey talk about seals and uncanny shopping! You tried to make me into an animal, didn't you?' Her voice rose and she shouted at Ottoline, who went on staring as if the sun had not come out at all. 'You tried to get at me, like an old bitch, trying to hunt me –'

'I do wish you wouldn't shout so,' Ottoline said crossly.

But the Girl was strung beyond governesses' tactics. She was red all over, shivering with anger, with fear, with the release of fear, so that she imparted, to Ottoline, a hot, sour stink which made her turn her head away gently, as if she were tired or a little ill.

'You must understand,' Ottoline said patiently, like an invalid explaining confidence in an unusual treatment, 'that I am not at all antagonistic towards you. At least –' she peered at the Girl, and hesitated, 'no, definitely not towards YOU, or indeed towards my son. But Coimheadach is a PLACE – it is not a person. You can't take its temperature and ask if its birth certificate is in order. Let alone take away specimens in a stainless steel birdcage. It is a PLACE ... a PLACE –' she went on repeating the word, rubbing her head against the faded cyclamen and leaving the Girl isolated in a crystal of unused vigour.

The Girl felt the isolation and shouldered it away with a clumsy shrug. She wanted to break the isolation, which was terrible, by rolling the crystal violently around the stone floor – surely that would break it, surely?

Ottoline saw her in the isolation, rolling about in it, knocking witlessly against the stones, against the quartz, mica, felspars on the beach; rolled witlessly and waywardly by the waves, knocking, knocking –

'Rory's in, You,' said Aelebel stridently. 'You gone deaf?'

Ottoline yelled, 'I was bloody thinking, you old black fool –'

'Funny way to think, quiet like that. What are you up to?'

The Girl began to laugh, madly, far out beyond the reach of the two older women.

'O, for God's only sake,' she shouted, 'you have it made, you two, you really do have it set up!' She slapped her thighs and glinted at them from beneath her brows. 'Talk about history –' she cried boisterously, ' – what do you think is going to turn up in all the archives better than this?'

Still outside them, for they were very close, she began to walk again, twisting her head to watch them. Ottoline sat up straighter, her knees together, prim. Beside her Aelebel glowered and snuffled, her loose mouth open, turning from Ottoline to the Girl and back.

'I mean, what a set-up!' the Girl cried, shaking her head seriously like an American student. 'Madame O' unpronounceable and her Dogberry out of the sty – I mean –!'

'What do you mean?' said Ottoline Bonaparte, very soft.

'Like it's a seaside show, a pier act or something ... the two of you in this PLACE – Pig and Whistle!' She began to really laugh, now pointing from one to the other. 'The Whistle all hot air, and Pig, here,' to Aelebel.

Ottoline Atlantica rose to her feet. The Girl stopped talking and looked at her.

Ottoline pointed to the door. 'I will rid my servant of your vulgarity,' and she spat accurately upon the flagstones.

The Girl went out. She opened and closed the door for herself, quietly. Ottoline's spittle gleamed in the sun.

'Which boat is Rory in?' she asked.

'The big one.'

'Tell him to take the separator. The garage will mend it for us.'

'So.' At the door Aelebel half-turned. 'Thanks, so —' she muttered.

Ottoline screamed, leaping from her place beneath Robin, 'Don't thank me — you fool, you bloody fool! Don't thank me, ever —' and she struck out with the fly-swat.

The wire edge caught Aelebel on the neck. Squealing, she ran into the cloister the blood oozing between her fingers. 'BITCH! You old BITCH —!'

In the warming-room the sun was still out. Ottoline stood beneath the tapestry and ran her thin fingers up the brown thighs of the faded man, up and up. Outside on the gutter Gilles, father, was there.

'Father, Robin —' said Ottoline, not hearing herself in the settling dust. 'Father, Robin, why?'

'*Venes après moi*, Ottoline Atlantica, my love, my bitch, my son,' they sang.

Differential preservation had acted arbitrarily upon the graves. Ottoline had lied, slyly, calculatingly, when she had told the Girl that there was no soil in all Coimheadach; there was, and it was in the graves of the monks. The brethren had fought for these graves, battling with inadequate tools, wooden shovels, bound baskets and iron picks passed from hand to hand until the shallow depressions had been sufficient to disguise the brief coffins. Granite chips, soiled débris from the outbuildings, hanks of heather-tight turf and refuse had gone on top of the little boxes; grasses had grown upon them, sorrels, docks, nettles, purple and white plantains, who with their tonsure of white about their dark pates resembled mysterious, exquisite long-headed academicians, exercising their dialectics in the sun and wind, in endless debate on the mysteries in miniature Lateran upon the graves, in camera of old bones. Or so it had been until Aelebel had let the Rhode-Island Reds in there to scratch. Which graves they selected, which old bones and black beads lay beneath their stations, was a matter of which poultry were masters alone. Gilles, the visiting herbalist from La Ferté, Silas's confessor who died frothing about the lips, Thomas who had tried to infect blisters on his hands to simulate the stigmata yet had died in a state of grace and septicaemia; the hens elected who to bare, who to leave privy. They ate the long-headed foreign invaders from the fat lands who talked and nodded in the sea wind; they broke and devoured the rusty, bloody sorrel until the surface of the breast of the hill was bare, riddled with marks and pits and graves and droppings, with smashed feathers and empty husks, with overturned broken jam jars that had once held Scottish Mincemeat, Whiskey-flavoured, or Golliberry Bramble, seedless, with, beneath the fence where they escaped, one human incisor, and against the east wall of the church a chick's wing-bones, articulated and white.

Into this four-cornered place only two winds blew: off-shore and on-shore; therefore the old bones could not rattle and click into place like Mr Punch, and the red face of the Girl, when she came into the graveyard caused no quartet of ventic spirits to operate as her long skirts whispered like a prophet's drab upon the dust.

The Girl was sad because she had no frame to her rage. The anger had dissipated after the glob of spit had plopped on the floor beside her feet. The hysteria broke like a boil or a bran bag, and the effluvium drained hygienically away. But the sadness did not drain off. It lay inside her, lumpish and uncouth, waiting for her thick muscles or her heavy tongue to release it. She stood in the henrun, or the graveyard, shapelessly, with her stomach slouching roundly and her weight on one hip. Piebald hen shit and grey granite, grey stones, anonymity gave her nothing. She had no notion, no signal of herself from which to begin. Around herself her body was assembled but not coherent. She had no freedom in her wrists or in her neck to make gestures, to exhibit herself; she had no sense of identity with her eyes or with her fingers, no training, no discipline within which to channel herself so that the sadness could become formalised, articulate, used. There were no sounds abroad on the afternoon which she could meet and inform, or become informed by. She could not speak because there was no one there to receive her words and make them valid. She just stood there, in the hen-run, sad.

The Girl was not accustomed to thinking of herself as incapable of action, but she had not yet thought of feeling as an active process. Feeling was a thing which was generated from within, by unlovely and hidden ingredients, as menstruation or ear-wax was and just as unexpected and as implacable. She tolerated emotion on the same level as such phenomena, as a thing totally personal but beyond control. She admitted its existence, indeed, for she was a formidable person; permitted it to exist within her and suffered its waxing and waning, dismissing it from her consciousness upon its cessation. She had never taken possession of it, never taken it in her short hands and moulded it to fit her. She had never tried to colour it in, or listen to it, or use it as a thigh muscle with which to leap or posture. It was not an element within which to exist, but an element which existed within her. She rested her buttocks against the slats of an old coop, tip-tilted and long abandoned. The shadows of the church reached out across the run and deprived it of warmth or well-being. She drew in the dirt with the toe of her sandal. The coop supported her weight, as if within her she had slung a hammock from hip bone to hip bone and the dull sorrow lay in it, dragging her spine, her belly and ultimately her head to the pellets of the red hens. The gaping roof held the hammock up, so that the weights did not break it and stream out around her feet. If they had, of course, they would have been utilized; something, some place, could have been built of them, but she was unaware of the possibility.

Rebelliously she shook her head and the Rhode Islands shrieked raucously and fled for safety behind an illegitimate stillbirth of the gate-post period. 'Grerr!' she yelled at them.

The sound of her own voice mingled with that of Aelebel who was still screeching 'Bitch!' and mopping at her neck with the corner of her pinny.

'Yeah!' replied the Girl at the top of her lungs. 'Yeah! BITCH!'

She bounced off the hen coop, and the strings of seeds leapt and clicked. The sadness drifted out across the hen-run, and she lost sight of it quickly because she had no interest in it.

I will not be forced into this absurd performance of the old witch's, she thought. I won't be manipulated as a butt in her dreams and fantasies, set up as a target for her little poisoned darts of desire; a ball-alley for her to run amok against like a mad cow.

She strode rapidly over the bare earth, stubbing her toe in the holes dug by last week's chicken pie who had held ambitions to fecundity and made innumerable little pities in the unreceiving earth in which to hatch mythical and appalling eggs. The bitterness of abuse was welcome to the Girl: it was virile, active. She flickered her fingers in anticipation and mussed her hair.

Mary-Rose had been dragged up to the abbey by a great need to see Ottoline. After the sordidity of the conversation with Sigerson she had gone home, stroked wildly with a brush upon her eyebrows, and then sat for some time regarding her whorish expression with satisfaction. The instinct to whorishness had been coming upon her regularly at monthly intervals since her divorce. She could time it almost exactly. Whilst it repelled her in theory, it filled her at the same time with a tremendous urge to be physically active, and to be beautiful, and she would suffer a suffusion of a sort of wild glee which was profoundly creative and at the same time unreal. She distrusted herself in these times, and in between them was slightly nervous, but she had never made use of the mood, largely because there had been no opportunity to do so.

Now the unsettled vigour was with her again. She had been shocked and affronted by Sigerson, not for declaring passion but for not declaring it. In some way she felt that the desire he implied was a desire for the mood she exhibited and not for her. She knew that she was likely to appear more beautiful, and contrarily more severe, at these times than at others, largely because the habit of suppressing the inner excitement was reflected in her face as a mirror-image of chastity, of withdrawal. It was this to which she imagined that Sigerson was responding. His sudden gobbet of acidity spat at her with the words, 'What else have I got to do but talk?' She had taken them as a direct implication that he expected her to refuse him. Yet he had not asked. Had he asked, what would she, in this mood, have said?

They had parted at the cliff top without word or reference, both too grown up now to make anything of it. And that was why Mary-Rose had needed to see Ottoline: in her unobservant way she thought of Ottoline as being totally childlike, and she needed the conflict of her own consciously directed intentions and Ottoline's undivertable whimsy to strengthen her attitude to Ottoline's son. So she had taken infinite care with her face and her clothes and now appeared in the slype in a white trouser suit of pristine calico and the white plastic sunglasses. In the shadowy tunnel she glowed like a faintly illuminated siren with black pits for eyes.

Coming from the poultry run, the Girl almost walked into Mary-Rose in the dark slype before she saw her lurking against the dank stones like a white cloud across the moon. She did not so much populate the slype as inhabit it, as if by being there she gave to that passage-way an importance greater than access: she gave it a meaning, a function, as other rooms, pantries, gun-rooms, libraries, have functions created by their content. So the slype through which Mihilanus had drawn the dead bodies and the quick souls to the moon-coloured granite became a placing for the moon-coloured Mary-Rose with her blacked-in eyes. It became a place where a thing was which was obscured as the moon by the whitening cloud; a place where fugitive and transitory things would happen, which were not direct, nor permanent, either in operation or in effect. The mood of Mary-Rose, the passing, moon-aligned mood of whoredom, this moon-mood filled up the slype, ran jaggedly between the thin stones, dripped like dew with the damp from the vaulted roof and echoed about the dark as it fell, interminably slowly, on the broken chips and chill stone of the floor. No sunlight ever came into the slype. The slype sat around Mary-Rose and she was there – being – within it. Yet to the Girl, when she came up against her, not quite properly being. The Girl stumbled on the uneven, puddled floor, close to Mary-Rose, and it seemed, when she looked up and saw her there, that the slype had taken Mary-Rose, and made of her a thing of its own when she had chosen to stand within it.

'This bloody place –' the Girl said viciously, regaining her balance and glaring at Mary-Rose in the shadows, dressed for Goodwood or Badminton or some aqueous activity on Thames or Isis. 'It gets you one way or another. It has a spirit of downright belligerent intent, never mind the personification of it. ...'

'Poor dear,' said Mary-Rose easily, her lips moving quickly and glistening with the restlessness of her mood, 'you are having a bad time!'

The ease of the words told the Girl that Mary-Rose was not having a bad time and that there was enmity somewhere, not only in Ottoline. She was surprised, this not being a quarter where she had expected to have to fight against disdain. Rapidly she said, 'Far from it. I have the situation pretty well taped now. ... I have only to make up my mind whether it is worth bothering any further –' She let the sentence hang in the chill passageway.

Mary-Rose crushed it out with her light, neighing laugh. 'I suppose it can give one a sort of framework,' she conceded, lounging against the stones, 'but I wouldn't have thought that you would need that. You have seemed so very confident right from the start –'

'Of what?' said the Girl quietly, looking up to the plastic-rimmed eyes and unable to see them.

'Of your ability to get it all taped. Now I would have said that Coimheadach presented some problems to anyone wanting to get something out of it – I mean, Ottoline isn't exactly forthcoming, or can you handle her?'

The question was so direct that the Girl was startled, and she turned, shrugging and fiddling with the rough stone. 'O, I don't say it's easy to get things out of her –'

'Look,' said Mary-Rose suddenly, leaning forward and putting herself close to the Girl so that the gleam of her lips was clear and wet. 'Ottoline is riding it light at the moment. Don't upset things, will you? Are you with me? She's tricky. A lot of things get tricky here in the summer. ... There are too many of the wrong things to do – I mean, all these long evenings and nothing happening in them – and she gets a bit tied up in herself. You must have noticed. ... Don't upset the applecart, will you?'

'What's the matter? Why are you getting at me? I haven't done anything to upset her –'

Mary-Rose snorted, 'Classic, adolescent classic. Sorry to offend, my dear, but what a remark. When did you leave school? Talk about defensive!'

'You pretty well told me I was on the verge of upsetting her, now tell me why?'

'I'm sorry, my dear, I forgot you were so young. ... No, you haven't done anything. It's just that life here can be very intense, with Ottoline's moods and so on, and I thought that perhaps you might be getting a bit — well, you know, well — pressing, if you follow me.'

The slype, dank as the trestles in Whitehall, leaped around the Girl. Yah! cried her angry bosom, her indigestion, her constipation from the flat, unslaking water, her burn from the Tilly, the shivers, the chill of the linen sheets and the frigid eyes of the old bitch — here was a frame for the anger and the sorrow.

'Mrs Deckle,' she said furiously, her head lowered as if to charge and peering up at Mary-Rose from beneath the forelock of hanks, 'I AM pressing. I am pressing that — that — to let me look at a few old bits of paper. Just old, old bits of paper. And she is so avaricious that she can't let them out of the strong-box for her own son to touch. She prevaricates, she lies, she malingers in bed when I am ready for work. She even threatens me with physical violence —'

'God, I'd be careful of that —'

'Thank you very MUCH, Mrs Deckle, I am comforted by your reassurances —'

'My God, you are angry! You've gone red with rage —'

'I'm surprised you can see it in this mausoleum —'

The redness surged hotly all over her, taking hold of her pulse, of her breathing, of her eyesight, wringing sweat and gripes and tears out of her, clutching at her muscles in spasms and sweeps, and then coolly, remorselessly letting go, dwindling as the chill came back into the stale air.

'O, for God's sake,' she said desperately, 'I'm going. I'll go tomorrow. I hate this bloody place. I've never been anywhere where there is so much — incest!' she cried at last.

The voices of the girls drifted up to Ottoline where she sat in her conservatory over their heads. She had left the warming-room too edgy to pull Robin out of the tapestry to keep her company, too peaceless to talk to Father Gilles on the gutter. Somewhere Aelebel was running amok calling her a bitch, and Sigerson was feeling peculiar, running his hand over his hair and offering her money to buy her papers; she had gone up to her own austere rooms and lain on the great bed, picking at the damask and smoking the cheap, minute cigarettes until she had been urged by her own restlessness to go in among the wild plants to her writing table where she had intended to wrench her grammar into a composition from which the harbour-master would understand that she would be expecting heavy machinery by freight from the garage yard sometime in the next fortnight. Her grammar had refused to be so wrought, and instead she had slumped back in the wicker chair and listened to the girls arguing beneath her. She did not understand the words, merely the tone: the aggressive, vulgar note that occasionally crept into Mary-Rose's voice and the high squealing anguish of the Girl. She smiled at the thought that there was an assignation in the slype after all, even if it was not Sigerson's, and thought that a little activity like this was a good thing in a house full of women.

She wondered which of them would get Sigerson in the end and thought the Girl probably would. There would be the initial problem of twisting Sigerson by the bollocks until he understood.

It all sounded very vigorous. She dozed, thinking that perhaps when she woke up it would be amusing to twist Sigerson. ... It was pleasant to hear the girls so bitter about her own son. She forgot Sigerson and concentrated on the idea of it. That she had women in her house fighting over her son. That, at least, was satisfactory. It lifted the blanket of inertia which settled over her every time she thought about him. It was a happening, a reflection of vigour, or even of vice; a showing of something by people about her. It was part of the tedium of her existence that no one around her ever made displays to her. She alone displayed, preening and pluming in her coloured clothes, posturing and defiant before her house, her son, her father, anyone. But her son did not respond to her. Nothing happened. Anything that ever happened at Coimheadach happened because she made it do so. She crept up on her house, on Gilles, fingering them, milking them, sucking at them until she dreamed or screamed and an event had taken place. And at every event her love for them drove in deeper, into them, into her, a wild, hermaphrodite worm eating at the heart of Coimheadach, among the wax petals, carmine, peach and pearl. ... But now! O, that the worm would become a serpent! Something suffused with grandeur and anonymity — a fierce fatal thing, unguessable and mysterious in its needs to twine and grip and devour finely the things which rode her! Some mad passion on its way, slithering out of the tunnel of the slype to savage her son ... Pinell's son.

A corner of the blanket of inertia lifted in the draught of the voices from below; the hollow sound of Mary-Rose echoing in the slype; a voice, Mary-Rose's, which was always an echo of something else, something from away back sounding down the long underground way from her blank black past into the high space of Coimheadach. Poor, uninhabitable Mary-Rose. And the higher sound of the Girl, resounding up through the walls, along the top of the old nightstair, between the draughty gaps in her window frames. This voice was full, stuffed, a bladder of confusions about to burst and spill out into her house where it would do no more damage than the split drain had done, which was now flushing so sweetly; lovely work, lovely effective work, thought Ottoline, opening her eyes and gazing sleepily at the high windows, because she had not quite gone to sleep with the girls squabbling like this so close to her. ...

Down in the slype Mary-Rose looked sideways at the Girl who was trying to pass her. Mary-Rose stood in the centre of the passage, so that the Girl would have to brush against her, or cringe to the wall or ask permission to get by. She stood proudly, like an unexpected statue in a formal garden. She stood like a model for herself, for who she was that afternoon: a woman of pride, a woman who had put on vanity and chastity for unchaste purposes. The energy that was inside her taughtened her shoulders, which were usually rounded and sloping, and her breasts, low and Gothic in shirts, became aggressive points of personality which the white suiting might not conceal. At last she put out her hand. The Girl turned away from it, but Mary-Rose touched her on the upper arms and drew her closer, making a slow, tender movement, perhaps a caress, perhaps a threat.

Smiling slightly Mary-Rose said, 'It is a pity you have to work so hard. ... Wouldn't you like to enjoy yourself, too?' and she released the Girl and added astonishingly, 'Don't you play any games?'

'Not your sort!' the Girl shouted, jumping back as soon as she was free.

'And what do you think MY sort is?' questioned Mary-Rose,

again coming closer so that the Girl edged and dithered, and embarrassment took the point out of her anger.

'I don't know – I don't understand any of you –'

'Want to go home?'

'Mrs Deckle, I don't know what you want from me, but I'm going to my room now. Can I get by, please?'

Mary-Rose stepped forward and, flattening herself politely, slipped around the Girl, then strode to the far end of the passageway. 'Of course!' she cried over her shoulder, stepping out high into the arc of light; momentarily a silhouette, a blackness against the light.

Circumnavigated, the Girl stood alone in the slype, facing the wrong way.

Sigerson walked down the long corridor. He was familiar with it. He knew every unevenness, every projection, in the sharp stone; every failing of light, lowering of headroom, burst of whistling air in the long, rank draughts. At the end it was very dark, and there was a small room, vaulted, its ceiling ambiguous in the darkness because it was difficult to tell exactly beneath which point of the parabola he was standing. But even that he was used to, moving about in it with a conditioned caution. On his way to it, his footsteps rose from the stone floor and flew about in the air; mythical, pointless sounds, alienated from the soft padding of his sandals, the separation between the sounds so great that the connection was lost to him. He moved quickly, talking as he went and moving his arms and hands in little flat explanatory gestures.

'I need him, I need him terribly badly. There are times when I have to go to him, almost as if he was a woman! The urge builds up inside me, and I can't rest for – not thinking about it exactly – so much as needing to think about it, instead of just feeling this desire –'

'Slow down, it's getting dark,' said Geoffrey, pulling at him slightly. The touch of Geoffrey's hand quietened his pace, and he laughed self-consciously.

'I know, but I know my way so well –'

'You come down here a lot, do you?'

'When I was a boy I did. ... You've no idea what it was like being a boy, Geoffrey, here –'

'You talk about it a lot. ... I have a slight idea –'

'D. said it was rubbish, the way I keep going back to it. ... D. is very harsh, isn't he? A stream of imperatives and then he lets go of you and leaves you in a void without ever telling you which directive to follow –'

'O, D.'s all right. He just likes to keep things clean, don't you D.?'

Behind Sigerson D.'s footsteps made no echo so that he was unsure how close to them D. was walking. But he heard his gentle laugh, and the slight timidity that D. always made him feel was diminished and he felt somehow more secure, as if D. had agreed with him or promised to be a bit more direct – helpful perhaps. He looked over his shoulder but could only see the thin shape and not any details. In his mind he filled in the straight dark hair, the thin temples, the brown stains about the eyes and the feverish, monkey glitter that flickered about D. when he was at rest. When he was active the glitter became steady and focused, arc-lights from which there was no escape. If D. choose to light up like that down here, there would be no escape; the hot brilliance would vibrate from stone to stone, mesmerising him, reducing him to a rabbit, to a worm of a man in a torture chamber – an element designed by the man who had designed this passage – what a good torture chamber it would make! The icy chill and the light from D. perpetually searing through the eyeballs, through the skin, through the stripped private parts, exposing the phalaria beneath the membranes, the secrets in the armpits and the circles in the skull – how the screams would echo! Round and round in madrigal from etched stone to mouldy cornice, and not a sound, not the faintest tinkle, would creep upstairs!

'You won't, will you, D.?' he asked, anxiously, still trying to see him clearly.

D. laughed again, but it was a happy sound and Sigerson felt sweat come out on his top lip. Gracious, what a dreadful idea that had been ... yet –

The three men walked on, Sigerson slightly ahead, Geoffrey in the middle. Geoffrey kept his hand on Sigerson's sleeve, and the warmth of it made Sigerson want to put his own hand on top of it. He could feel Geoffrey's body beside him, the heat that the energy generated; at last, with a deprecating giggle, he put his own fingers on the back of the comforting hand. Geoffrey said nothing and they walked on in silence. Sigerson had a wonderful feeling of being helped, of being secure in a sphere of mutual understanding and sympathy. He knew that his own weaknesses would not cause a disaster for which he would be alone to blame – indeed, there could be no disaster for the two men with him were so close and so friendly, they would foresee when he was about to fail and interpose their own strength and perspicacity. He would not need to excuse and justify himself from them. ... They were with him; on, as it were, his side. ... As they passed the spring (he had forgotten it was there, and the sudden clear light around it and the rushing, clean sound and the cool breath which came up off it made him jump a little, and he was afraid he had whimpered) –

'Do you want a wash?' D. asked, pausing expectantly behind them.

'No, no,' Sigerson said, hurrying on. He heard D. splash the water and then the sounds receded. But D. was still there – he could feel him –

Hurrying now, definitely in a hurry. 'I have this sort of necessity to be face to face with him,' he went on to Geoffrey, lowering his voice as if D. was not there or as if he almost did not want him to participate in the conversation now. 'I always stand so that I am looking at him, face to face, you know? He never comes behind me, that's always been true – he is a very direct person. Even when he is taking me somewhere we walk side by side so that we can see each other, like this –' he tugged on Geoffrey's arm and brought him up right alongside so that his cheek was almost in touch with the long sideburns. Alone of the three he had no silky hair on the side of his cheeks –

Behind him D.'s footsteps had taken a more definite sound, perhaps he had wet his feet at the spring. Sigerson began to trot, pulling at Geoffrey.

'Come on, come on,' he said in a whisper, 'we're nearly there –'

The feet of Sigerson and Geoffrey were running now; Geoffrey more heavily, more firm, out of step, so that they joggled each other and bumped their shoulders.

'It's all right, there is nothing chasing us!' Geoffrey said.

To spin round, 'Ha!' if he had the strength in his eyes, flatten D. like a bug against the sun! How the screams would ride and never rise. 'Ha!'

'Mihilanus, I'm coming!' he shouted down the passage. 'Coming!' and broke from them as if he were afraid, running down the stones to where Mihilanus stood in the dark room waiting for him, his arms stretched out to catch Sigerson, to hold him close to his breast, to cherish, to cherish. Sigerson put his head on his arms and retched against the table. The hard wood knocked at his temples, spittle trickled from his nose and mouth and tears from his eyes. He coughed and grunted and twisted his knees as if he had colic. His hair clung wetly to his forehead and his eyes wouldn't focus. Shivering, he dragged his dressing-gown around him and stared vacantly at the weave. Outside his window the grey of evening quietened the sea and the terns and the world.

When Mary-Rose came in he said quietly to her, 'Come and hold my hand. I am afraid I am going mad.'

For a few minutes Mary-Rose stood beside Sigerson's table, then she reached out and touched his shoulders. He sat still in the dressing-gown, untidy, hunched, cold, his eyes cast down onto the blank blotter in front of him where the stains of his lips and mouth betrayed him. As she stood there, not saying anything at all, the passage receded back in him, dwindling and diminishing until he was no longer aware of it but only of her. He looked up at her. She was wearing white suiting and she was beautiful. She would not hold his hand. It was clammy. He must wash ... O, D. –

'What's wrong,' she asked, drawing away slightly, watching him.

Feeling that he must answer her, and answer her in some way directly, he stroked the naked shaven flesh in front of his ears and said with tremendous difficulty, 'I think I am lonely. I'm unhappy, Mary-Rose, at the moment. I feel so cut off –' he stopped, uncertain whether she would answer.

Mary-Rose walked away from him in a circle and said, with her back to him, 'Go and wash. That will help.' Her voice was muffled. Anxiously he saw how straight her back was; rigid, one might say.

When he stood up his knees were weak, and he had to lean on the edge of the table. Pettishly he thought, she has no idea how difficult this is for me! He staggered into the bathroom, where the new lavatory sparkled and declared its purpose – his mother was right, he thought gloomily, it was not somewhere to cry. Oh, gracious, the mess he was in! He gazed at the mirror. That, that should be him! The stupid look, the damp pallor, the twitching mouth. And how he could care! How could he care, at this second when passages and madness were driving like Ben Hur about him, when hidden springs, denoting God knew what psychological horrors, were flushing alongside Ottoline's lavatory, and Mary-Rose in white and Mihilanus in white stood offering caresses and emoluments in his bedroom? All he was wondering was whether he was mad.

'Jesus Christ,' he said to the man in the mirror, 'what are you?'

He couldn't make up his mind. He was a vacillating, mental hypochondriac stroking his cheek in the mirror – or was he a madman dragging at any level of remaining reality? There were pains in his head – should he take aspirin and behave himself, or go to the nearest asylum, crawling on his knees for Valium?

'Sigerson? Are you all right?' Mary-Rose called from the passage.

'Yes, yes, I'm just coming –' He smoothed his hair in the mirror, moistened his finger like a woman and ran it along his eyebrows – they were rough. Dry Scalp –

He hurried back to his room. She was again standing by the window, her back to him. Suddenly he was afraid. Her voice had been so harsh, so sharp. ... She stood as if reluctant to admit that she had heard him coming in.

'I'm here,' he said nervously. 'Mary-Rose?'

She did not turn around and assess him. Relief and disappointment made him cower. He had forgotten to relieve himself and suddenly felt the need. There was nothing yet there between him and this woman which would allow him to speak of any of these things. If there was ever to be, then he had to make it.

He looked humbly at her hostile back and thought, she does not want me to make anything between us. He was too ignorant now to know how to begin. Dreaming had made him ignorant.

But there was a little pride left in Sigerson, and the idea that his precious dreams could make him, of all things, ignorant, was something so awful to him that his head snapped up and a little life crept back into his eyes. He wiped his face; that automatic, reflective gesture that assured him that, clean and smooth, he was ready to go into combat – if only for his dreams.

Still, Mary-Rose expressed enmity. Or it might be reluctance or fear in the tense carriage. Some element of competition crept into his mind; some vague idea that to protect his dreams and the validity of them he had to prove them against her. It was an incoherent thought, and there was no time to follow it. It was mixed with the desire to be cherished, to be held and wrapped up in her desire for him. As if her need would build something indestructible about him which would make him safe. It came to him unpleasantly that he was in the position of an army which would force that of the enemy which it had conquered to provide cannon-fodder in its own front-lines, while it consolidated its own position and advanced insidiously in safety and impunity. Geoffrey would understand the tactic, the terms, he thought. It made his need for her very sharp, very focused. The vagueness and the nightmare inconsequentiality of the evening faded out; everything faded out except the woman in white calico and the necessity of providing himself with safety, which was the same thing.

Mary-Rose stood very still, waiting like a cat. He was not ill; he could not be ill. It was not possible to her, in her lunatic whoredom, that his body, which was all she had come for and that not explicitly but only as a declaration, as a symbol, should reveal itself in the actuality of malfunction. She had been repelled by the sight of his face; of the sick, stupid look he had worn, of the weakness when he rose. She had heard him fumbling and stumbling, and irritation had shot through her, charging her with a violent animosity against him, that he should be coarse enough to be unwell when she was there. As if he allowed a lower thing, a physical thing, an animality, to come up against her and against her simulated chastity. It showed that he could not understand her or any of her needs. It was not the real thing she wanted but the image of it. Could he not see, not feel from her very appearance that the image was as low as he could bring her? But the image was necessary now! It was vital, in the pure old-fashioned sense, that her restlessness and glee should be consummated to her own, private satisfaction. A quiver of anticipation shivered up through her loins, and her knuckles whitened.

'Are you better?' she asked in a low voice, not yet turning.

'Entirely,' he said briskly, his tone high and insincere with the effort to be sincere.

'I am so sorry, I have made a complete ass of myself. ... I had been having awful nightmares –' Treason, it twitched at him, so far off that his conscience was barely affected. Certainly not enough to inhibit him. D. a nightmare? Would to God that that was all he was! 'It comes of dozing in the afternoon in this sultry weather ... and perhaps of being a trifle unsettled. ...' he added coquettishly.

The lightness of his tone spun Mary-Rose around as a delicate cast spins under the fingertips of a master craftsman. And that was how she felt: a cartoon of herself waiting for the final sophistication. So she looked at him with hope; a sudden lightening and sparkling, a river-gleam which he misread as something directed towards himself.

Behind Sigerson the imposing Directoire four-poster simplified the context in a way in which Ottoline's feverish furnishings could never have done. Mary-Rose gazed at the stringent emblems in the polished woods: the lictors, the flails. They were sufficient; she did not need the bed so long as those fertile, punitive symbols embossed it. The glow which had illumined her mirror in the Grange shone in her slanting eyes. For a moment she was near delight. Soon she would be satisfied.

'I must go,' she said. Her voice was uncertain. She turned towards the door, the movement of a woman who is easily tired.

Sigerson, who was watching her closely, trying to spy into her, dogging every muscular twitch, every inflection, was not to be flushed that easily.

'You don't need to go,' he said. 'You can sit down here.'

He had seen the sudden torpor. Submission, he thought wildly, is always exhausting. The offer made him gracious, made him gentle in the way that women make minute comforts of great compassion and imagination.

Immediately the flavour of the room changed. Mary-Rose hesitated by the chaise-longue and then laid herself upon it. It was covered in green velvet, the colour of English elm leaves in late summer, and to Sigerson the sight of her there was so secure and inland that it brought him suddenly forward to kneel beside her and he reached out and took her brown hands in his. Her rings lay placidly in his palms amid their aroma of Ambre-Solaire.

'This is how it should be,' he said unclearly, meaning this new, decorous, anglican thing.

'Yes,' said Mary-Rose, smiling at him, quite comfortable now that the crisis was over and he was kneeling beside her. She took off her sunglasses and tucked them safely under his chest so that they would not fall to the floor, an action so intimate and trustful that Sigerson immediately felt that he had consummated some great achievement. As if by shielding her precious plastic glasses he had assumed another right of guardianship and all its implied dependability.

'We seem very far from the rocks, here in the middle of them,' he told her.

'Yes!' she said quickly, her long lips smiling with a sort of excitement. 'As if we had made a place here for ourselves which has nothing to do with Coimheadach – which is really like other places –'

'Are you very lonely?' he asked her gently, assuming the state, wondering only as to its degree.

'At times –' she said, incompletely. He waited for her to go on, to fill in the details of the familiar outline, but she would not and he accepted that their intimacy was very young and its shortcomings not yet clear to them.

'It is comfortable in here –' he suggested.

'O, it is! But perhaps I would interfere with your work –' She hurried to make the speech, establishing as early as possible an excuse for herself, attributing to him alternative and compelling demands which would relieve her of him whenever she wanted to use them.

'I doubt it! But how generous and complete of you to think of it. So few real women understand the nature of work.' He had stressed the adjective so slightly that they both responded to it simultaneously.

'Like Dorothy Lambert —' she evaded.

'Like Dorothy!'

And they both laughed, together, slightly malicious. They did not mention Ottoline. Both of them, suddenly, obviously, thought of Ottoline, but there was no room, here in this new room which they had put together, for Ottoline Atlantica. But in their eyes they could each see where she had been shut out, and the duplicate image bonded them to each other, both afraid for the same reason, at the same time. They moved slightly, but deliberately, like grown-ups; quiet, informed movements for mutual protection, not at all the sudden, arbitrary gestures of children, and so grew closer together.

Sigerson held Mary-Rose's wrists very tightly and said unexpectedly, 'Thank God you are a woman.'

'You are surprised?'

A new suspicion was reflected in the faint lines of her face. When Mary-Rose became afraid the lack of clarity in the shape of her jaw-line became apparent; a minute crassness of age which in some women will turn into vulgarity, in others into immemorial vitality. In Mary-Rose it was as yet a thickening with no indication of which, if either, direction it would take.

Sigerson was strangely moved by this showing of herself, and he leaned forward and placed his lips upon her throat where for him some transcendent concept of reality engorged her.

Against the touch of his mouth, as natural as leather bands to the skin, Mary-Rose suddenly stiffened and turned her face away so that the thing he was seeking from her throat suddenly went, and he reached out, panicking, in a blind grasping made by lust and rage. ... Beneath his chest the white, plastic sunglasses scrunched as they shattered.

'You've broken them,' she shouted at him.

The thing he had been seeking from her throat ... what was it? His hands moved about without direction, seeking the appropriate sensation. The chill fingers of wrack or tangleweed, rootlessly, silently feeling in the dark water — what shall we do for our ancient sister the seaweed, for she hath no roots? Streams and currents moved on around his hands until they blurred like the hands of drowned children beneath the wavering, violent sea — a-CUSH-la, a-CUSH-la. The Beloved One reached up for him outside the window panes, twisting and writhing in the air which should have been there beyond the frame but which was expunged by the presence around him. He saw the great Atlantic wavering beyond the glass like a wistful lover or a spirit or a woman born of dreams or a spy — peering darkly in and claiming a hideous intimacy.

Tripping, Sigerson lurched across the room from the chaise-longue to the window and slammed the shutter. He forgot the tilted pile of paperbacks on the sill and the shutter slammed against it, twisting and tearing the shiny covers, and would not close. He scrabbled wildly at the trapped paper and the stiff, cracked spines until they thumped, open, to the floor, and then he swung the shutter to with a crash and dropped into its bracket the great iron bar which held the two leaves together.

Panting and jerking he leaned his back against the wall and stared at the broken books, one of them his own. In the half-dark he had created he was safe. He wiped the spittle carefully from the corner of his mouth where it had collected. The room echoed to faint cries he did not remember making. The boards of the shutters were of oak brought over once in long black boats and fitted so tightly together that hardly any light filtered through the damp-swollen hinges. The bar was of cast iron as simple and indomitable as a gun barrel. As his breathing slowed he felt the sweat cool on his forehead and neck and dribble haltingly between the hairs on his chest. He scratched through the woolly dressing-gown and smoothed down his hair. As his left hand soothed the back of his head it came round and rested around his throat — a woman's gesture. He let it lie there: it would not harm him. It felt the pulse and the moving gullet beneath the palm, and this sensation drove out the last recollection of the meaningless currents which had swayed it when it was drowned. The blood coursed in his jugular vein, pounded under his fingers, thrashed forwards by the heart. He could appreciate its warmth.

For a long time he stood there, until he was calmer. His eyes were soothed by the wooden shutter and the iron bar, and his hand was the hand of a Lazarus, holding in the precious blood.

Then he moved slowly from the blank window and sat on the chaise-longue, on the velvet which was the colour of English elms in summer. Between his feet were fragments of splintered white plastic and smoked glass. It was there that the Girl found him when she came to tell him that she was leaving.

The world the Girl lived in was thick with people. It was a dense world, full of moving masses; an amoeba-world, slow, fluctuating, choked with plasma and with cells. There were no gaps, no vacancies in the gel; all was conjoined. Where the Girl lived, in Wilberforce Close, in college, in her head, group merged with group, flowed on from group to group without distinction or particularity. And all the groups were masses of people and all the people were real. When the Girl was alone she was never alone, she was merely absent in a peculiarly carnal sense from the presence of the others, all the real others. But she still belonged to them, was full of them and surrounded by them. All of her, deeds, sensations, apprehensions, flowed through her and to her and from her in participation with the gel. Isolation was sharp and unbreathable, a killer among the elements as air to the mackerel or sea-deep to the crow. It was the Thing Outside, the Dark of space. She was too young to fear it as Grandpa had feared it. Grandpa was Out There now, but Grandpa was dead and she only thought of him when she heard your Hundred Best Tunes remotely on someone else's wireless and a fleeting acknowledgement would touch her, but no apprehension, that one day she would be old and fear the Dark element, the dark grave. But for the present the periphery of the world of real people was out of view. There were no loopholes in the head, in Wilberforce Close, in college, in the future. As her bones grew from Nursery School to Infants to Primary; as her breasts grew through Direct Grant School to university she had never stopped to stare at an unsold piano in a shop window, never lain awake beside a sleeping man. D., who was only real in some senses, could be broken by light, by its presence or absence or conformation; but the Girl recognized the Thing of light only as something which reflected or did not reflect some thing which was or was not there. The surface of the gel was intact; the mass of the gel was intact.

So she passed with ease from the corridor into Sigerson's room, which was in fact barricaded from within by strips of light as bright as aluminium hung from the hinges of the shutters to the doorway and which were pinning D. back in the shadowy part of the room where Sigerson was lying on the chaise-longue, as easily as she passed from the encounter with Mary-Rose in the slype to an encounter with the slovenly man lying down under the weight of his Dry Scalp. To her their situations were adjacent, comingling at the verges. He lived here, Mary-Rose lived here; they communicated on some plane with each other, smelt each other, took tea; this was enough. She shared this with them both. There was no barricade, no chasm, no need to make a great stride from the state of being with Mary-Rose to the state of being with Sigerson. Sigerson, D. and Mihilanus, Pinell and parts of Mary-Rose lay ordered behind the barricade, wrapped in grey gowns, inert. The Girl still wore the uniform in which she had battled with Ottoline Bonaparte; scarlet and embossed.

'Dr Ottraine?' she called, peering in like Quintus to check up on the deceased, a Quintus becoming suspicious of tombs and still forms in grey wrapping –

'*Hic jacet*. ...'

Quintus, not welcoming whimsicalities, but wanting to be certain, Rock-of-Peter sure –

'Where? O, on the couch. I'm leaving.'

'O?'

'Like we're not making out. This thing won't leave the ground at all. I'm tired of the hostility to start with. There's not a single person in this place who is prepared to make any sort of relationship with anyone other than him or herself and even then there's no real work-out; it's all little isolationist fantasies and no contact with reality. Do you get me? Like your mother just now, do you know what she's been doing? She's been playing soldiers! No, for real, she has! Feinting around on some battlement, trying to make out how I'm laying siege to her papers! She's not going to let me see them, you know. Not for anything. As I see it, what's the point? I'd do better in the university library, wouldn't I?'

'O, gracious!' Sigerson said softly, looking at her, at her solidity and emotion. 'O, Dorothy, what are we going to do?'

'We?' said the Girl, indignantly. 'That's the first time I've heard that pronoun since I came here –'

'Nonsense! It's all plural here. ... Look at us, all tangled up in each other's needs, and no room to manoeuvre. ... Don't be ridiculous, Dorothy!'

He sounded so like his mother that he was surprised himself.

The Girl looked at him with compassion. 'Jeeze!' she whispered, 'you sounded just like her –'

Sigerson sat up hurriedly, acknowledging the fact. He made a rough movement and plucked the dressing-gown back off his arms, struggling to get out of it. 'Look,' he said, 'I'll go and talk to her. ... I'll tell her all about your thesis and why you have to see the papers. I'll tell her I think you ought to have them. ... I'll tell her to hand them over to me and we will examine them together – don't you think?'

Under the dressing-gown his jersey was too short; it left a gap of shirt wrinkled around his waist. The ribbing was frayed, and there were moss stains on the elbows; the scarf about his neck was very slightly greasy. He was not pleasant to look at. The Girl, not noticing, stepped smartly closer to him, her little stomach jostled under the soft viyella of the long skirt with its constipated little flowerets. It was rounder than any breast or buttock; it looked very solid.

Fixing his eyes on her stomach he said, 'I would have thought. ... They are only two old women. ... I would think that we –'

'Ummn?' said the Girl, too cross to part her lips.

'Damn it,' he said consciously. 'I say, they are only two old women – Ottoline and that frightful old Aelebel. We ought to be able to combat them. ... O dear, now I am being military, too but they cover us, Dorothy, like a – a cock treads a hen. ... Excuse me –'

For the metaphor had called up the redness, and it trod her and her little round ball of a tummy, and he could smell the deodorant in her armpits and it was warm, warmer than any rutting musk of Mary-Rose's. He stared at her, at a blackhead beside her nose, at the thick tacky hair, and he could smell it, too, so he stared at the carpet as if he would lean down and touch the faded pattern in the brown wools.

The Girl stared as if he had touched her, but she did not move away. Her eyes flooded and reddened, and heat streamed through her. She wiped her hands on her skirt, the same gesture, as if they were wet or dirtied or smirched, down again and again over the soft woolly flowers. 'I won't be trodden down like this. ... I won't. I'm not doing any harm to any one, I haven't said anything. ... You are all sour and lonely people and the sooner I get away from the lot of you the better I will be pleased! I want to go home now; I want to get back to work and back to my own group and get out of this filthy broken down farmyard where you can't even go to a shop!'

Startled, Sigerson said, 'Is there something you want? There are ways of ordering things from the mainland. ... Can I help you –'

'I don't want ANYTHING in ANY shop; I just want to go shopping!' she shouted.

'But what for?' he said uselessly.

'Shit, that's not the point! I want to get back to a normal life! Like you said, this is a Home for Mad Awful Old Women, and I'm not staying in it – I hate it! I hate the sea all round me like this and the ghastly food – mackerel and tough beef and more mackerel and more tough beef, and your mother hacking at the bones and giggling, and Mrs Deckle making like she's up for grabs and getting high on painting seaweed! It's crazy – it's all down the river – it's a bloody madhouse and I'm going.'

She started to quiver and the tears began to show, and she wobbled and wept and began to stamp one foot rhythmically on the brown wools where Sigerson was staring as if he were watching her herself.

'Dorothy,' he begged the carpet, 'let's be reasonable. ... Let's approach this thing sensibly, as if we were in England, or somewhere. It's only the atmosphere that is creating this – this hysteria we are suffering. The atmosphere and the draughts. ... I don't know about you but I can't think when I'm cold and I've never been warm at Coimheadach that I can remember. Even these turf fires,' he added vaguely, 'they make a wonderful general heat, but you can't get hot by them. ... Now Mrs Deckle burns wood at the Grange. ... She collects drift in the summer when she is sketching on the rocks, I understand – there are so many wrecks here, you know, and I find I am much more like myself in her drawing room than I ever am here. ...The wood, you see–'

'Ummn?' said the Girl again. She sucked up his words as if she would feed on them, on their rambling inconsequence, on their inapplicability to her tears, on their uselessness. Her eyes glowered at him, threatening him that if he stopped chatting some punishment would come to them both.

'I think, you know, that if you and I and Mrs Deckle could sort of, talk things out, perhaps,' he hurried on, oblivious of the futility of the matter, 'we could in some way get out of this trap – er, this sort of hold that the old women have ... establish some sort of enclave. ... O dear, it sounds like the Boy Scouts, but a sort of Normal Patrol within the – the –' He giggled, and for a minute he looked up. Then he saw her.

From their place up on the Baun the Old Cattle saw him coming in. He was alone, a young bull, cruising, unready to haul up so early but feeling somewhere the first draw of the hard rocks after the long months at sea. His eyes were vast with fish, with dim, shifting light, with subsistence in everlasting flitting gloom. His body was beautiful with fat but not yet magnificent; and very pure. He had never been wounded. Within him the two hard little balls of unshed sperm snuggled deep in the fat, omnipresent, perpetual, peaceless. His stench lay on the water where he surfaced. The cormorant savaged the wave tops and left in a long, sulky flight, ugly and dispossessed, along the race beyond the headland. The Old Cattle turned their heads away, but the offshore breeze was stiff and spiced with heather and land-chill in the evening and they had nowhere to look that was not either dank with the island or sourced with the rutting rotten presence of the young bull in the rounded evening sea. Clumsily they moved down the side of the earthwork; the cows lay down by the wire fence, the bull remained standing, the first, solemn star too pale to light his horns.

When the Girl had left him Sigerson moved to and fro between the bars of light which had separated the part of the room where D. had been from the place where the Girl had stood. As he broke the strands the barbs of light glittered in the broken fragments of Mary-Rose's glasses. He could not feel the strands parting as he walked amongst them. Once or twice he put out his hands to touch one, but he could not hold on to it. There was nothing to hold on to; nothing to construe. All outside fluctuated imperceptibly with the unsecular tide, with the uncharted shifting of the shoals; the very walls about him were breached by the comings and goings of antique beings, and the glance of a man was meaningless to them. In the ashen rooms and empty courts the rudimentary eyes of blind Cyril peered at the alien yams and cacao flowers; at the busy termites hunting in Pinell's silent mouth. The rowels of Ottoline's spurs and the flattened bullets tinkled beyond the dark corners of the passage-ways, and Sigerson turned his lips from one side of the light strands to the other, seeking for the brown breasts of Ursula, strapped flat against the sweaty ribs or for the nipples of Aelebel, clogged with Ottoline's tears.

'Mamma, mamma, feed us.'

There was nothing to hold on to, nowhere to go except to follow the sound of his own words and he left the splintered room.

He moved through the abbey timorously, pressed against the cold walls and into dark recesses which he felt for with an outstretched, dexterous hand whilst his sinister hand reached back for the old touch of Geoffrey or Mihilanus or D. So he came down the great emptiness of the chapter with both hands stretched out to her.

She looked at him out of her violet eyes and made a strange gesture, laying her arms across her body and hanging them limply across the arm of the chair furthest from him. Listlessly she said, 'There is no one left who can make me afraid.'

She turned her head and looked past him, out of the great windows. The dying sky was thick with the sulphurous shades of the coming storm.

Then she said, 'There is no one left to kill –' and turned back to the deep corners of the chimney, slow tears like pearls drifting down with the silver ash. When she held out her hand he could not see who took it. Perhaps no one took it for she said, 'My daughters?'

Almost sure that he had heard her say, 'My daughters –' he took a sudden step towards her. Her beautiful, porcelain face was turned away.

'My daughters, my daughters –' she whispered.

He was alone. He lurched forwards at her, his arms swinging, 'Mamma – Mamma –'

'DON'T CALL ME THAT!'

The first lightning flickered far out at sea, beyond the broken roof of the gatehouse. Beyond Coimheadach. It took her attention away.

'Don't call me that,' she repeated petulantly.

'Ottoline, Ottoline Atlantica –' He kneeled by her chair. He did not know if he could take her in his arms or if she could take him in hers.

Is anyone laughing?
Is there anyone there to laugh?